BOOK 1:

A KING'S RETURN

KINGDOMS OF ISLANDIA TRILOGY

BY JACOB JOHNSON

Identifiers:

Library of Congress Control Number: 2020910566

ISBN: 978-1-64746-321-2 (paperback)
ISBN: 978-1-64746-322-9 (hardback)
ISBN: 978-1-64746-323-6 (ebook)

Available in paperback, hardback, e-book

Book design by JetLaunch. Illustrations by Igor Olszewski.

Cover Art By Kimmo Hellstrom

This book is dedicated in loving memory to
Danette Tropansky.

Without your love and support Danette this book
would not be possible. I cherish the day we can see
each other face to face once again.

TABLE OF CONTENTS

ACKNOWLEDGMENTS

Thank you to my loving wife and daughter for allowing me the countless hours to make this dream become reality. I also want to bring special attention to every person who helped give feedback and critique. Jeanette Liebsack, thank you for putting in the effort to help craft this book into what it is today. Thank you to my friends and family for your amazing support. Without your belief in me and this story no one would be reading it today. Last, but certainly not least, I want to give glory to the Name above all names. He is the true morning star and the dawn bringer of our story. His name is King Jesus. He deserves all the honor, glory, and praise.

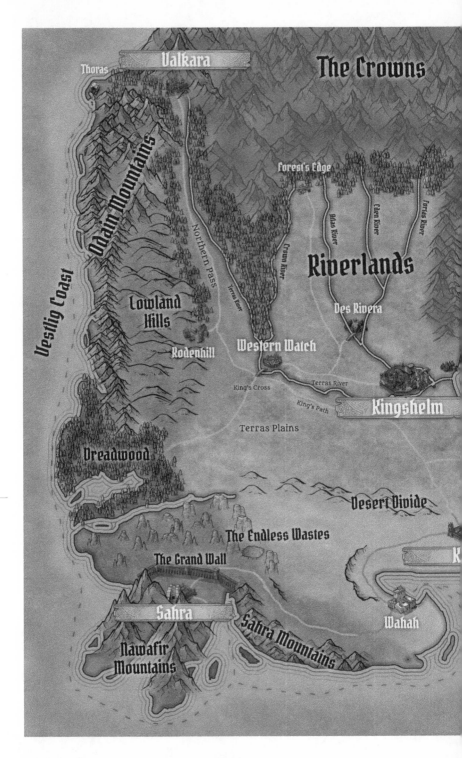

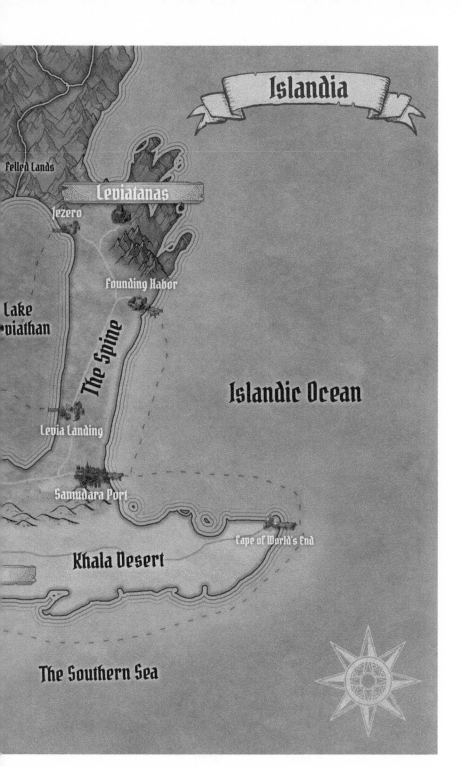

PRELUDE

My Dear Son Titus,

I write this to you, son, for one day you may reign in my stead. It is troubling times in Islandia. Rumors of war and discord fill the air. Many of it fueled by the story you will have heard countless times by the age you can read this. But now I feel the need to share our histories with you in greater detail for someday you will need to know them, to understand this present age. It has to do with High King Eloy and his strange departure.

A little over 10 years ago he left us. Many were shocked and dismayed by his sudden departure, myself being included in that company. It was not until he took me aside that I discovered the necessity of his journey. First, I feel I must digress to a bit of history. To what we in Islandia call The Founding.

It was some 2,000 years ago that our ancestors, The Founders, left their home and landed on the shores of Islandia. Upon their arrival, they began to colonize the lands of the eastern shore. What we call in our time, Leviatanas. They eventually reached our home, the Riverlands. To their surprise, much of the land was unpopulated. Sure, there were some small villages, but nothing to the extent of their original home. It was these small villages that told our ancestors of the present powerful kingdoms. In the South, what we call today Sahra.

In the Northwest, the name given by us is Valkara. These two kingdoms, the records tell us, kept mainly to themselves.

Our ancestors changed all that. Representatives of both realms came to The Founders to discover their intentions. In this exchange, Yeshu, the great king of Sahra, laid eyes on Saria, a noblewoman of The Founders. Yeshu offered a uniting of the kingdoms in exchange for her hand in marriage. Our ancestors agreed on the terms that they would rule from the centralized location of the Riverlands. Thus Kingshelm, where we dwell today, was formed. It is from this unbroken line that the kings of Islandia are born. The latest being our King Eloy.

Now, as you could imagine, Valkara felt cheated in this exchange. The two kingdoms offered concessions that Valkara accepted knowing that they could not win in an open conflict, but tensions have remained to this day.

Our family comes from a line of Stewards to the King. We served as his armor-bearer in conflict and his royal advisors in court. Our line, like the king, has stayed in place to this day. The other Founders scattered to different locations throughout the Riverlands, and the other noble families to Leviatanas.

As the years passed, the line born from Yeshu and Saria varied in greatness. Like all reigns from bloodlines they come with their high watermarks and their low. It was some 100 years after Yeshu that the first great conflict arose. It was under the reign of King Marcian. He saw the plight of the Khalan people in the south, a clan of men born in the south who had been under the control of Sahra. They were treated poorly and made to serve in harsh conditions. A great city named Khala was being built on the labor of their backs. Deep holes were drilled to reach reservoirs below the desert ground. It would be an oasis on the long road to the north, but the Khalans, who slaved to build it, would have no share or say in the new city. Their ancestral home was taken from them by their own labors.

Marcian set out to end this abuse. Now, 500 years from his Sahra roots, he showed no favoritism in this act. Sahra, as you can imagine, did not respond well. They called upon the old resentments of Valkara to raise up war against Kingshelm. The conflict was known as the First War of Islandia. Leviatanas came to the aid of Kingshelm. With this aid and the Khalans in support, King Marcian helped bring an end to the oppression. Khala was officially made an independent realm with a Khalan to rule at its head. Khosi is the name given to this ruler.

Sahra's jurisdiction was pushed back to the city of Wahah where it remains to this day. Valkara lost the vital King's Cross city, then named Lokirus. Kingshelm claimed this point as their own and renamed it Western Watch, where it has stood as a defense against Valkaran aggression to this day. Sadly, this war would not be the last. It only started a deep rift in the kingdoms of Islandia.

The next 500 years were a low watermark of small rebellions against various kings in Kingshelm. It all reached a climax when They came, the dreaded ones that no one speaks of. Our ancestors named them The Felled Ones. Dark creatures like men, but twisted, vile, and deformed. They came from the mountains in the North. It was at this moment that all Islandia seemed doomed to darkness. The ruling king at the time, named Bailian, was forced to retreat behind the Grand Wall of Sahra in the South. All of Islandia's people made their final stand.

But a light came from the mountains of Nawafir. Bailian, and a few of his greatest craftsmen, formed a weapon that could withstand the oncoming tide, what we call the Dawn Blades. Forged in deep fires and given a power by The Founders now lost to us, these blades radiated with light and could tear through any armor or weapon with ease. Five weapons were made, one for each realm. Valkara was given the Longsword Dawnbreaker, Sahra the scimitar Dawn's Light, Khala possessed the spear Daybreaker, Leviatanas was given Dawn's Deliverer, and lastly, Bailian was given the greatest of them all, Morning's Dawn. It was with these blades that they held the darkness at bay, but at a cost.

They fought on the ramparts of the Grand Wall. It was here that The Endless Wastes got their name. Destruction and death destroyed that land. The ruler of Sahra, Saladar, was lost to the great chasm there along with his blade. Valkara's ruler, Thoranus, was also slain, and his blade was taken by the enemy. Imaran of Khala survived the conflict along with Tiberius of Leviatanas. Bailian barely made it out with his life, losing his left arm in the conflict. The day was won with great sacrifice and The Felled Ones retreated to whence they came. The dreaded king of The Felled Ones, if you can call him such, escaped with a grave injury.

Islandia was in shambles and the rebuilding took centuries. The next 500 years were a striving for long lost days of glory. It was in this time much of the histories were recorded for fear of being lost in another conflict. Much of life continued as is until, like all of history, it seemed to repeat itself.

Another brutal war erupted between Valkara and Kingshelm. This time over what we today call the Hillmen, those who dwell in the Lowland Hills. Several tribes who, even up until our own time, have avoided joining the rest of Islandia in one united rule. Valkara had spent many years raiding and pillaging these peoples. The King in Kingshelm, named Jeruh, stood against them for such reckless assaults. He had a desire to bring them under Kingshelm's domain, but knew aggression would only create more resentment toward outsiders. No resolution could be found, and so war broke out again. This time those in the south stayed neutral while Leviatanas The Faithful came to the aid of Kingshelm. With their combined force they crushed Valkara. After this, they set many restrictions upon them, which has left them diminished of their ancestral strength.

There is more to this time that I will come back to shortly, but, to continue the histories. The next 500 years were a time of peace. Islandia could finally lick her wounds and, in fact, she began to thrive. Under the reign of Eloy's father we saw an expansion to Kingshelm that had not been seen since the days of King Valelian The Wise. Eloy's father, Yehua, was one of the greatest to rule. So great promise was upon Eloy when it was his time to rule. Eloy was diligent in study. He searched and studied the ancient texts like no one I had ever seen. He desired to be a wise and strong ruler. It was because of this study, however, that we were left kingless.

One day, King Eloy drew together a council of utmost secrecy. He relayed to Leon, Fahim, Doran, Imbata, and myself an ancient warning given by Bailian and recorded by a later king that preceded Jeruh. The warning was of The Felled Ones return 1,000 years from their defeat. It went on to say that the Dawn Blades would not be sufficient in stopping them this time. The secret to their ultimate defeat could only be discovered from where The Founders had come, the name and location lost to the histories. Of course, many in our council disregarded it as an old legend, that if some dark force called The Felled Ones did exist at one point, they were long gone. Eloy was not so convinced. You see the writings of ancient Kings are regarded highly among their predecessors. This particular warning had just been discovered in an uncovered site below the castle full of ancient scrolls.

This warning, along with the timing, (it being the beginnings of the next thousand years) was enough to convince Eloy of his urgent need to discover The Founder's homeland. Those of us in the king's council hesitated at such a move. For 2,000 years one from Eloy's line had sat on the throne. Should now, in our potentially darkest hour, the throne sit empty? He would not be moved in his decision to go, and so we consented after much debate.

It was in this meeting that Eloy placed the greatest honor one could receive on me. I was to be Steward King in his place while he was gone. Imbata agreed with this council along with

Leon. Doran and Fahim conceded, citing that I would be the most "neutral" choice. It was not two weeks later that Eloy and five hundred of the king's men sailed out into the Islandic Ocean.

It is now our great task, my son, to hold the realm together in his absence. What seemed a king's folly to many, I believe will be our salvation. You see, before Eloy left he gave me his council. He told me that he was not mad, that there had been signs to confirm a time of great significance was drawing near. As the king's steward I was a witness to a few of these as well. Before he departed he bestowed on me Morning's Dawn. "A sword to hold the realm together," he said. I have put my faith in him, that he will return. It has been some years now, but I still believe we will see him again. If not me, then you, my son, will carry this burden as well.

It is a burden and an honor to lead Islandia, so I will leave you with this guidance. Leon is a faithful friend. I hope someday his son Lancelin and yourself will become trusted companions. Kingshelm has always relied on Leviatanas as our ally. Imbata is also a man of honor. The customs of the south differ from our own, but in him you will find a true leader. As for Doran, I fear I see old tensions rising again. He has begun to raid the Lowland Hills like his ancestors before him. He has suffered great loss in the process, but I believe all wounds can be mended. Even deep ones. Lastly, Fahim is a man of many faces. Be careful of him for his words are like honey. He will speak the words you wish to hear, but there is always something to be benefited for himself.

My son, I take great pride in being your father. We are of a line not often in the spotlight of history, but I see now a time where many fates hinge on how we act. So, I say this to you, be faithful in your service, honor the king, and do what is right at all cost. I love you, Titus.

Your Father,
Steward King Richard

1

TITUS

Rain sent a dreary echo throughout his room. Titus awoke and rubbed his eyes.

"Today is the day," he thought with sleep still clinging to his voice. As he sat up, he could not tell from the dimness of his room what time it was, but he was certain the ceremony preparations would begin soon. Today was the Day of Remembrance. Each year people from all over Islandia would gather into the royal city of Kingshelm. Kingshelm was the crown of Islandia. A sparkling gem of grandeur and trade. The city itself sat between the mighty Terras and Atlas Rivers, creating a hub of trade for the Riverlands. It also created a magnificent sight for the residents of the great city. But the greatest sight of them all was the marvelous palace of the king a sparkling white structure filled with the finest art and greenest gardens. Many from far and wide traveled to gaze at all Kingshelm had to offer. That is why so many were shocked thirty years ago when High King Eloy had set off for his journey and placed Titus' father, Richard, on the throne as Steward King of Islandia. It was this very moment that would be remembered today.

Each year, the Steward King is honored as the temporary replacement of King Eloy until his promised return. As the years have gone on, however, the kingdoms of Islandia wavered in their belief of Eloy's return. Titus and his father's house had remained loyal to Eloy, believing he would return soon. Others doubted and began to question whether they should listen to Eloy's commands after all these years. Each year that passed has led to ever-increasing tension during the Day of Remembrance. The days leading up to the Day of Remembrance made Titus' stomach churn with dread. A knock came crashing against his door pulling him abruptly from his thoughts.

"Is our charming Prince Titus awake?" a mocking voice said.

"Shut it, Lancelin. I've been awake," Titus said as he rose from his bed.

The door burst open and there stood a lean, but muscled, figure. His dark green armor bore the symbol of a leviathan curled into a striking position. His face was handsome and stubbled with a smug smile and his green eyes flickered with mischief.

"Well, your highness, I am here to make sure you are prepped and ready for your father's big day," Lancelin said, with that same mocking tone.

"I am sure if that were the case, they wouldn't have sent you," Titus said with a wiry smile.

They both embraced, and Lancelin grabbed him by the shoulders.

"Now friend that hurts. Truly," he said with a grin stretching across his face. "I thought all those times training together as young princes would have convinced you by now that I am the man for the job." He smirked.

"Hardly, I've seen your skill and princely etiquette. It lacks refinement," Titus said with a friendly shove. Lancelin scowled in reply.

"We best hurry, Titus, the festivities are starting."

They briskly walked through the white marble hallway. Alternating banners hung on each wall. The first was a purple field and golden lion cub of Titus' family, then the sigil of

King Eloy, a white lion on a silver field. Men stood guarding a large oak door at the end of the hall. They were dressed in the royal guard attire, which was dark gray armor with a lion's face etched into the breastplate along with a purple cloak with gold edging draped over their shoulders. Both men carried a stern look on their faces.

Without a word, as both young men approached, they opened the door. As they walked by, Lancelin leaned over and whispered, "Someone forgot to mention to those guys today is supposed to be a celebration."

Both men snickered as they entered a large lobby filled with guests still filing in. The same banners hung from the vaulted stone ceilings along with the sigil of the other four kingdoms of Islandia; the Black Ram horn on a postal blue field for the house of King Doran who reigned in the northern kingdom of Valkara, a yellow leopard paw displayed on a black field which represented Khosi Imari and his southern kingdom, Khala, a yellow sun and red field representing the southwestern kingdom of Sahra ruled by Sulta Fahim, and lastly, the leviathan on a gray field for Leviatanas, the same as represented on Lancelin's armor ruled by King Leon.

The guests began to notice the royal sons who had just entered.

"Greetings guests! While we would love to stay and chat, I have a prince to deliver," Lancelin proclaimed comically. The guests chuckled, and Titus was thankful to dodge the formalities.

"Thanks for that," Titus mumbled.

"I made a promise I intend to keep," Lancelin said with a sly smile.

They hurried through the crowd to the throne room door and ascended the right side of the double stairway. Marble doors of the throne room stood before them covered with carvings of past deeds. Another two guards covered in the royal garb manned their posts and opened the doors for the two princes to the grand throne room. Ten black marble columns lined both sides of the hall. The floor was white marble and led to ascending marble stairs. A crowned throne sat at the top of the stairs. Two black marble lions guarded the armrests. The rest of the throne was white with three lions splayed out on the sides rising to the top of the backrest, their paws in a pouncing position. King Richard sat on his throne, his face painted with frustration. At the bottom of the stairs stood the advisory court with head advisory, Eli, pacing back and forth.

"We should not have invited King Doran's sons here! We are on the verge of war, and you bring our enemy onto our doorstep," Eli said in a chastising tone.

"If we cannot even celebrate our kingdom's common heritage, how can we expect to broker for peace? Besides, no one has declared war yet," King Richard said in his booming voice. That voice had always brought comfort to Titus. The voice that taught him to be compassionate and generous but also strong and committed. He had to be willing to listen and take good council, yet make a decision when necessary. This was his father, not a perfect king, but one who led well.

"Peace is a fragile thing, Eli, and you know, as well as I, if I had not invited them the tension might well push the North past the edge," persisted King Richard. Eli frowned in reply, and turned to the two royal sons.

"Greetings, royal princes. Your King has been expecting you, especially one of you." Eli's gaze focused on Titus.

"Sorry. It was the rain. I mean, who doesn't sleep in on a rainy day?" Titus croaked.

"Princes who have a sacred duty to uphold," boomed King Richard with a grim look. In a flash, that look changed to a giant grin. "But I suppose it's better late than never, especially with this son of mine," the King said jokingly.

"Now, if my royal advisory would excuse us, I have a royal prince to speak with."

The advisory team dispersed to the back of the throne room in silence.

"Were you discussing the rift between us and Valkara?" inquired Titus to the King.

"Unfortunately, yes," the King replied, as his shoulders slumped. "It seems more and more of the regent kings grow restless over Eloy's absence. This year especially. Something has happened in the North and they have grown more and more hostile to our kingdom. More than simple border disputes. Something darker is happening…"

Titus frowned. "Will it be full-scale war, then?"

"I do not know, but cheer up, my prince, for today is to be one of celebration and reflection. The future holds what it will, but we should be mindful to remain in the present. No outcome is assured as of yet."

"Beg my pardon, my King, but would you like me to lead the Prince to the armory to prepare for the ceremony?" Lancelin asked.

"Yes, good thinking, Lancelin! It is almost time, and I have yet to get fully ready myself. Be off with him," the King exclaimed with a playful smile.

Lancelin clasped Titus by the shoulder, "Shall we?"

Titus glanced over to his father noticing the sorrow hiding behind his eyes. "Yes of course," he responded distantly.

"Well, come then!" said Lancelin slapping him on the shoulder and pulling him a few feet down the hall.

"Just one moment, actually," came the King's voice behind them. "Come close, Titus." Titus stepped forward with Lancelin waiting patiently behind him.

"My son, there may be conflict and darkness ahead. I want you to remember what Eloy told me before he left. 'Darkness may come, the night may be long, but I will return and something greater is ahead.' I want you to remember this, my son. Life is full of peril and difficult times, but there is something greater ahead. Many lose perspective of this. They seek what

5

they can hold here and now. They take, they kill, and they desire what is not theirs. Let it not be with you, no matter what it looks like. Do you understand?"

"Yes, I do, Father. You have set out that example well, but why tell me this now? Is something going to happen?"

"I cannot say for sure," replied Richard, stroking his chin, "but you must remember regardless, a man is not defined by his status. It is what he leaves behind him that truly shows who he is. I just want to affirm what I leave behind stands well. Do you understand me?"

"I do. I will make you proud."

"I know you will. Now hurry, don't make Lancelin wait any longer. Eloy knows you have already." With that, the King sent Titus off with a smile and a small chuckle, but Titus could sense it was masking something much more burdensome underneath.

The two princes made their way into the armory. The dark armor of the royal guard hung from their individual alcoves. At the end of the room, the royal armor of Prince Titus was displayed. A dark grey breastplate with a gold outlined lion cub's head. Attached was a gold cloak fringed with white. In the center rested a purple lion's head identical to his breastplate. Lancelin helped him clasp it around his torso. Titus slid the dark metal bracers around his wrists.

"What about the helmet?" Lancelin said, gesturing to the helmet hanging from the wall a few feet away. It looked as if a lion's mouth was opening its jaws to consume the wearer. In the back, a golden mane flowed down to the wearer's shoulders.

"That pompous thing? Forget it," Titus scoffed.

"I don't know, it has a certain quality I can appreciate," chuckled Lancelin.

Both men stood as two guards entered the room.

"Princes, it's time," one of the men commanded.

"So it is. Are you ready?" asked Lancelin.

"The royal princes are ready," Titus said to the man.

The guards led them to the large doors guarding the throne room. The guests had already filed in and were awaiting the royal court of each kingdom to enter. In the front stood the two sons of Doran, King of Valkara. Aiden, the oldest son, and Brayan. Representatives from Khala stood next to their conquerors from Sahra.

"That has to be awkward for them," Lancelin gestured.

Sahra, a few years back, had taken control of Khala in a surprise attack. King Richard had spoken against the action, but tensions with Valkara, even then, left his hands tied to send any retaliating forces.

Titus looked over at them with sympathy. "What they did was treacherous. We should have responded."

"I agree. To add insult to injury they bring the Khala representatives here, and display them like nothing happened."

Both men moved toward their respective places in line. Lancelin finding his place behind the southern men. Titus moved to his place next to his father's side who stood with an inviting smile.

Trumpets blared and the royal procession began. Many onlookers cheered or stood in awe at the royal court. The young maidens in the crowd stared and whispered as the princes passed by. Titus could focus on only one thing, the knot building in his stomach. Something seemed off.

In a blink, he found himself along with the others in the procession overlooking the entire throne room. He took his place standing next to his father.

"We welcome the royal families as we celebrate this Day of Remembrance," proclaimed the royal announcer.

A moment of silence filled the air to remember all who had passed since King Eloy's departure. This was the moment Titus and his father always lamented. Thoughts of the late Queen came flooding to his mind, and he was sure his father's as well. Tears welled up in Titus' eyes, and he fought to hold them back.

"A prince must remain dignified," thought Titus, but then he glanced over at his father. The strongest man he knew had tears streaming down his face. He had never seen his father respond in this way before. Then, he noticed something like a smile on his father's face. Confusion began to permeate his thoughts.

"Why is father smiling?" Before he could find a rational explanation the next part of the ceremony began.

"And now, for the recommissioning of the Steward King!" exclaimed the royal announcer.

"Bring forth the steward's crown and King Eloy's sword, Morning's Dawn." Morning's Dawn was a weapon like no other left behind for Titus' father in the case of dire need. Morning's Dawn had a golden hilt, wrapped with a white leather grip. The blade, when unsheathed, glowed with a white hot light around its edge. It was said that it could slice through any armor as if the wearer rode to battle unprotected. Only five blades had been made like Morning's Dawn in ancient days. The others were lost in the great war against The Felled Ones or were lost to history. Eloy's royal line, however, had carried their's since the day it was forged.

The crown was not audacious. It was a simple ring of gold with seven protruding spikes. No gems or adornment was added to it. Simple, but firm. The sword in its sheath was wrapped around King Richard's waist. The crown gently lowered onto his head. Lastly the royal robe was placed on his shoulders. It was adorned with the lion of Eloy and the cub of King Richard's house.

The crowd cheered and began to give shouts of, "Long live the Steward King!"

King Richard raised his hand to silence them. As he began to speak his face became distorted. Pain filled his eyes. Black lines began stretching from his neck onto his face. He let out a shriek of agony. In a flash, swords were drawn and the room sprang into chaos. Screams filled the air.

The royal guards shouted, "Grab those sons of the North!"

Titus was in a daze. Stupefied he stood, unmoving in the surrounding storm. Cries from below the throne were followed with the clanging of steel.

"Faa..aa..ther?" muttered Titus as he fell before the writhing king on the ground. He stretched out a hand, but before he could grasp his father he was jerked back.

"Don't!!!" came a voice.

"It's the robe! It has been poisoned!" exclaimed the familiar voice of Lancelin. Titus was jerked up to his feet. Before he could say a word, he watched as he was dragged in a daze farther and farther away from his father. The crowd began to hamper his view, but through the crowd of panicked bodies Titus saw the last breath leave the king.

2

IMARI

Imari stared at the parchment with the same sinking feeling in his stomach. The words 'Steward King Richard is dead' flooded his mind back to that horrid day. The day Imari lost everything. The betrayal was a cold dagger to the back. The kingdom known as Sahra, west of Imari's homeland Khala, had betrayed his family in the deepest way. Nabila, daughter of Fahim, had been pledged to him in marriage to unite the two kingdom's of the South. It was a day of celebration and rejoicing, until it wasn't. Nabila had caught the eye of many, Imari's especially.

She was a slender woman who carried herself in a regal fashion. Her dark olive skin and deep brown eyes had gazed into Imari's with the same affection his carried for her. Her radiant form captivating all who had attended their union. He stood her opposite. A thin, but muscled, warrior of ebony complexion. His hair cut short for honorary custom. His golden dashiki glistened in the torchlight. The ceremony flashed by. They shared the night laughing, rejoicing, and sharing their new found love. The short lived moment was a place Imari wished he could return to.

"No, a king does not dwell on the past," Imari reprimanded himself. But the truth was, he would trade anything to go back before that evil day. The day that Sahra, in its deception, sent a surprise force to surround Khala. The wedding had been a rouse to get into the kingdom palace. With forces inside, Fahim sent men to open the gates and flood Khala with its enemy. Imari's father, Imbata, the king, and his radiant mother, Khali, were slaughtered. For some unknown vengeance, to send a message, or from a heart of pure evil Imari did not know.

At the death of their king, the elite guards, called the Bomani, rescued Imari, his brother Imbaku, and his sister Khaleena. They fought their way out of the city and escaped into the eastern desert of the Khala. It was six years ago when Fahim had taken over the great city. Six years since Imari was robbed of his greatest loves.

"Khosi! I have news."

Imari turned to see Impatu bent over breathless. He was a young, unproven Khalan warrior still carrying the lean muscle of his years. His hair a short beaded display.

"Ah Impatu, what is it that you feel the need to rush and tell me?"

"There has been another raiding just north of the Herdsmen's Valley."

"Another? This is not the season, nor is it their way to strike in the same area. This is strange indeed. Grab me my camel and muster a force together. I will meet you in a moment."

"Yes Khosi," Impatu turned to leave, then faced Imari again.

"Yes?" asked Imari.

"Khosi, I know I am a young boy still, but may I join you on this scouting?" he pleaded.

"I think this will be good training for you, yes. Reach out to my brother Imbaku as well. He should know about this."

Without another word, Impatu scrambled out of the tent entrance to gather the men. Imari turned and walked over to a wooden table set up in his bedouin tent. He placed the parchment with the news of Steward King Richard down on the table and sighed.

"When will these trials end?" he thought to himself. He then reached over and grabbed his spear that had been leaning against the table. Next to it rested the painted-hourglass shaped shield that all Khalan warriors carried. After gathering the rest of the supplies he needed, he turned to the tent opening.

The desert sun blinded his vision for a moment. When clarity returned, he could see Impatu already returning with at least a dozen men and Imari's brother, Imbaku, at his side. His brother carried the posture of a seasoned fighter. His arms were a form of tight muscles and his face always bore a stern look. He had the hair of many Bomani warriors, shaved on the sides with the top decorated by elaborate beads.

"I hope this is worth our time," grumbled Imbaku. "We were just about to go on a hunt. The camp is running low on food again, and who knows when the next herd will pass by."

"I understand your anxiety brother, but I do believe this is important," Imari replied in a deescalating tone. "There has been another raid in Herdsmen's Valley. I believe this is something more than wild Bedouin."

"What makes you think that?" impatience and doubt radiated from Imbaku's response.

"It is neither the way, nor the season, of the Bedouins. Herdsmen's Valley is much too close to Khala for them to venture."

"So you think it could be Fahim? If so, why would we even think of going near there! We have spent the past six years avoiding such an encounter, and now you want to go straight to him! Are you."

"I do not know who it is, brother, but we cannot live like this forever. What we need is information," interrupted Imari. "We have had no pulse on what has happened in Sahra since our exile. That could change today."

"This better not be about that traitor wife of yours," Imbaku scowled.

Imari let the sting of the insult roll off him before he responded. "No, brother, Nabila is lost to me. I have no idealistic dreams of our reunion. What I want is not to lead 300 starving warriors in the desert for another six years until we all waste away."

Imari motioned silently with his spear for the men to mount up. Imbaku fell in line with the rest, and Impatu still carried his childish grin. The trip to Herdsmen's Valley would take two days of travel. The men of their camp freshened up their camels and stocked up on final provisions. By mid-morning they set out.

***

Imari admired the sand-swept edges of the ravine flickered by the light of their campfire. Impatu, along with the rest of the men, worked to prep for the next morning's journey. The day had been uneventful, hours traversing over sand dunes scorched by the tireless sun. They reached the end of the Khala Desert and reached the unique, rocky Banu Ravine that evening. The next few hours of sunlight were spent collecting what firewood they could find and scouting for any unwanted guests. When everything had cleared, Imari invited Imbaku to sit with him over the meal he had prepared. The tension from earlier floating in the air. The tension between them had never really left Imbaku since the disappearance of their sister Khaleena. A disappearance he squarely placed on Imari's shoulders. "It seems everything rests on my shoulders," reflected Imari to himself.

"So, brother, did you invite me to sit in silence, or do you have something you'd wish to speak to me about?"

In the background, Impatu and a handful of men began to play a few instruments they had brought along for the journey. A melody of drumbeats and smooth voices filled the air. Both brothers turned to glance at the musicians, and then returned their gaze to the fire.

"We must fix this tension between us," said Imari passively.

"There is nothing to fix. You are the Khosi, and I will follow you. That is the end of it."

"Esshhk! Will I never be forgiven for my mistakes, Imbaku? Should my every decision be blamed for destroying our family?" asked Imari. The musicians stopped for a moment to stare at the brothers, but found it wiser to pretend to not hear and continued to play.

"If that is how you see it," Imbaku mumbled staring into the flames. "You speak as though you should not be the one who is held accountable for all this." His eyes lifted to look at Imari.

"Was it not you who brought that vile woman and her father into our home? Was it not you, brother, who made us flee as Father and Mother were slaughtered in their own bed?" Imbaku was standing now. The rage evident in his face and tensed muscles. "Was it not you who, after years of wandering, sent our sister back to Khala, likely ending her life? For what? A vain hope that your traitorous wife might not be the Shuka that she is?"

At that, Imari was on his feet gripping Imbaku's beaded breastplate. "I may be your brother, but do not forget I am also your Khosi, Imbaku, and if you ever speak to me in such a way again, you may come to regret it." Imari let Imbaku go and took a step back. With a deep sigh he spoke again. "You have shared your mind, brother, I cannot fault you for this. However, if you do not trust me to lead us well, you are free to leave." Imbaku brushed himself off in defiance.

"I cannot leave the fate of our people in your hands alone. How will I know where you will eventually take us if I leave?" With that Imbaku spat and walked into his tent. Imari felt the gaze of all the men resting on him. He turned to see Impatu place a hand on his shoulder.

"My Khosi, don't let his words cut too deep. He speaks as one wounded himself. He feels the blame as much as you."

"What should I do with such a man? He is my blood, but what am I as a Khosi if my own family will not follow me?" sighed Imari.

"If I may be so bold, Khosi. Family is more than blood. We will follow you to the death. Something tells me behind his anger, so would Imbaku."

"Thank you for the kind words, Impatu. When did you become a sage in your youth?" teased Imari.

"I told you, Khosi! I have come of age," grinned Impatu. Both men let out a breath of laughter.

"I will rest easier tonight because of you, my young warrior. Now, I must get some rest. Make sure you and the men do the same." With that Imari clasped his hand on Impatu's shoulder and made his way to his tent.

When Imari awoke, the sun began to peak into the ravine. Violet hues mixed with scarlet splashed across a morning canvas. The other Bomani warriors stirred in their tents as well. They made short work of disassembling the camp and, soon after, headed on their way, all traces of a camp erased from the desert floor. From Imari's assessment they would arrive at the Herdsmen's Valley by midday.

The Valley was essential to the nomadic Bedouin camps in the area. It was one of the few places their herds could find the resources they needed in this parched land. It also meant it was notorious for being ambushed. Imari knew it was likely that this journey would end in bloodshed. The other Bomani could sense it as well.

The remaining travel was taken in relative silence. Besides a jest here and there, the men prepared for a potential conflict in ancient fashion, silent mediation. The sun hung in the sky signaling midday, Imari could see the valley floor resting just within sight. They closed the distance noticing a few scattered tents. As they reached the small camp each man dismounted, pulling his spear and shield from their mount. An eerie silence hung in the air.

Empty tents flapped in the wind. Small cooking pots lay smashed and scattered. Even a few fresh corpses could be seen strewn on the ground. It seemed as if the small camp never saw the ambush coming.

"There has definitely been an attack," stated Imbaku, breaking the silence. "The question remains, by who?"

Imari shifted through a few remains with the end of his spear. At that moment a whistle rang in Imari's ears. The Bomani behind him cried out at something in the distance. Shouts then filled the air as a group of camel riders came flying over the valley's peak.

"Bomani, assemble!" ordered Imari.

Without hesitation, the trained warriors interlocked shields and dropped into formation. Between the gap of each Khalan warrior's shield protruded a six-foot spear. In a matter of seconds, the Bomani had assembled into a circular pattern, protecting them from all sides. The camel riders did not hesitate, they ramped up their speed and came full force at Imari and his men. Imari gripped his painted shield and braced for impact. Right before the two sides would crash into each other he heard a voice.

"Holt!" came the cry of a woman's voice.

The line of descending camel riders pulled on the reigns at the last possible second. They maneuvered to surround Imari and his men. The petite, but chiseled, warrior who had given the order, dismounted. She removed her helmet made of bone to reveal the face of a beautiful, dark skinned woman with black and blonde braids intertwined into a bun. Her chestnut colored eyes carried a penetrating stare. She had a small upturned nose, and dimples that creased her smile. There was also a barely visible scar streaked across her right cheek. It was the same face of Imari and Imbaku's sister. The sister they had not seen in four years.

"Kha…Khaleena?!" choked Imari in surprise.

"Sister!" exclaimed Imbaku dropping his weapons and moving to approach her.

"Eeiish!" barked Khaleena as she moved her spear point to stop Imbaku. With shock gripping his face, Imbaku stopped and raised his hands in a gesture of surrender.

"Sister, we thought you were dead! What a blessing it is to see you!" he said.

Khaleena gave them both a distrusting glance, then melted into a grin and cackled out a laugh.

"My brothers! I did not know if you two could keep each other alive this long." She moved to embrace them both. The warriors on both sides visibly dropped their guards.

"How, how are you alive? We believed you to be taken by raiders, or worse," Imari asked with a joyful smile.

"Ah, it is the truth, my brothers, at least about the raiders, but those raiders did not carry me off as bounty or kill me for sport. They embraced my warrior skills. As things would have it, they follow only the strong, so my time came, and I proved my strength to them."

"But what is this now? And why did you never come to us before?" questioned Imbaku with a little anger tinting his voice.

"Yes, I am sorry I never reached out before. As I said, I had to earn my place, and this was not in a day as you can understand, brothers. This particular group, the Masisi, only follow the strongest warrior. I followed wherever they would go, fighting, raiding, and doing what it took to learn their ways till one day I found that they followed those who could prove their skill. So, I proved who was the greatest warrior among them." A wiry smile crept up Khaleena's face.

"Yes, we understand that, but why did you not try to find us after?" asked Imari.

"I did, brother, but you are always on the move. The same way you survived against Fahim's agents searching for you. I looked for many months, but found no trace of you, till now, and what perfect timing it is."

"How so?" Imbaku asked.

"I have news from Sahra. There is discontent in the kingdom. It would seem Nabila is planning a coup."

"That witch? I could not believe it even if I was a coconspirator myself," spat Imbaku with disdain.

"Well…you see, that could potentially be exactly what you are." That same, wiry smile creeping up Khaleena's face again.

"If you think that we would ever join the cause of any Sahra Shuka, you are wrong!" raged Imbaku.

Khaleena turned to Imari. "You are silent on this matter, brother? I thought you might be excited to hear of your long-lost wife?"

The truth was Imari didn't have the slightest clue how to feel. In the last minute he was struck with the truth of his sister's fate, and now the hope that maybe Nabila didn't betray him. It all seemed too good to be true.

"I don't know what to think, sister, but tell me what you know and I can make a better decision."

"You seriously can't be considering this, Imari? Oh yes, you would do anything for that Shuka wife of yours, even lead us into the grave!"

With that reply, Imari turned and sent Imbaku on his back. Imari firmly placed his foot on his chest.

"You forget your place, little brother, and don't forget who the greater warrior among us is. I doubt you would like to try to win your kingship as Khaleena has. It would not end well for you." Imari's tone was firm, but not tinted with the anger he felt. He released his foot from Imbaku's chest to allow him to scramble back to his feet.

"I see you two have not missed a beat since my absence," jested Khaleena to break the obvious tension. "When I could not find you, I traveled west near The Endless Waste. I ended up at the port city of Wahah. There, I stumbled across Nabila. She was sent to meet some ambassadors from the northern kingdom of Valkara. I thought this strange, and followed her till I could get her alone."

"Valkara, here in the south? Why would they go all the way to Wahah?" Imari asked.

"I thought it very strange as well, so when I cornered Nabila, I interrogated her. She told me of a plot to take Kingshelm, and ultimately, Islandia. She also told me she had her suspicions that something else was at work, and that is what she went to discover."

"And? Did she find out?" pressed Imari.

"I was getting there, brother, patience. She said there was another party involved in all this and that Doran, king of Valkara, was not even aware of this plot. That confirmed the strangeness she sensed in the royal palace in Sahra as well."

"What would cause her to consider a coup, then? To betray her own father?" Imari mused.

"She told me she would return to her father and see his response. I waited in Wahah for her. A month later she returned to me trembling. Fahim was more than pleased, and provided a special gift for King Richard to be presented by these men who had come to visit from Valkara. Later that evening, she overheard her father in his room consulting with someone. She acted as if she did not hear and barged in. What she saw struck fear into her heart. A man of all shadow stood with her father. When she entered the room, the shadowy figure disappeared into thin air. Fahim acted as if nothing out of the ordinary had just taken place."

"A shadow...that sounds like," said Imari.

"The Felled Ones," interrupted Khaleena.

"That can't be. It is just an ancient myth," Impatu said behind Imari.

"This is dark news indeed," Imari reflected.

"I have been searching for you ever since. I had heard rumors of you in the east, so I have been raiding out of fashion hoping to get your attention. Hoping you would come to me.

The truth is, Nabila believes something sinister is happening. She is worried that if her father remains on the throne, darkness could be brought to Islandia. So I came to ask for your help."

"Darkness has already fallen, sister. King Richard is dead. Poisoned, it would seem, by this special 'gift'," Imari said somberly.

"Then there is no time! We must return to Nabila and help her before Fahim can make his next move."

"We don't even know what that might be, let alone if Nabila can be trusted," Imbaku said, daring to make his voice known again.

"Imari, this is your decision. I will take my men to help Nabila, but this could be our chance. Nabila, I'm sure, would let us return to Khala. We could be home again, no longer on the run."

Imari soaked this in. He had waited a long time for this moment, to see his sister alive and to hear of Nabila. It all seemed like a dream. Dreams could be deceiving, however. This was a moment that would shape his future forever, and Imari knew it. He could potentially be reunited with his wife, Nabila, become Khosi over all Khala, and no longer live on the run. Or, it could end with a decisive betrayal he was all too familiar with. It hinged on this decision.

"Gather the rest of the Bomani. We will go to Sahra," Khosi Imari commanded.

3
GERALT

The spring winds filled the air with the fresh smell of pine trees. Geralt was on his daily task of overseeing the two royal daughters, Nara and Lydia. This afternoon was filled with the young Valkara princesses practicing their swordsmanship and spotting wild deer to later hunt in the western woods. Geralt, for many years, found these tasks demeaning until one evening when he approached King Doran about such "missions". It was in that conversation King Doran confessed to him that his most precious treasures were guarded by his most loyal servants. Geralt had been taken aback at first. He was, in fact, no more than a captured slave of war when Doran first found him. His peoples had been one of many tribes of the Lowland Hills. When his village was attacked for retribution of past raids, he was taken to serve in the royal palace. As fate would have it, he grew to be quite the warrior. So much so that no man in the royal guard could match him. This allowed him to join the ranks of the military. He had his detractors, sure. Many rose in opposition of him, but, like every man who ever tried, they all came to an end one way or another.

This was Geralt; no more no less, a warrior, a sword, and a quiet presence. That is why the king's words shocked him. He had done no political appeasements. He had not desired to get close to the king, in fact he avoided him when he could. Yet maybe that was why the king chose him. As his observations would reveal time and time again, the men most eager to be near the throne should be the ones kept far from it.

"Geralt, did you see that shot?" came the cry of Nara.

"Ah sis, I'm sure he wouldn't be impressed by your shoddy bow skills," quipped Lydia.

"I am sorry. I didn't see the shot, but I am sure it improved from yesterday's outing." Geralt was never good at jokes, but at times he attempted them. Even as this one left his mouth he was unsure if it would carry his intended meeting.

"Just what I need! You taking the side of Lydia," replied an exasperated Nara.

"Come, sis, you know I'm only pesterin' ya. We all know you're at least the hundredth best bowmen in the women's ranks," Lydia burst into an abrupt laugh.

Nara began to pout and stomp off much like twelve-year-old girls seemed to do, at least to Geralt. He enjoyed the days, now, where the girls talked less and trained more.

"Now come, Geralt, care to finally show me a real warrior's dual?" Lydia asked.

He let out a dismissive grunt that meant no.

"How many more times do I have to ask? We all know you're the greatest warrior in the kingdom, or so they say. You could at least try to prove it to me," She begged.

"The greatest warriors don't have to prove anything. Besides, you're beginning to sound like the whiny sister," He replied.

Her face scrunched in disgust.

"You know better than to believe that, Geralt!" In a blink she had pulled out a wooden training sword and darted at him. "Maybe I just need to force you to show me."

She leaped off a small boulder and sent a slash down at his head. He quickly sidestepped out of the way causing Lydia to crash onto the forest floor. He casually kicked her wooden sword aside as she rose to her feet covered in pine needles.

"You think you proved something?" Anger flushed into her cheeks.

"My only thought was how I can explain why the royal princess is covered in pine needles to the king?"

"Good show, good show," clapped the now returned Nara. Behind her stood two men, Jorn and Lokir, two of the king's head advisors.

"It seems the king has found ways to keep you busy, hasn't he, Geralt?" Jorn smirked.

"Yes, here soon the royal daughters may be our greatest warriors when you're done with them," Lokir chirped.

"Like you would know what it meant to even hold a sword," Lydia stated as she spat some blood from her mouth.

Geralt could see the flash of rage fill both men as quickly as it faded behind their carefully guarded mask.

"Politicians," he thought. These were the exact type of men who should remain far from the throne.

"We have important news to bring to the king. Would you care to escort us back to Valkara?" asked Jorn.

"Come, ladies, we have had enough leisure for one day." Geralt motioned for the sisters to follow him with his head.

The small company arrived under the shadow of Valkara. The city was encompassed by a wall that was built into the western formation of The Crowns, a ridge of mountains that blocked all of Islandia from the north of the island. The Crowns ran the length of Islandia and ended in the realm of Leviathanas. They also created a barrier east of Valkara, cutting them off from the Riverlands. The city of Valkara was nestled into a peaceful valley below the mountain range's shadow. Valkara, and the region surrounding, carried a mystical presence as if you had been raptured into a forested tale of strange creatures and snowy mountain peaks. Many of Valkara's people had created legends to suit the nature of this land. Geralt felt differently. It was a place that was charming as it could be, but like any other land it had its warts.

The fact was many of the stone walls and homes had not seen repairs for many winters. The order given was not to "destroy" the history of the legendary city. Geralt knew this "preservation" was due more to the coffers being dried up than with any historical sentiment on King Doran's part. Geralt was jolted from his reflection when a sharp whistle filled the air. Without realizing it, they had already reached the towering city gate. Jorn had whistled to let the gatekeepers know they desired to come in. With a few seconds delay, the gate flung open to receive the small band of palace officials and royalty.

"The city on lockdown?" Lokir inquired of the attending guard.

"Nah, sir, boss just said to keep an eye out today. Strange guests been afoot," replied the guard in a thick accent. Geralt secretly hated the accents that many in Valkara possessed. What the guard said, however, took him aback.

"Strange guests? What kind of strange guests?" grunted Geralt.

"Ahhh, now they wouldn't be strange if I knew them, ya see?" moaned the guard.

"Enough! We are wasting our time. Let's just see for ourselves, shall we?" Jorn said with restrained annoyance.

They swiftly moved through the bustling main road up to the Fortress, the home of King Doran. As they made their approach, the looming inner fortress wall greeted them. Many merchant booths were camped along the inner wall displaying the black and blue colors of Valkara. Many of the exotic exports could be found at these booths close to the kingly abode.

The small party passed under this second gateway after giving the royal signal via a horn blown. They stepped into the lush royal courtyard where the smell of finely trimmed grass and lush vegetation encompassed them. Different displays of statues stood honoring past kings and royal friends. In the middle of the courtyard was a large fountain with a large black ram as its centerpiece. From its snout came the flow of water into the pool below. On a bench next to the fountain sat King Doran and a darkly cloaked guest.

King Doran and his guest both turned to greet the returning men and the king's daughters.

"Ah, my sweet girls, you've returned!" smiled King Doran in his deep raspy voice. He was a large man built by years of conflict and toil, but the years as king had added some weight to that muscle. His warrior's face was scarred and pocketed by the life he had led as commander of the Valkaran armies. His red hair had streaks of grey and was braided in the ancient way of all Valkaran men. For a warrior, the creases on his face would show a man who smiled more than he frowned. That was King Doran, a hard warrior whose heartbeat was for those he would do anything to protect.

"I see my faith in you has not failed yet. Thank you for returning my daughters safely home."

Geralt gave a nod in reply, and Lydia and Nara rolled their eyes.

"As if we need a babysitter anymore, father. We are capable warriors," Lydia complained.

"Even the greatest warrior can fall to a lucky blow. These days there are many who would be willing to do us harm. That is why Geralt accompanies you."

Jorn let out a subtle cough.

"Yes, Jorn I see you sit, you too, Lokir," Doran grumbled.

"May I ask who our honored guest is?" prodded Lokir.

"Where are my manners? Men of Valkara, I introduce you to Balzara, a man who is new to my presence, but informs me of some interesting news."

Both Jorn and Lokir turned to look at each other.

"What news could that be?" inquired Jorn.

"Why should I speak for you, Balzara, go ahead and tell these men what you told me."

Balzar stood and bowed in greeting to each present. He still had not removed the hood from his head, and with good reason it seemed to Geralt. Underneath he could see a man who looked to have no hair and pale skin. His eyes were similar to that of a cat and glowed with a silver sheen. as such. He was somewhat bent over, but due to his deformities, Geralt could not peg his age. When he spoke it was almost like a hiss.

"Yes…but my guess is these two men would know already… They have come to tell you what I know."

"What would that be?" replied Lokir quizzically.

Balzara let out what might have been a laugh, but sounded more like a cough.

"What I have told the good king is the fate of Steward King Richard."

"Then you have come to share the same news, but you may not know the whole story," said Jorn. "My King, there is more that you must know."

"Is it about the king's sons? I was just about to tell him as you arrived," hissed Balzara.

"Yes, in fact, that is what we need to speak to the king about. I am curious how you know all this, and why you would want to help us? Who are you, and where do you come from?" asked Jorn sternly.

"I was sent from the king in the South. You may know him as Fahim." Balzara now stared at the two men as if he knew something the rest didn't. Both Jorn and Lokir squirmed visibly.

"Interesting how you could get that information so quickly when we had just returned from Sahra ourselves," Lokir's stance moved to that of the aggressor.

"Now, now, gentleman, no need to show hostility to a guest, especially one who has come to help," chided King Doran.

"Careful who you think are welcome guests, my king. I don't know if I would trust a man that looks a serpent!" spat Jorn.

"Enough! Now, what is this information about my sons? That is my real concern," boomed the king.

After some silence Lokir spoke up.

"My king, we believe Aiden and Brayan have been taken captive by Kingshelm. The blame of King Richard's death is being placed on them due to our past tensions."

The king was quiet for a moment. "So they would take my sons under the assumption that I would commit such a cowardly act! Do they not know the ways of the Valkarans?" The king's hot temper was beginning to show. "Muster every man including those in the Lowlands. We will march to Kingshelm and demand their release. Geralt, I want you to…"

"My lord," interrupted Jorn, "I do believe we should discuss this before we drive Valkara into a war."

"Ha! That would be your council, you weak politician. We will not bow to a false king on an empty throne. Who is the ruler now? A child? How long will we let some meadow frolicking boys tell us in the North how to rule?"

Geralt cleared his throat. "My King, I will do what you desire, however, if we are to go to war I do suggest we take our time and make preparations. If we take this fight to the Riverlands, we will not have the advantage."

"Now, there is some advice I can follow," said the king gruffly. His anger dissolving as quickly as it came.

"If there is to be a war, father, I want to join the shield-maidens!" blurted Lydia.

"I will not lose both daughter and son to these river folk. No, you will stay here."

"Father, you know I am capable," Lydia complained.

"Silence! Now go to your chamber. You are no warrior yet. Maybe next season, in the Lowlands, when I can join." Doran then motioned with his hand for the girls to go. Begrudgingly they obeyed without another protest. Doran then turned his attention back to Balzara.

"So, now that you have brought this to me, what is it you want?" he inquired.

Balzara bowed his head. "I will return to Fahim in the South. He will want to know if you wish to take action against Kingshelm. He, too, feels this a betrayal of trust, and an opportunity to rule independent from their influence. With your seal I can inform him of a possible alliance against the Riverlands."

"That would be a very strategic maneuver," Jorn said, "but would Fahim be so bold as to act on his promise?"

"Of all of us, you and Lokir might know," replied Balzar with a cold stare. A silence hung in the air as the two Valkarans locked eyes with Balzara.

"I don't understand your meaning," snarled Jorn.

"I just meant you are the ambassadors for Valkara. You two, of all people, should have a pulse on the happenings of the kingdom and its rulers."

"Tell Fahim if he wishes to have a say in the new Islandia, to meet us in the Riverlands. We can make their rivers run red together," Doran stated coldly.

"I will offer him this proposal, my lord." Balzara bowed and made as if to leave but stopped abruptly. "It is not my place to ask a king, but I have always wondered what a king should have to fear. So I ask, what are you afraid of King Doran?"

Geralt shifted his eyes to Doran to see how he would respond to such a question.

"I fear a Valkara without a son to sit on its throne," growled Doran. "Now go. I believe you have a message to deliver."

"Yes, indeed, my lord." Balzara bowed again and this time made his way to the fortress gate.

"Should I go prepare the men, my king?" asked Geralt.

"No, wait a moment. As for you, Jorn and Lokir, you can retire for the evening. I am sure your journey has worn on you," the king commanded cooly.

"Of course, my lord, we appreciate your kindness," Jorn replied. Both men bowed curtly and turned toward the Fortress chambers.

"I don't trust them," confided the king. "When they have settled in this evening, I want you to spy on them. Find out what they are withholding from me."

"Of course, my king. What would you have me do if I should find something?"

"Bring them to me. I will deal with them directly."

Geralt bowed. "It will be as you have spoken." Geralt turned to depart to his own chambers when the king's voice rang over his shoulder.

"Thank you, Geralt, you are the only one I trust."

Geralt stopped for a moment. "It is my duty." With that he continued forward, fighting back the memories of his capture, the face of the man who murdered his parents. The face of the king.

***

Geralt jerked awake from his sleep glancing around his chambers. The candle he had lit, now melted on its stand, was out. The evening cool had crept into his room and a soft breeze entered from the window to his left. The sun was now about to slip beneath the horizon leaving his room dimly lit. He arose from his bed with a grunt.

"I slept way too long," he thought to himself. He walked over to a water basin set in the corner of his room. Taking his hands, he dipped them in the basin and splashed the water onto his face then reached for a cloth to wipe away the excess water. When he raised his head he caught a glimpse of himself in the mirror above the basin. It was the weathered face of an old warrior. A scar stretched from his cheek down to his chin where grey stubble was beginning to grow. His slicked-back hair was missing the jet black of its youth. Like him, it looked worn and tired. His green eyes held a cold gaze. He gave his arms a stretch and spoke aloud to no one, "At least I still have the body of a warrior even if I have the face of an old man." He took a step and then experienced a cramp in his right leg. It dropped him to his knees. "Right...what was I saying," he chuckled in a mocking tone. After the cramping subsided, he made his way to the door. His long sword sheath hung on the wall. He proceeded to grab it and fling it over his shoulder.

"Let's hope I don't have to use this," he muttered to himself.

With that, he made his way through the stone halls of the king's Fortress. Paintings of past men of valor hung in the hall. Geralt's quarters lay in the king's guard section of the Fortress. Each hall represented great men and women of the past in their respective roles. He would need to cross the courtyard to reach the hall of diplomats, where Jorn and Lokir would reside.

As he recalled the events earlier, a continuing dread filled his gut. He could sense something was happening in Islandia, something foreboding. A sense of darkness was creeping in. Balzara, however "helpful" he had seemed, rubbed Geralt the wrong way. The comment he had made about Jorn and Lokir knowing what Fahim would do seemed to be more about a knowledge they shared than a mock of the two men. Jorn and Lokir had just arrived from the Day of Remembrance, so how would they know what Sahra was up to?

"But wait," Geralt said aloud as he stopped in his tracks. Now things weren't adding up. "If they had been in Kingshelm, they likely would have been apprehended by the guards there along with Aiden and Brayan. Besides that, they returned from the port in Thoras. A port that only sails to Sahra." Now he recalled them speaking of their journey there...

He turned to rush to the king's chambers. He dashed passed the Fortress servants in the colonnade entryway to the King's Hall. He flung the doors open to the Grand Throne Room. It was the familiar sight of timber beams lining the walls each showing a tale of valor by the men of Valkara lit by firelight. Eight columns stretched down the hall parallel with each other. An embroidered rug weaved with the colors of the kingdom sat between the columns. Like a jewel to a crown sat the throne of Valkara three steps higher than the rest of the room. It too was made of timber and carved into the shape of two rams as the armrests. The back of the throne was carved into two wings folded into each other. Geralt glanced around the Throne Room to spot anyone who could be hiding in the shadows.

Near the bed chambers of the king he could make out dancing shadows from a nearby torch. He could also hear the sound of indistinct voices. He crept to the right of the columns, keeping to the shadows. Four armed men stood facing outward from the king's door. Geralt was taken aback when he realized these where not the king's guard. Then he heard the distinct voice of Jorn.

"You see, Doran, your reign is done. You have ruled from emotion and allowed Kingshelm to rule us for too long. Those spawns of yours will be dead soon along with your bloodline. We have made our own allegiance with Fahim. He will join us in conquering Kingshelm, and we will build a new kingdom together over its ashes. We, of course, meaning Lokir and my new rule. We have watched as you sit in your Fortress day and night forgetting to look outside of your four walls. You are a line of wasted kings waiting and hoping for something that will never return. We see the faint hope you have for Eloy. It's over, Doran, a new era is here and we are going to make it."

Geralt didn't wait for another word. He leaped from the shadows pulling his long sword from its sheath. He sent a deadly blow to the unsuspecting guard. His sword caught the guard's neck and sent him tumbling to the ground. Before the other three could discover what happened, Geralt sent another upward slash sending the tip of his sword through the chin of the next man.

The other two had recovered from their shock and stood to counter his next blow. He feigned a slash to the right bringing the man's guard up too quickly leaving his right flank exposed. Geralt's real strike caught him center mass creating a gash from rib to hip, nearly taking off his leg. The final man left sent a furious thrust at Geralt. Using the momentum of the collapsing guard he just incapacitated, Geralt pushed him into the oncoming thrust. The guard's sword pierced his comrade which caused him to let out a terrible shriek. Both men went tumbling backward and collapsed on the ground.

Geralt strolled over to the now-dead guard sprawled over his companion. Fear filled the man's eyes as he saw his murderer approach. "Mercy... Mercy," he began to moan. Without a word, Geralt sent his blade through the chest cavity of both men. The faint cry for mercy faded along with the light from the guard's eyes. He took a moment to observe the clothing of the bodies. They looked to be disloyal Valkarans. Jorn and Lokir likely convinced them of their place in this "new era". Their dreams of power now dead with them.

He threw the doors open. Both Lokir and Jorn threw a glance toward the unexpected visitor.

"I told you four would not be enough," complained Lokir.

"I thought the toxin we slipped into his room would have lasted longer," shrugged Jorn turning his full attention to Geralt. "We were hoping to convince you to our side when all this was said and done. Your prowess as a warrior could help us form a new kingdom. One, I might add, without the murderer of your family." Jorn had a hint of solace on his face.

Geralt was taken aback. How did Jorn know that? The king would not have confided in these men.

"So what do you say, Geralt? Want to help us?" suggested Lokir.

Geralt, for a moment, wasn't sure what to do. They were right. This was his moment to get revenge if there ever was one. Before he could reply, the booming voice of Doran broke the silence.

"Enough of this treachery! Lucky for you, Balzara left me a parting gift." King Doran reached beside his bed and pulled out a sword. The hilt was a dark steel with a navy blue grip. The sheath had dark runes and symbols on it. He proceeded to draw the blade. It was like nothing Geralt had ever seen. The blade was black as night, but the edges had a faint glow to them. A sickly mist seemed to radiate from it.

"Is that one of the lost blades of The Founders?" Jorn stammered.

Doran smirked. "A blade once lost, now found." With that, he bull-rushed Lokir. Geralt, noticing Jorn's distraction, took advantage. He rushed at him and sent a flying slash his way. Jorn reacted at the last second and deflected with his own blade. Both men took a swing at each other, knocking both blades back. Geralt took the brief pause to glance at the king and Lokir. It looked as if Lokir was lost. The king's first swing cleaved the tip off of Lokir's sword. Lokir, recognizing he had no defense, kept dodging the slashes thrown at him, but he could not keep that up for long.

Geralt's observation was broken when Jorn sent a slash to his left. He deflected the blow and sent a counter strike to Jorn's waist. Like a cat, Jorn side-stepped the attack and hurled a thrust at Geralt's shoulder. Geralt deflected it, but the edge of Lokir's sword grazed his shoulder.

"It is not too late, Geralt, you can join us. Why fight for this man who took everything from you."

"You are a better swordsman than I imagined," Geralt panted ignoring his suggestion.

Both men turned their attention when they heard a shriek. Lokir's left hand lay on the ground next to him. He had been backed into a corner, and there was nowhere for him to go. It was over. With an enraged growl, Doran lifted the sword above his head and sent it crashing down onto Lokir's uplifted blade.

The sword passed through metal and flesh as if it had met no resistance. Lokir was rent in two. Geralt turned to face Jorn. The man stood dumbfounded at his partner's death. He sent a testing slash that shook him from his stupor. Jorn parried the blow and sent his own strike in return. Geralt blocked it, but could feel the strength of his left arm fading with the flow of blood.

"Geralt, catch," came the voice of the king.

He turned to see the dark blade flying in his direction. In one move he blocked the slash Jorn sent his way with his left hand and caught the incoming sword with his right. While locking Jorn's blade with his own, he swiftly sent a slash with the dark sword at Jorn's sword arm. It came sweeping down cleaving the arm at the elbow. Jorn rolled to the ground with a shout of pain.

"Very good, Geralt, now be done with him," ordered Doran.

Geralt stepped toward the shriveled man. Suddenly, he smelled smoke, and before he could react, there was a flash in the room. When his vision came to, it was only King Doran and him. Geralt starred at the sword in his hand. There was a hum of energy that was running up his arm. He thought about the power he was holding. Power to defeat any foe. He looked up at the king who was intently staring at him. He truly trusted Geralt. He had placed his life in his hands intentionally. To test his loyalty? For an instant the thought crossed his mind. Without a word he tossed the sword back to the king.

"I believe this belongs to you."

"Once again, you have proven your loyalty to me." The king kicked the slumped half of Lokir, "What a Valkan mess this is."

"What should we do about Jorn?" Geralt asked.

"Let him slither back to his new master, Fahim. We will get our chance at him again someday."

"What should we do from here? Should we reconsider the march on Kingshelm?"

The King stopped and with a dark fire in his eyes said, "No. Before you arrived these animals revealed to me that they have taken Lydia and Nara and sent them with some men as trade to Kingshelm. We will march on them and demand my family back, and if not, we will have war."

4

TITUS

It had been a month. A month since that dreaded day when Titus had witnessed his father, King Richard, die in agony. It had been a whirlwind ever since. He had been thrust into a seat of authority long before he thought it would be his time. His days had become full of council meetings, discussions on how to proceed, and what to do with Valkara's sons. Titus had no answers before his father's passing, and now, in the midst of the fire, he felt even more lost.

The sound of trumpets blaring jolted him from his thoughts. As if he had returned from another world, he realized he was sitting on the throne surrounded by a host of people. He had felt this way many times in the last few weeks, lost in another world passing through this one in blurry scenes.

"All rise to proclaim our new Steward King," came a voice behind him.

The host of people stood to their feet in silence. Two men approached Titus on either side. One held the crown of Eloy, the same crown that dawned his father's head. In the other man's hand was Morning's Dawn, the blade crafted by The Founders of Islandia. A sword forged by the line from which Eloy descended.

Eli then stood before Titus who was seated on the throne. "With this crown, do you, Titus, swear to uphold justice and peace so long as Eloy does not reign on his throne?"

"I will," Titus mustered in his best kingly voice.

Eli plucked the crown from the royal guard's hand and gently placed it on Titus' brow.

"With this sword, do you promise to keep the darkness at bay and only use it in dire need?"

"I swear," the new Steward King responded.

"Then, as the elder of the council and with all the witnesses here today, I proclaim you Steward King of Islandia. May you reign till Eloy's return."

The room erupted in a chant of "May he return soon!"

Eli then bowed, "Now, Steward King Titus, arise. May you rule well."

Titus arose to his feet and unsheathed Morning's Dawn. A light flashed as it was being drawn. A sight Titus had only heard tales of was revealed before his eyes. The blade was a dark silver, engraved in the ancient language of The Founders. The edges of the blade hummed with a brilliant light, like the sun's rays peaking over a crested hill. The crowd stood in awe at a sight not seen since King Richard's coronation.

"I promise by the light of Eloy and by the edge of this blade, we will have peace in the Kingdom again," Titus sheathed the blade and turned to nod to Eli.

"We welcome all in attendance to enjoy a feast of celebration on this historic day. Eat and be merry for we have much to prepare for in the days ahead!" Eli proclaimed to the crowd. The host of people began to disperse to the various exits no doubt wanting to be placed in the finest seats first.

Titus turned to exit behind the throne when Eli grabbed his arm, "A word, my lord."

Both men descended from the throne into a discreet hallway.

"Have you decided how you would like to proceed with the two sons we have locked up?" Eli inquired impatience evident in his tone.

"I have not. It's something I don't want to be hasty to act upon. It could tip us into full scale war."

"We are already in a full-scale war. The formalities just haven't happened yet."

"Are you aware of something I am not?" leered Titus. "If so, do tell." As if on cue Lancelin appeared from the throne room doorway.

"Am I interrupting something, my lord?" Lancelin asked.

"Nothing that cannot be discussed later," Titus responded with a clear hint for Eli to drop the subject.

Eli bowed in frustrated submission, "I will join the other guests and await your presence, my king."

Titus dismissed him with a curt nod.

"Thanks for the help getting out of that one," sighed Titus.

"Anytime, friend," Lancelin said. His smirk quickly faded when he saw the distress hanging over Titus.

"What am I to do, Lancelin? If I take any action against Aiden and Brayan it will surely drag us into conflict with Valkara. To leave them unpunished would present to The Five Kingdoms that I am a weak king, not ready to make the hard decisions which in turn could create even more rebellion."

"It may be too late to stop it alread," Lancelin said with an unusual firmness.

"What do you mean? What news have you heard?" Titus asked.

"There has been a report of rebellion in the South. There is a group that has risen against Fahim. Leviatanas scouts have also informed me of stirrings in the North. Apparently there was an assault on King Doran."

"Is the world falling apart?" Titus was pacing now. "It's as if someone was setting this all up. Any action against the North would be seen as a retaliation."

"My informants tell me it was a splinter group of Northmen who wanted Valkara to themselves, so your fears of a setup may be misguided. However, if you want my opinion, we must act."

"Define act, Lancelin," Titus' gaze was stern as he pondered his friend's words.

"For this not to spiral out of control, we must take the fight to Valkara. Show them that this behavior is not acceptable and the kingdom should remain together. I am not suggesting a battle. I think a show of force will be enough. Plus, we have two bargaining chips." He gestured to the chambers behind him where the Valkaran sons were held.

"We? Levaitanas means to join us?" excitement filled Titus' eyes.

"Yes, that is why I wanted to speak with you. My plan is to return to father. I will speak with him as best I can in his state. We will muster a force to join you. Then, we can march against Valkara together."

Titus embraced Lancelin, "You don't know what this means to me, friend."

A grin crossed Lancelin's face, "Don't thank me yet. I still have to convince father, and that is not a walk in the meadowlands."

"Either or, I finally feel confident on how we should act. For that, I am thankful."

"With your permission, my king, I will ride to Levaitanas as soon as possible." Lancelin gave a half mocking bow.

"Would you stop! With no crowd around I am still your friend, there is no need for formalities, and yes, quit stalling. If we are to win a kingdom I'll need to still be a young man by the time you get back."

"With that encouragement, I will be on my way."

With one more half bow, and his infamous grin, Lancelin departed to the doorway. Titus turned his thoughts to the feast that was awaiting him. He made his way down a few winding hallways until he could see the flickering of candlelight and silhouettes dancing on the walls. Shouts and cheers echoed down to where he stood. The smell of ale and meat cooking could not be missed. He took a deep breath and entered into the room. His entrance was instantly met with a toast by one of the high council members, Jorath.

"A toast to the new king!" he shouted with a slight slur.

"A few pints in already," Titus thought to himself.

The Dining Hall erupted in a cheer, "All hail the king."

They returned to their merriment in a blink. The room was filled with music, cheers, laughing, and more than a few intoxicated guests. Titus glanced around to find his seat. At the end of the royal banquet table sat an empty seat. The king's seat. His father's seat. Now his seat. He slipped through a crowd of guests giving his royal courtesies and gratitudes. When he finally reached the chair he slouched down in an attempt to dodge any unneeded conversation.

To his left sat Elorah, general of the Riverlands military. Typically he dwelled at the Western Watch, but due to the ceremony he had been called to Kingshelm. He was close to middle age, his hair cut trim for practicality and speckled with grey. A scar ran from his left temple down to his cheek and he had a stern face that left him looking upset most of the time.

"Greetings, my king," Elorah nodded as Titus took a seat, "I see you're hoping to ignore as much of this as I am."

Titus gave a curt nod in response. The truth was he wanted to be as far away from here as possible. To be out of this seat that did not belong to him and chuck this whole cursed conflict into Lake Leviathan.

"Finally you could make it, dear king," came Eli's voice to his right. Titus turned to face him.

"I have just been informed of more news," Eli whispered as he sat in the chair next to him, "You will need to know this too, Elorah." Elorah maneuvered to face Eli, half interested.

"Go on then," he snorted.

"A messenger has just reached Kingshelm and informed me that the North is on the move."

Suddenly both Titus and Elorah shifted in their seats listening intently.

"How would you know this before me?" Elorah asked, "My men would send word as soon as they spotted anything."

"Lets just say there are some working for me that are deeper into Northern territory than the Western Watch, and not soldiers."

"I have a lot of catching up to do in my knowledge of how Islandia is run, apparently," stated Titus.

"Some things King Richard left up to my discretion," Eli responded.

"In any case, Valkara is on the move, and we should act accordingly. If you want my advice, we should strike first. Hit them on the road. If they don't expect an attack, then we can decimate their forces. They will have no option but to give up this rebellion or whatever they are calling it." Elorah suggested.

"I believe they are coining it as a break for independence," Eli turned to Titus, "but regardless, Elorah's advice does make a bit of sense."

Before Titus could respond, their conversation was interrupted by a soldier approaching Elorah.

"Sir, the Western Watch is reporting in," informed the soldier.

"Well, go on then, report."

"It, uhhh, seems that a group of Valkara breakaways have offered us a gift sir."

"What kind of gift?" Titus asked.

"They have given us the daughters of Doran. As hostages, I believe, were their intentions."

"Great, thanks for informing us of your opinion," Elorah snapped, "Now go and tell a messenger that they are not to be harmed. We will be there as soon as we can."

The man, without another word, rushed off to deliver the order.

"This day keeps getting worse," Titus slumped in his seat, "This will only aggravate Valkara even more."

"May I speak freely, my king?" Elorah asked.

"Yes, although I doubt I want to hear it," sighed Titus.

"We are at war. Whether it looks like it right now or not has no bearing on the reality. If we do not act we will be in a bloody conflict here in the Riverlands. If we do act we can take the fight to them. It is as simple as that." Elorah was standing now, and a few bystanders were staring at them. He pulled at his tunic.

"Forgive me, my lord, I just feel this would be the best course of action."

The onlookers returned to their conversation, but with an obvious eye on the three men.

"Way to keep that discreet, Elorah," Eli said with rolled eyes.

"He's right," Titus bemoaned. "I hate it, but he's right. We need to muster the forces here at Kingshelm. Gather all the men we can spare and take them to the Western Watch. We can create a plan from there."

Both men stood in surprise as if they had expected a different answer.

"You have spoken wisely, my king. I will gather the men as quickly as I can." Elorah bowed and hurried over to some guards standing watch. He motioned with indistinguishable commands and they began to hurriedly scatter across the room.

"It seems we have no time to waste. I will inform the rest of the council, my king." Eli nodded and went to leave.

"Wait a moment, Eli," halted Titus with a hand, "I am going with Elorah to the Western Watch."

"My king, I advice against..."

"It's already decided," interrupted Titus, "I need to see if we can reason with Valkara. Doran's daughters may give me some indication of the situation in Valkara. It seems there is more than meets the eye in Doran's court."

"Wise words, my lord. Who shall stay in your stead?"

"I will have you watch over the throne. I grant you the power to make the decisions you need. Also you should know Lancelin is working to gather Leviatanas forces to join us. I fear I can't wait for him, but if he should return soon, send him on to the Western Watch."

"It will be done, my king." With that Eli was off.

"What have we started? Father, what would you do?" Titus pondered. Silence was his only companion.

***

The next morning, Titus awoke just as the sun was peeking into his window. He had decided to stay in his room for now. It was sufficient for his needs, and the thought of staying in his father's chambers seemed wrong to him. He went to a table that carried a few personal items. He slipped on the ring his father had always worn. It had the face of a lion cub pressed into a gold ring. Next he slid over his neck, the necklace his mother had given him as a young boy. It was a silver seven pointed star pendant. Her words echoed in his head.

"Someday, my love, you will have to rule," Queen Eva laid the necklace around Titus' neck.

"But Eloy will return before then, surely? Right mother?" Titus was confused on why she thought he would ever be king.

"I fear he may be gone longer than any of us think." She looked down at Titus thoughtfully, "Being a ruler is not easy, my love. There will be times when you won't know what to do. Do you remember the importance of the seven pointed star?"

"Yes, of course, mother! It always hangs in the sky day and night. It is the compass that we all use to find our way." Titus grinned knowing this was the answer his mother was looking for.

"Very good. That is exactly why I gave you this pendant. There are going to be days in the future where you will not know the way to go. This necklace is to remind you to look for the star. It will show you what path you should follow."

"The star? But mother, how is a star to help me to make important decisions?"

"I don't mean the physical star, my boy. You will know when the time comes what path leads to peace. Even if it is difficult, don't run from that road. It is the only one that can lead you back home."

Titus sighed aloud, stirring himself from his memory.

"Your words ring true, Mother, although I don't know what star to follow. In my heart something seems off, but it feels as if this path is the one set in stone."

He gripped the pendant in memory of her, then tucked it under his tunic. He grabbed Morning's Dawn, wrapped it around his waist, and proceeded to the armory. The Castle was already bustling with life, armored soldiers prepping in every manner for the task ahead. The Elite Calvary unit, headed by Elorah himself, were grooming their steeds for the two-day ride to the Western Watch. Their horses shining in polished armor, hooves tearing at the dirt in anxious expectation. They could sense the unease and excitement that filled men before battle.

Titus weaved his way past several groups of soldiers who either greeted him as "my king" with a polite bow or tried to avoid him altogether.

"I am king now," a thought that still didn't seem real to him.

He soon reached the inner chamber of the armory. It was filled the with frantic motion of soldiers scurrying from place to place as if in a controlled panic. Titus searched and found Elorah giving orders to two of his captains amid all of the commotion. As Titus approached, Elorah gave his men a nod of dismissal and turned to greet him.

"Good morning, King Titus."

"Good morning, general. I see preparation is in full swing."

"Yes, we hope to leave by mid-morning, my king. I also hear you are planning to join us? I don't suppose I can dissuade you?"

"You would be correct in your assumption," Titus said.

"I thought not, in that case I have made arrangements."

"Arrangements? How so?"

"As active general I do hope you take my advice on this, but I believe it prudent, with your lack of combat experience, that we pull some unorthodox tactics."

"Go on. You've got me curious."

"I believe it wise that we create a decoy if we are to ride into battle. Simply put, you riding out in your gold plated armor with that helmet that screams 'kill me, I am the king' would not be advantageous to your health or our kingdom."

"Alright, you have my attention. I hate that helmet by the way." Titus leered at it hanging just a few feet away.

"Well, I am glad you're not too attached. Here is my plan; you will dress as a standard soldier in my calvary unit. I have heard of your skill as a rider, and it should be adequate to keep up with us. We will then have another captain dress up in your armor and lead a separate ground units force. While they draw in Valkara's army, we shall circle behind them undetected and smash into the rear of their forces. They should route quickly seeing as they have minimal calvary to counter us."

"I like the plan. But what does it say of a king that hides while another man takes on the risk of losing his own life? I can't stand by and let someone die just so I'm not a target!"

"Of course you can. You are the king. Each and every man in this army will give his life for yours. I have already selected the captain and he's prepared to serve and die, if need be, for his kingdom and king."

"But that is not the purpose of a king! He serves the people, not the other way around."

"My lord, I ask that you understand as king you must make these hard decisions. Yes, this captain may die. His family will mourn him. There will be those who criticize you, maybe even mock you. That is your burden, not for everyone to love you, but to do what is best for the kingdom. You dying will throw us into chaos, and chaos will destroy the fragile kingdom we are holding together right now."

Titus was silent for a moment. He clutched the pendant under his tunic.

"May I meet this captain?" he finally replied.

"I don't know if that's wise," Elorah stammered in a bit of shock.

"If you want me to follow your plan, then I must meet him. Those are my terms."

Elorah whistled, then called out, "Dios, the king wishes to speak to you."

A captain, who could not have been older than thirty and who had been giving orders to his men some twenty yards away, approached them. He knelt before Titus.

"At your service, my lord."

"Please stand," motioned Titus with his hand. "I don't have words to say. What you're willing to do goes beyond valor."

"I believe in this kingdom, sir, and I believe in you," the young captain replied.

"Know this, no matter what happens, your family will be looked after. If you are to make a great sacrifice, I promise it will not go without the highest honor."

The young captain smiled, "Thank you, my lord, you don't know what that means. To know my family is safe is all I need."

"You are dismissed, soldier," came the command from Elorah.

The young man stood, and with another huge grin, bowed and made his way back over to his men.

"Hope is a dangerous thing, my king," Elorah scolded.

"Hope is all we have, general. If we lose that we might as well quit now."

"How optimistic…if you will excuse me, my lord, I shouldn't delay any longer if we are to depart on time." Elorah motioned to some young men, "See that he is fit with proper armor."

"See you on the road," Titus said as Elorah began to make his departure.

"Yes, see you then, my king."

The young men scurried to grab the different plates of armor. They first sized Titus for a coat of chainmail. Finding a size that would fit, they began placing the plate armor. The gauntlets were a basic silver polish along with his bracers. The chest plate was also a steel base, with a faint etching of a roaring lion. The greaves followed suit. Lastly, they placed a purple and gold trimmed tunic over him. In the middle was the symbol of the roaring lion cub of his family. He made his way over to a mirror to inspect the young men's work.

Here was the king, not a soldier. He was a toned, but untested, youth. His light brown hair recently trimmed on the sides leaving some length on the top. A faint shadow of a beard starting to come through on his handsome face. His light green eyes burned with a fire to prove himself, but to who? His father? He was gone. To his men? Like Elorah said, he would have to let some of them down. To himself? He didn't even know how to go about that question. Was it to Eloy? He had never met the man yet his kingdom was under Titus' authority. If he was even still alive what would he come back to? Something inside of Titus knew that he was still out there, still coming back. He was determined to give him a kingdom intact on his return.

Lastly, he was handed his helmet. It wasn't the gaudy one he hated. It was simply made. Steel, with a slight nose guard and two guards that came down past his cheeks. Etched on each side was that familiar lion. A line from the outer parts of the nose guard stretched to form another layer on the top of the helmet. Engraved on these lines were the words: "A lion's roar they hear. They fear his cry. They fear to die. They know the men of Eloy are here."

Observing the words Titus put the helmet on with a shrug, "I guess we ought to go prove those words."

5

IMARI

S and. That's what the last week had consisted of. Since being reunited with Khaleena and hearing the news of Nabila's potential coup, the past few days had been very uneventful. Crossing the Khala desert by the unknown paths had caused their journey to double in length. The rolling dunes were a treacherous path to any unfamiliar with their ways. This journey had given Imari time to think, to process all that had happened to him.

Tensions with Imbaku had died down since Khaleena's return. She had always been a calming presence between the two of them. It was strange, however, the sister that had returned to them was a different woman than the one they'd known. Her warrior exterior and bravado played well to the Bomani and Masisi, but Imari saw that there were scars and wounds not visibly seen, things done that she may never want to share with them. Imari might ask her about them one day when all this was over. That, he was hoping, would be sooner rather than later.

The sun was a little lower than midday as their caravan of 200 reached the final stretch to Wahah. It was the cratered edge of the Endless Wastes that loomed over them. To the west lay the expanse of the Southern Sea. This road was known as the Causeway to the Wastes. It also was an indication that Wahah was close.

"Holt!" came the order from Khaleena. She raised her spear in the air as a physical command. All the Masisi warriors stopped in their tracks.

"What is it, sister?" inquired Imari as he strolled up next to her.

"This is a dangerous area. Raiders set up ambushes here often, and there are dangerous foes to our cause that we should concern ourselves with here."

"We should be fine with this many armed men, right?" Imbaku chimed in.

"Nevertheless, we need to keep our guard up from here on out. We are in enemy territory. What I truly fear more than raiders is Fahim's spies," she trailed off.

That instilled a solemn fear in them all. If Fahim were to find out who was in their party, he would send a large force after them, potentially even the Sycar. They journeyed on until the sun set over the crater's edge above them.

"We should make camp tonight," suggested Imbaku. "We will reach Wahah in the morning."

"No, we need to keep going. If we stop now we are still exposed," Khaleena countered.

"By the time we get to Wahah it will be late. Where will we find a place to stay for all the men and supplies?" Imbaku argued.

"They will need to stay on the edge of the city, regardless. If we go marching in with them, Wahah will think us coming to conquer it," informed Khaleena. "Brother, you are Khosi here, what do you say?"

Imari contemplated the decision. Both had valid points.

"Imbaku is right, it has been a long day. I would rather we walk in knowing the situation in daylight than approach Wahah blind."

"Thank you, Imari. For once we agree," Imbaku said with a half mocking grin.

"Fine, Khosi, but I will send the Masisi to set up a parameter. I don't want any prying eyes on our camp. Especially now that we are on a main road."

"I will assist them. I agree, sister, we should not make it easy for Fahim to find us. That also means knowing our terrain." This was Imbaku's attempt at resolution with Khaleena, or so Imari guessed.

All three departed to their respective assignments. Imari went to announce the news to the Bomani. He could see the relief in their faces knowing they would not need to march in the dead of night. He assisted them in setting up the tents. After a few hours, the camp was prepped for the evening. The stars had filled the sky in a vast array. The desert was a lonely place, but in solitude there can be found extravagant beauty. The star-filled sky brought Imari back to that fateful night of his wedding.

"Nabila, my love, we are finally together," Imari was grinning ear to ear.

Nabila stood before him, her back turned, in a thin white gown. She turned her head with a rueful smile.

"Now, what will we do with our time together?" a seductive smile filled her face.

"Here, let me show you." Imari leaned in, embracing her with a kiss. The pent-up passion of months bursting forth in a moment.

Imari soaked in the memory, one he had not let himself drift to in many years. The idea that they soon could be reunited, that maybe, just maybe, Nabila had no part in what happened to his family were dangerous thoughts. Ones Imari had dismissed long ago. Yet here they came, creeping in again. He was stirred from his memories when Impatu planted himself down beside him pulling him back to the present where he was gathered with the others around a fire.

"Am I disturbing you, Khosi?" Impatu seemed to have something weighing on his mind.

"No, young warrior. What is it? I can see something concerns you. It's painted on your face."

"It's just…how do we know we aren't walking into our deaths? I mean we have no assurances that Princess Nabila will be any different than her father."

Imari was troubled to see Impatu concerned. Had he not thought this through? Was he leading them all to death?

"Do not worry, Impatu. Khaleena has spoken with her. If she wanted my family dead, she would have done it by now."

"That's the thing, Khosi. Every great hunter knows you don't kill one prey in haste when you can have the herd with patience. What if she used Khaleena to bring you all here?"

"Eeesh, Impatu, I swear, when did you become a wise old man? It is true we could have made a grave mistake, but something tells me we have not."

"You know I trust you, Khosi, just know, some of the Bomani have doubts."

Imari placed a hand on Impatu's shoulder, "I hope I never lose the trust of such a wise friend."

Impatu's smile stretched across his face, "Friend? Thank you, Khosi, you are too kind."

Before Imari could respond, a Masisi warrior approached them from behind. His face covered in tribal piercings in line with Masisi custom.

"Khaleena wishes to see you," his deep voice bellowed from the dark.

"Must be important if she didn't come herself," jested Imari.

The Masisi warrior only grunted in reply.

"Their people were bred without jokes we have found," Impatu said with a grin.

The man glared at Impatu. His demeanor showing his impatience.

"Lead the way," Imari gestured to the Masisi warrior.

They traveled in silence through the camp, passing Bomani huddled around their traditional fires. Men glanced up disinterestedly from their conversations as the two men passed by.

"No panic in the camp at least," thought Imari to himself. The camp had been built in a giant semi-circle off the main road with the Southern Sea to its back. The Masisi created a parameter on the outskirts. In the middle of the semi-circle rested Khaleena's tent.

The men approached the red canopy flap of the tent that lay open and ducked into the dimly lit entry. Khaleena stood hunched over a makeshift table, parchments scattered out in front of her. In the corner stood two Masisi warriors and a slouched man in a black cloak.

"He's here," grunted the soldier as they stood in the entrance.

Khaleena turned around with a look of frustration, "I told you we should have traveled straight to Wahah." She was pointing at the slouched man.

"Who is our esteemed guest?" Imari asked.

"This is no time for jokes. Our "guest" is an elite Sahra spy, a part of the Sycar branch."

Hearing the word Sycar made Imari's blood run cold. "So what does this mean?"

"It means," Khaleena responded with a pause, "It means we are in big trouble. Sahra must be on high alert already if the Sycar are all the way out here. It means Fahim may soon know we are coming, AND," she said drawing out the word, "getting into Wahah unseen may be close to impossible."

"That is a lot of bad scenarios, but you did miss the bright side of this," Imari retorted.

"Which is?" Khaleena said rolling her eyes.

"We would have walked into Wahah blind to this reality, but now we can prepare our approach knowing Fahim will be watching."

"I have considered this, and that is what I have been mulling over. How we can get into the city unseen?"

"For all we know, Fahim has yet to detect us. We have caught his spy," Imbaku stepped out from the shadows behind Imari.

"Wise words, brother. How can we be certain that Fahim even knows of our presence?" Imari asked.

"He may not know at the moment, but a missing Sycar will not escape his attention. He will know something is amiss." A cold fear could be seen in Khaleena's eyes, "We must move now. There is no time to wait. We will tell the men to move to the outskirts of Wahah in the morning. We must go tonight."

"Is that necessary?" Imbaku said with an appeasing gesture.

"I would rather arrive in Sahra with my head still on my shoulders with extra caution, then die by taking the risk of staying put."

"I agree, precaution cannot hurt. We move in an hour. The rest of the men will arrive and set up camp outside town tomorrow on the Khosi's order," Imari commanded.

"Tell the Masisi the same on their chief's command," Khaleena motioned with her head to one of the men guarding the dead Sycar warrior.

Imbaku ducked under the tent opening to give the order when Imari followed him grabbing him by the arm, "Brother, grab Impatu and inform him that he is to go with us. I need men I can trust."

"Only him?" Imbaku said with a raised eyebrow, "I know at least half the group of Bomani with greater skill than young Impatu."

"Yes, him. I said men I trust, not great warriors. Between you, Khaleena, and myself we should be able to handle any small force."

With a respectful nod, Imbaku went to find Impatu and inform the captains of their assigned task in the morning. A few minutes later the small band was assembled consisting of

Imari, Khaleena, two of her trusted Masisi warriors, Imbaku, and Impatu. They gathered on the edge of the camp with the hopes of not drawing too much attention to themselves. They packed their small number of belongings onto their camels and set off down the road.

The evening grew dark with cloud cover, but every once in awhile you could catch a glimpse of the dazzlingly display of stars hidden above. A few hours down the road, Imari began to notice small fires off to the side of the road in the distance.

"Are these other travelers, as well?" Imari asked Khaleena.

"Yes, many come via this road to reach Wahah and ultimately Sahra. They are pilgrims going to the great city."

"Pilgrims?" Impatu inquired.

"Do they not teach the young men any history now? Eissssh. I suppose you've barely grown up in Khala. Yes, the great city of Sahra is believed by many in the south to house the tomb of Yeshu, the great king before The Founders," replied Khaleena.

"What made him so great?" curiosity now gripping the young Impatu.

"He is believed to be the father of Eloy's family tree. As the legend goes, he and a Founder woman named Saria were the first to marry between the two peoples. All parties saw this as a sign of peace between them. Because they carried the bloodlines of both The Founders and Islandia, it was the consensus that their line should rule," instructed Imari.

"Ahhh yes, but there was another line of men from the North, the Valkara, who felt excluded from this union. You see, they too were native to Islandia, but had no ties to this marriage, so of course they opposed it," Khaleena added.

"This has created tensions between Kingshelm and Valkara even to this day," Imari continued.

"A war that still sends ripples to our own time, as you can clearly see," chimed in Khaleena.

"I understand the issues with Valkara, but what of Sahra? If Sahra and The Founders were so close, why would Fahim seek to betray Richard?" Impatu asked, with confusion in his voice.

"Many years have since past, wars, alliances, politics, not least the first great war fought between Kingshelm and Sahra for our people's freedom. With the history and bloodshed, the marriage of Yeshu and Saria faded into the background," Imari said soberly.

"It also doesn't help that as The Founders began to gain more and more power, Sahra's diminished," stated Khaleena.

"Yes, that will do it too," Imari said as he and Khaleena turned and smirked at each other.

"Sometimes the greatest loves, become the bitterest enemies," he added as his smile faded.

"If we are done with the history lesson, we might want to focus on what is ahead of us," came the voice of Imbaku. "Look up ahead."

In the darkness, the party could barely make out a line of torches that seemed to stretch across the road. As they closed the distance, they could make out the shapes of men wrapped in all black, the torch light reflecting off of silver masks.

"Sycar!" came the panicked voice of Khaleena, "Get off the road now!"

Before they could respond, a command came from one of the Sycar, "Holt! Wait there, travelers."

Imari could make out ten of them approaching.

"What do we do?" Imari looked to Khaleena, but she was panic-stricken.

"Stay calm. They likely will not recognize us," Imbaku said calmly.

Before they could make a move, the Sycar were already before them. One man grabbed the reigns of Imari's camel.

"Awfully late for a group of travelers on the road," the masked man holding the reigns stated. His mask carried a golden tint differentiating him from the others.

Another behind him followed with, "We are missing a man from the direction you came. Have you seen him?"

Imari stood regal, not showing the growing anxiety in his chest, "No, my khosi, we have not."

"Khosi? This is Sahra, not Khala, address us as we are, your sultas."

The rest of the men chuckled behind him.

"Sorry, Sulta, forgive my foreign tongue. We are just road weary and desiring to make Wahah by daybreak."

"It is a risk traveling the road so late. Would hate for any harm to come to you," replied the man holding the reigns. Imari was unsure if it was a veiled threat.

"We will heed your wise counsel. We have traveled far and wished to reach Wahah by morning." Imari was beginning to sweat.

The man stopped to examine him for a brief moment, then became disinterested. He began to motion with his hand, but jerked to a halt.

"What's wrong with her?" he was staring at Khaleena.

She was hiding her face behind her cloak, but beneath she was violently shaking. When the man's attention drew to her she froze.

"You have something to hide?" The man let go of the reigns and approached her camel. As he reached her he tugged at the cloak, "Show me your face," his voice grew firm. He gave the cloak another tug. The Masisi next to Khaleena took a step forward with their mounts.

"Did I tell you to move?" barked the Sycar, "Now take off that cloak!" He gave it one more yank to reveal Khaleena's face, now calmed, but Imari could still see the fear in her eyes.

"I…I am sorry, my Sulta, I am ill and did not want to expose you to it," she lied.

The man took a step back and spat, "Reeking Shuka. You pilgrims all seem to carry some new sickness." He had appeared to buy her story when Imari noticed his gaze fall to one of the Masisi's feet. On the warrior's leather sandal was a stain of blood. He acted as if he had not seen it, but Imari knew they were in trouble.

"Search them," the masked man commanded to the rest of the Sycar.

Without a word, they began to order each of them to dismount and began rummaging through their supplies. Some of the men motioned to the rations they carried, and not so discreetly, pocketed them for themselves.

As a Sycar approached Khaleena she warned him, "You do not want to get near me or my things. I fear you may become infected."

The man looked toward the Sycar who's golden mask distinguished himself as the leader. The leader motioned to Khaleena, letting his man know he was not excused. The Sycar soldier turned in dismay and motioned for Khaleena to dismount as he grabbed her reigns. She wrestled the reigns back from him and moved away from his grip.

"Come now, do as he says," Imari ordered.

One man was now gawking over Imari's spear.

"Now this is a kingly spear. Where would a peasant like you get such a fine weapon?" asked the Sycar.

The Sycar leader turned his attention to the weapon. "You're right, Isham, that is a fine weapon," he said, snatching it from the man's grip, "Kingly is exactly how I would describe it."

Imari could see the light of revelation fill the Sycar leader's eyes. Before he could make a move, Imari heard a commotion behind him. Khaleena let out a screech and plunged her spear into the chest of her examiner. The man fell limp as she wrenched her weapon free from his chest.

"RUN NOW!" she screamed, her camel darting down the road in a flash. Her two Masisi bodyguards mounted and raced behind her. Imari unsheathed a hidden blade under his tunic and thrust it into the main holding his camel's reigns.

He jumped, and with a crack of the reigns was off, trusting that the others would follow suit. He heard the cries of men behind him, and then the sound of thundering hooves.

"Good, they're following," he thought to himself. He heard a whistling sound and then a cry. He turned to see Imbaku hot on his trail with two more Sycar lying dead behind them. A short distance behind Imbaku was Impatu, but something was wrong. He was hunched over gripping his shoulder. Imari followed Impatu's hand to see the arrow protruding from his back. He hesitated slightly slowing down to ride parallel with them.

Imbaku barked, "Go! I will take care of him."

Imari hesitated for a moment, but then listened to Imbaku's words. He turned his vision back to Khaleena who had gained some distance on him.

"What a mess," he thought. Both Khaleena and Imbaku were right, this journey was much more dangerous than he imagined. Had he been naive to think it wouldn't cost him? Impatu may pay with his own life for this decision, but it was one he had to live with. It was done, and they had no choice but to make it to Wahah, and quickly.

***

The sun's rays broke over the edge of the sea in the east. Beams of light danced off the vast expanse of water. Khaleena had not let up and had vanished from his sight sometime earlier. Imari, once the distance seemed safe, had slowed to a pace where Imbaku and Impatu could catch up to him. They had not stopped to examine the wound, but at the moment Impatu appeared stable. The three of them passed over a large plateau. As they reached the edge, they could see Wahah laying on the coast below them. Khaleena was nowhere in sight.

"Great, now that Khaleena has disappeared, how are we supposed to find Nabila or her contacts?" grumbled Imbaku.

"She won't abandon us," Imari said more confidently than he felt. He couldn't help but hear Impatu's raspy breathing next to him. "Besides, we need to find help for him first." He could see the same weariness that gripped himself taking hold of Imbaku as well. "Come, we are almost there."

The three began their descent. It was a winding path down to the bottom. It created a stunning view of the Southern Sea as the sun's crest began to rise higher and higher over the water. Imari would have drunk in the beauty if the threat behind them didn't feel so present. They made their way in silence until they had made the full descent. Wahah was now only an hour or so away.

At the bottom, the three men stopped to assess their approach. Imari glanced over at Impatu. He was breathing heavily and losing coherency.

"We need to remove this arrow from his shoulder, otherwise there is no way we will make it into the city unnoticed," counseled Imbaku.

"I agree, but if we remove it I fear he may not have much time." Imari worried about the young man regardless of the arrow remaining or not, but he did not want to let that show to Impatu.

"I will be fine. Remove the arrow. I can't be the reason we fail," choked out Impatu between breaths.

Both brothers looked at each other with concern. Imbaku rummaged through the rucksack hanging on his mount and pulled out a small crop used for the camel. He handed it to Impatu, "You might want to bite down on this."

Imari placed his hand on Impatu's opposite shoulder. "Are you ready?" he asked. Impatu replied with a grimace and a nod. Imari gripped the arrow's shaft and with a hard yank, felt the arrow give. Blood spurt out of the wound. Impatu let out a cry of agony. Imbaku quickly followed with a clean bandage. After a few moments of silence, besides Impatu's partially withheld grunts of pain, the three men stood.

"We should hurry. We don't have any time to waste. We need to make it to the city before the Sycar put it on lockdown," stressed Imbaku.

The three men hopped onto their mounts again. It wasn't long before the skyline of buildings filled their view. The sun had made its full ascent over the horizon at this point, but had not yet become the tyrant of midday. The city gate drew nearer and nearer until it was a daunting arch above their heads.

"This is it," murmured Imbaku. "We make it through this and we might be able to find some help."

"One obstacle at a time, brother," Imari cautioned.

Before the gate stood a handful of city guards dressed in typical Sahra fashion. Violet red turbans draped around a golden helmet. The men wore iron breastplates that bore the symbol of a sun, the sigil of Sahra. In their hands were spears, and at their sides hung the scimitars carried by every man of war in Sahra.

The three men cautiously approached the gate hoping to draw no attention to themselves. They moved to blend in with a caravan just recently arriving into the city, men from the spice trades with carts full of goods. Some were shouting at each other in the typical market fashion. They moved to subtly sneak around them.

"Holt!" came the cry of the head guard distinguished by his golden Turban.

"Here we go," Imbaku said reaching for a hidden knife at his side.

"Stop, brother, wait a moment," Imari said in a stern hush.

"Welcome, travelers. What brings you to Wahah?" inquired the guard.

"We are here to visit the famed markets to find supplies for our encampment in the east," lied Imari.

"I see. Well, you have come to the right place. Did you have troubles on your journeys here?" He glanced over at Impatu who visibly showed signs of pain.

"I am afraid wild animals. My companion was attacked while relieving himself. He needs help."

"Ahh, not a story to tell the others," mocked the guard. "If you are looking for a doctor you will find them off the main market to the east. Fair warning, there has been some disruption as of late. I wouldn't stay out past evening if I were you."

"Thank you, you have been kind to us. We will seek out the doctor where you've said, and heed your advice." Imari and the guard exchanged a courteous nod to one another. The companions moved from under the entrance of the gate into the city.

"You see, Imbaku, not everything is solved with the edge of a knife," scolded Imari.

"That guard is on to us, he will have us followed," Imbaku looked over his shoulder.

"Even so, we have nothing to hide. We need to find the doctor just like we said."

"And as soon as we can, thank you," came the raspy voice of Impatu.

Imari nodded and steered them into the main road. Wahah was a vibrate city full of sights and sounds. Shops littered the streets, each one covered by a different spectrum of color. Men and women shouted and bartered. Streets were jam-packed by travelers from all corners of the southern kingdoms. Imari felt the need to cover his face in hopes of not being recognized by another Khalan.

The trio weaved their way through the crowded streets until they reached the main market. This was the place where all the crowds congregated. Hundreds of vendors had set up shop with all manner of goods on display. Exotic stands for weapons, food, supplies, and those of a less savory nature. Imari had never visited Wahah as a boy. All that he saw surpassed even his imagination. Vibrant colors of every kind were worn by vendors and buyers alike. The smell of fish, meat, and vegetables cooking filled his nostrils. The noise was deafening.

Voices rang out like a disjointed choir each with a description of how their product was "the best" or how it would bring about a "life-changing experience" to anyone who would buy it. It was all overwhelming to the uninitiated.

"We should find them quickly," came Imbaku's voice.

"How are we to find them in all of this?" Impatu's eyes were wide with amazement, "Even the Great Fountains of Khala do not match this madness."

Imari scanned the makeshift signs for any indication of a doctor. A small sign in the far end of the plaza bore the symbol of the staff and serpent. The sign for all who practice healing.

"Over there," pointed Imari.

Next to the plaza sign lay the bay on which Wahah was founded. It, too, was a dazzling sight, but something else caught Imari's eye as he looked out, ships, and a lot of them.

"Do you see that?" Imari asked.

"I do. Not good…it looks like a blockade," Imbaku said concerned.

Behind them, near the plaza's entrance, came a voice rising above the rest. Men, robed all in black, began to file into the plaza with weapons drawn. One in particular separated himself from the rest, his mask a gold tint. The same one that had stopped them the night before.

"Listen, citizens and visitors alike!" came the shrill voice of the masked man. "There have been attempts of sedition made in the last day that has caused all of Sahra to enter into high alert! The city will now be on lockdown until further notice. No one will be allowed in or out. Any attempt will be seen as an act of treason and met as such."

Imari could sense the unease begin to rise among the crowd.

One man cried out in obvious frustration, "How can we continue trade if we cannot leave?!"

In reply, the golden masked Sycar let out another decree, "If any are willing to bring forth the traitors, they will help us end this lockdown quickly. We are looking for a group out of Khala. Any found to be housing such traitors will be killed without mercy. Now, I suggest you help us end this soon for all our sakes."

A madness settled over the crowd, many turning to those of Khalan roots with malicious intent. Imari could see the panic fill their eyes. Then he noticed the eyes begin to turn to Imbaku, Impatu, and himself.

"Not good," Impatu muttered.

Imari suddenly felt himself being pulled from his camel. A swarm of hands began washing over him. He was being pulled this way and that. His vision blurring from the madness. Cries and shouts swirled into a cloud of confusion around him. Then, in a moment, it was all drowned out with a loud slam. His vision turned to black. A crack of light flickered in the darkness. Behind it was the face of a man, not one of the South, but of Kingshelm. A light from behind Imari suddenly revealed the man more fully. He was a skinny, but muscular figure, dressed in informal garb. A light tan tunic with a brown shemagh wrapped around his neck.

"Where are we?" blinked Imari.

The mysterious Northerner replied, "Off the plaza in an abandoned storehouse."

"Let go of me you shukas!" Imbaku cried beside him.

"Quiet, brother, before you alert the whole plaza," came the voice of Khaleena.

Imari turned, temporarily blinded by the light. When he could once again see, six others surrounded Imbaku, Impatu, and himself. Khaleena stepped into the light.

"Are you alright, brother?" she offered a hand to lift him up.

Imari grabbed it and hoisted himself up. "Khaleena! You're alive?"

"You thought me dead? Silly brother!" That wiry smile filled her face.

"Great, great, you're alive, but who are these shukas?" Imbaku said rubbing his face which seemed to have hit the ground earlier.

"These "shukas" as you have so elegantly put it," Khaleena rolled her eyes, "are my contacts for Nabila." She pointed to the Northerner revealed earlier.

"Names Henry. It's an honor, Khosi Imari," he bowed in deep respect.

"I'm not Khosi of anything as of yet," shrugged Imari.

"That's what we are here to change," replied Henry with a grin.

"You met my men, Boani and Lambaku, earlier," Khaleena pointed to the two Masisi. Both let out a grunt.

She gestured at another Northern man, "This is James, an associate of Henry."

"It's a pleasure, Khosi," he nodded with respect.

"Lastly, but not least, Moheem and Riah, the leaders of Nabila's rebellion."

"Rebellion is such a crude term," groaned Moheem, "I prefer civic uprising."

"Whatever you call it. You lead it," Khaleena said bluntly.

"What is wrong with your friend?" inquired Riah pointing at Impatu. His face was looking paler by the minute. The bandage on his back was soaked through to his tunic.

"He took an arrow. He needs help as soon as possible," concern filled Imari's voice.

"That could be difficult especially with this lockdown. I wouldn't advise leaving this place," said Moheem.

"We may not have a choice. If the city goes on lockdown our plans will be ruined," Riah retorted.

"What plan?" Imbaku asked.

"Well, we were hoping to get Imari and your company on a ship to Sahra to meet up with our forces there. Nabila was relying on your men to make this happen," Moheem let out a sigh.

"To make what happen exactly?" asked Imari.

"She planned to use your surprise force to overtake Fahim's palace. From there you would work to wrestle control from him and the Sycar. With the palace taken, the rest of the army would fall in line," chimed in Henry.

"What's a Northerner have to do with all this?" Imbaku blurted out, "and besides that, your plan is shot to shuka. They have already blocked the port. There is no way to Sahra."

"One question at a time brother," said Khaleena rolling her eyes again.

"As for the Northerner question, I will take that one." Henry took a step forward, "James and I were sent by King Richard a few months after your father's death. He understood he couldn't send an entire force in retaliation to what Fahim did."

"Have to love politics," James said.

"Yes…as I was saying, he knew a military force was not possible. With tensions rising between Valkara and the history between Sahra, he could not risk full-scale war. So he sent us to be his eyes and ears, and if the time should come, to be his justice."

"So you have been here for six years?"

"Yes, and we have waited for a moment like this. To see the reign of Fahim end. Sadly, we were not able to stop him before his assassination attempt." Deep mourning fell over Henry's face.

"I am sorry. Richard was a great king. Islandia will miss him," Imari said with empathy.

"As tragic as King Richard's loss is, we need to form a plan, and quick," Moheem informed the group.

"What plan is there? The city is already cut off and our only way out is by sea," Imbaku spat in frustration.

"It is not the only way. There is another," Riah said. "You can go through The Endless Waste."

"With what supplies? We may be desperate, but not suicidal," Imbaku protested.

"With these supplies." Henry removed a cloth that had been covering boxes full of food and urns filled with water. "We can load up what we can and travel light and quick. We could reach The Grand Wall in half a fortnight."

"I agree that is the only path to Sahra, but how are we to get out of the city? The Sycar have it on lockdown," Imari asked.

"We can create a distraction," a grin crossed James' face. He lifted a vat of oil, "I can reach out to some of our contacts. We light a bit of this stuff on fire near the west gate and create a commotion, it will be sure to draw a force away from the gate."

"What about Impatu, he is in no condition to leave," Imbaku looked over at the young man, his breathing unsettled and rapid.

"He will need to stay, but I will do all I can to help him," Riah's concern clearly seen.

"I...I can go. I cannot leave you, Khosi." Impatu tried to get up, but slumped back to the ground. Imari moved to lean over him.

"No, Impatu, you need to recover your strength. When the time comes you will help us in this fight." Imari turned to the others, "I only see one other issue. What about our men? You said you needed them. They don't even know what has happened to us."

"Ahh, brother, you think me that unprepared?" Khaleena asked. "The second I got to Wahah I sent a messenger back to the camp telling them to meet us southwest of the city. They should be there within two days."

"So it's settled. We will leave the city tonight via James' distraction. Imbaku, Khaleena, Boani, Lombaku, Henry, and I will leave for Sahra. We will meet up with our forces, and then march to the wall," Imari stated.

"That's the plan," Moheem said.

"A shuka of a plan, but a plan," Imbaku complained.

"We best get ready," Henry said.

***

Night soon fell, and preparations had been set. The plaza was deserted when the small band made their way from the warehouse. Through the dark alleys, small, torch-lit patrols were found wandering the streets. James had disappeared earlier to gather his "contacts", the plan all riding on his success. Sneaking past a band of Sycar and dodging from shadow to shadow, the west gate finally became visible to Imari.

Underneath its arch stood a group of guards whose numbers were no less than twenty. They were a mix of the local authorities and that of the Sycar. Henry was busy looking for the designated signal given to him by James. He motioned for the rest of the group trailing him to proceed. A small light was lit in the top window of the building adjacent to the city wall. Henry threw a stone that clacked against the wall a few yards away from the guards. They stirred like a kicked hornet's nest. Shouts of "Who's there!?" and commands barked by the captains filled the air. In a burst that took Imari by surprise, the building with the lit candle erupted in flames. Now a panic flooded the guards as they rushed to see what was happening.

A cry from the street next to the building was heard echoing down the alley they were in. Imari could make out at least fifty men armed with clubs, farming tools, and some swords. At their head stood James.

"What is he doing?! Doesn't he know that's suicide?" Imari cried in disbelief.

"He does, Khosi, but he knows what your people have endured, and he is willing to pay that price." Henry's face was somber.

"He knew! He knew this was the plan all along and he had me left in the dark about it," Imari fumed to himself.

The outcome was now inevitable, but he could not allow James' sacrifice to be in vain. A battle cry roared from the mob James was able to incite. They rushed the guards, and began to overwhelm the battalion placed at the gate.

"Come, now is our chance!" Henry rushed out of the alley into the final building before the gateway. He opened an unlatched door. Inside were several camels stocked with the supplies from earlier. James had come through again. They mounted up and quickly returned to the street. The fighting had turned into an all-out brawl. Men fought with makeshift weapons, slashing at any weak point they could find. The Sycar held their own and were cutting down the mob with relative ease. Fire now engulfed the neighboring buildings around them.

Imari saw James take notice of the Sycar decimating the mob. He turned his attention to a group that had surrounded a man wielding a shovel. With weapon drawn, he dodged an incoming blow and countered with his own cutting deep into the ribs of the Sycar warrior. Without hesitation he moved to the next one, parrying a blow and slashing away another. With an upward motion he caught the inner arm of the Sycar warrior rendering it nearly in half. The man clutched at the wound dropping his guard. James sent the finishing blow downward into his chest.

Only two remained, one of them the golden masked leader. He and his companion charged James at the same time. James deflected the first strike and sent a crushing blow to the golden masks' companion, but James neglected to see a secondary blade the golden mask had slipped into his left hand. He sent the dagger into James' side, dropping him to his knees. As he was falling down his eyes met Imari's. He mouthed the words "Go" then turned his gaze to the Sycar towering over him his golden mask reflecting the inferno all around. James gave the Sycar one last smirk before he drove his blade into James' abdomen.

Imari was thrust from his shock when he noticed Henry yanking on his reigns. "Come on!" he shouted as he pulled Imari forward. Without further thought, they rushed through the gate past the Sycar engaged in the small riot. Imari looked back to see the golden masked Sycar staring him down holding James up by his hair, the light fading from his eyes.

"I promise it won't be in vain," Imari whispered in quiet rage, and with that vow he fled into the pitch black of night.

6

GERALT

Rodenhill, a place for those who cared only for drink and merriment. It wasn't the place Geralt would seek out himself, especially because of its locale. Rodenhill sat on the edge of the Lowland Hills and was the last town in Valkara's territory. It was a rundown dump. A final stop for travelers either leaving for the Riverlands, or, in the rare case, the first stop on the way to the city of Valkara itself. Geralt found himself here for the former. King Doran had not relented in his fury the days following Jorn and Lokir's betrayal. If anything, it grew deeper and darker.

He had placed almost the entire Valkaran army under the command of Geralt and another general named Ferir. The order was simple, march into the Riverlands and demand the royal family's return or all-out war would ensue. It was brash and reckless even for the temper of Doran, but Geralt followed orders. What choice did he really have? What did surprise him was the king's insistence he wield the dark blade into battle. Geralt felt uneasy about the foul weapon. Even holding it in is his grip for a brief moment sent a flood of craving for something...dark. He couldn't put his finger on it, but the blade was something he would only choose to wield in absolute necessity.

He was shaken from his thoughts as the cheers and jests of men erupted beside him. The dingy tavern was packed full of Valkaran warriors drinking themselves into a stupor on the eve of their final march. Some with desires of ale, others women, and for the commanders, a night without complication. Through the hoots and howls of the men, Geralt could see Ferir weaving his way toward him. Ferir was a fair tempered man. Smaller in stature than one would think for a general in a kingdom built on a warrior ethos. What Ferir lacked in apparent size he more than made up for it with his strategic abilities. Unmatched by any commander in tactical advantage, he rose up the ranks at an early age. Surprising, even to Geralt, that he didn't seem to let it go to his head. Ferir plopped down next to him at the bar.

"Scouts just returned," Ferir muttered while scratching his stubbled chin.

"And the report?" asked Geralt.

"Not good. At least 7,000 foot soldiers have been mustered at the Western Watch not including another 2,000 calvary. It's going to be a massacre." Ferir was clearly agitated at the situation. "What was Doran expecting us to do? We don't have the numbers to intimidate Kingshelm into any sort of action."

"The last count of our own was 5,000?" inquired Geralt.

"Yes, just about, and only 500 calvary. Not nearly enough even with a significant terrain advantage, which we don't have."

"Hmmm," Geralt rubbed his chin mulling over the circumstances. He then realized he hadn't even taken the time to shave in the last week.

"That's all you have for me?" Ferir grunted, "Just hmmmm? I need a little more than that."

Geralt paused for a moment then asked, "When do we suspect the encounter to happen?"

"Marching orders are to arrive at King's Cross in 3 days. Should take us no more than two to arrive and draw battle lines."

"One more question," Geralt swirled his drink and took a deep draw from his cup. This next question was the one he feared to ask, mostly because he knew what he must do. "How many do you need?"

"How many what?" snorted Ferir.

"How many men? How many do we need to even the odds?" Geralt's face was all business.

Ferir let out a slight chuckle, "I mean, 5,000 more men would be nice, but in all seriousness, we need at least 2,000 more calvary if we are to stand a chance. This battle will be fought on the Terras Plains. Calvary will win the day, and right now, we are greatly outnumbered."

Geralt let out a deep sigh, "I can get you the calvary."

Now Ferir let out a real laugh, "Have you been keeping a secret army from me? Where do you plan to find them? Valkara is not known for its riders, and we have called on almost every available man already."

"The Hillmen have the cavalry, that's where I'll get them."

"The Hillmen?! They haven't answered a king's call in a hundred years. I know you're one of them, but it's been a while since you were running half-naked through the hills."

Geralt let the insult roll off his shoulders, "You're correct, they have not answered a call, but those kings did not have a Dawn Blade."

Ferir sat up, "Valkara hasn't seen one of those in 500 years at least. You claim to have one?" his voice was in a hushed tone.

"I do, gifted to me by Doran. They will answer to that blade for it is of the same kind that defeated them before."

Silence hung in the air between them. Ferir fell back into his chair in deep thought. Geralt internally dreading every moment that was to come. He knew someday he would have to return, but it didn't make it any easier.

"We don't have much of a choice," Ferir finally said. "Go, see what you can do. We march with or without you."

"Understood."

"Do you want anyone else to accompany you? We are already outnumbered, but I can't imagine you going to the Hills alone."

"I only need one."

"So be it. Whoever you need. Good luck, Geralt, you'll need it." Farir pushed himself from the bar and with a curt nod left the same way he came.

Geralt took one last sip of his drink and rubbed his face to buy just a few more precious seconds. He stood to his feet and followed Ferir out of the bar and onto the streets. Evening had already settled with lamps lit to light the streets. Rodenhill was as dingy outside as it was in the Rodenhill Tavern. The dark stoned streets seemed to be coated with a grime that years of scrubbing could not remove. Drunken men stumbled along the sides of the road, accompanied by a bounty of beggars. At this time of day no respectable woman would be found outside her home, but those you did see were not of the respectable nature.

In Geralt's youth, that temptation may have arisen, but he was older now. Time had been the greatest teacher that all those women wanted was the coin in your pocket. He was going to need his. He strode through several streets until he found a dump of an inn aptly named The Sleepy Hills. Geralt moved to the back entrance, and without knocking, opened the door.

The room was pitch black. A foul odor permeated the air. That smell was exactly who Geralt was looking for. With a long known knowledge of the place, he reached to the side of the door and found a torch, unlit, mounted on the wall. He lit the torch and held it up to reveal the contents of the room. On the floor lay a sleeping man surrounded by empty bottles of ale. Dry vomit stains on his shirt.

"Wake up, you slug," Geralt said as he kicked the sleeping man.

The man's eyes shot open in shock. He bounced up into a sitting position.

"Ahhh good to see you too, ya Lacka!" the man rubbed his side where Geralt had kicked him.

"I'm calling in that favor."

"We've been even seven times over!" shouted the man. "Go get a favor from someone else."

"It's time to go home, brother," Geralt said evenly.

The man's eyes shifted from annoyance to dread. "What's happened now?"

"King Doran's army needs the Hillmen, and I am going to convince them to fight for us."

Geralt's brother let out an obnoxious laugh, "Good luck, lad! Do you get to take the whole army on a side trip with you? Cause you're gonna need it." He rolled back over to sleep.

"I don't need an army, I have this." Geralt moved his cloak to reveal the blade resting on his back. He gripped the hilt and drew it from its sheath, the blade radiating a sickly green colored aurora.

"That...that can't be.." stammered his brother.

"It is, Valkin, and we are going to use it to claim what is rightfully ours."

Valkin rose to his feet, "Which is?"

"Our father was the chief of clan Harnfell. His was the rightful claim to command all the Hillmen tribes. We are going to claim that title once again."

Valkin grabbed a mug of ale from a nearby table and took a long swig. He slammed the mug back down and wiped his unkempt beard. "What makes you think they are going to listen to the son of a long-dead chief who's now no more than a Northman to them?"

"This blade is what. It will command them because it was the blade that subdued them once before."

"You'll need more than a fancy sword to convince Thumdrin to surrender his entire army to you."

"That's why you're coming with me. You are my witness to legitimacy. A rightful claim can be made to challenge his power. As for convincing him to accept that challenge, you let me worry about that." Geralt put the sword back in its sheath.

Valkin stood with his eyes half glazed over. Geralt had almost thought he'd fallen asleep again when he finally responded.

"We all die, and as you can see, I have a lot going on right now, so I guess now is as good a time as ever. Just let me pack my things." He turned and picked up his sword and grabbed a canteen that Geralt could only suspect held more ale. "Alright, I'm ready."

Geralt rolled his eyes. "Just try not to die from alcohol poisoning before we arrive."

***

The two brothers set off just before midnight, the full moon shining off the cobblestone streets. Lanterns lit their path until they diverged from the main road. Many were still carousing through the night, most in a drunken stupor. Geralt examined his brother. It had been several years since his last visit. The man was thin, too thin. His sandy blonde hair a tattered mess that was only rivaled by his beard. He wore a plain brown tunic and black trousers that hung loosely from his frame.

The death of their parents had taken its toll on Valkin. Even after thirty years the raid still left its mark on both of them. Geralt had not even known Valkin survived for many years until one day he happened upon him in Rodenhill. The two men were drawn to different paths after that fateful night and could not have been molded any differently. Raised in the royal courts of Valkara, Geralt had learned a life of dignity. Valkin, on the other hand, had been sold to a local landowner named Shamus. Valkin had learned the ways of the streets due to his owner's unsavory business endeavors. Pickpocketing, spying, and muggings were a daily rhythm to his life.

Geralt couldn't help but feel a faint sense of pity for this brother of his, but Valkin would see it very differently. He viewed Geralt as the one to be pitied having been raised in the home of his parent's murderers, trained like a loyal dog to such a man. That was truly something to be pitied. Geralt, deep down, wrestled with that reality himself. Maybe he was the one who should truly be pitied after all.

"This way," came the quiet voice of Valkin as he turned down a dark alley. He was leading them to a tunnel out of the city. While Geralt's mission was nothing to keep fully under wraps, the element of surprise was needed to not inform Kingshelm of what he was up to. They, after all, had informants of their own.

"Shamus going to be okay with you taking this little adventure?" questioned Geralt as the two men reached the tunnel entrance.

"That Lacka owes me a few favors, besides, he won't miss me." He leaned over to remove a large stone that sat at the end of the alley they entered.

Geralt took that as, "What Shamus doesn't know won't hurt him." Underneath the stone was a hole about five feet in diameter.

Valkin motioned toward the entrance, "After you."

Geralt knelt and lowered himself into the opening. To his surprise, there was a fully lit tunnel with several other people seemingly doing "business" of their own.

"Don't mind us, lads, just finding our way out," came Valkin's voice behind him.

The shady figures all turned their backs to ignore them. Valkin motioned for Geralt to follow. It wasn't another twenty minutes before they both stopped and Valkin began to remove an object from the ceiling.

"Here we are," he said as a ray of moonlight shone through the opening.

Both men made their way up, and Geralt found himself standing several hundred yards away from the city, the lanterns flickering in the distance. To the east he could make out the Valkaran armies' camp, grey canvases barely visible in the night. The two of them set off again for, what seemed to Geralt, an hour or two. After some time, he could see where Valkin was leading them. A small farm, not far from where they were, sat peacefully among small rolling hills. As they approached, an older man with two mounts approached them.

"Heading out again already?" asked the old man to Valkin.

"Just business," he replied cooly.

"Alright, Alright, I don't mean to cause no trouble." The old man looked Geralt up and down and muttered something under his breath. There was a quick exchange of coin and the two men were off again.

"What did he mean by 'heading out again'?" Geralt asked after some time had passed.

Valkin was silent for a moment. "Old Shamus sends me out a time or two to the Hills for business. Nothing special."

Geralt wasn't convinced. For the years he had known Shamus and his "work", none of it had to do with the Lowland Hills. He often gave Geralt the vibe that the men dwelling there were not the sort to do business with. In any case, he let it go for the moment. They began their first real ascent into the hill country. The journey was not so much done on roads, but old trodden pathways. Geralt and Valkin's clan came from the Southern Hills near the Dreadwood. The path that Valkin seemed to be leading them on was straight to the feet of the Odain Mountains, the land of Shunderhill, the home of Thumdrin.

After some time, Geralt broke their silence with another question, "I haven't returned since our captivity. What has changed in The Hills?"

Valkin let out a light chuckle, "Everything, and nothing." He shifted in his saddle, "Thumdrin's father, Valkor, moved in to claim the chieftain role after Father's murder. He submitted tribute to Valkara for close to twenty years before he passed. In the last ten years, Thumdrin stepped in to fill the void."

"So, why did Thumdrin decide to go against Valkara again after so many years of peace?"

"Peace? Ha! If you call enslavement, forced labor, and gutting The Hills of every resource we have, peace. Then yes, why would we ever want to rebel?" Valkin retorted snarkily.

The picture Valkin painted wasn't exactly true. Yes, harsh measures had been meted out to the Hillmen, but, living in Valkara, Geralt had seen the devastation The Hills had laid out themselves.

"War is a tricky thing, Valkin," Geralt replied.

"HA! Here you are, after all these years, defending the Lackas! Brother, these people devastated our family, our heritage, and our future, and now you fight for them?"

"Your future," thought Geralt to himself. "Brother, The Hills have caused devastation by their acts of pillaging long before and long after Valkara ever got involved. What they did was wrong, our family paid the price, but do you even know what our father did?"

"Lead a strong and free-willed people, and raised a lacka son, it looks like."

"He raided Valkaran lands, took whatever women pleased him, and slaughtered children. His hands are not clean." Geralt's voice began to rise, "You want to know why Doran killed our family? Why he marched an army the farthest south it had gone in 500 years? Because our father killed his firstborn in a raid on a royal embassy. He murdered a baby in cold blood."

There was a stunned silence between the two of them.

"It seems that Northern king truly has his claws in you now," came Valkin's reply. "So much so, you'd betray your own family and create lies to do so."

Geralt wouldn't even give that reply the satisfaction of an answer. If his brother wanted to wallow in a gutter for another thirty years, let him.

They traveled for a few more hours before the peaks of the Odain Mountains glimmered on the horizon. At this time of year barely any snow rested on their heights. Behind the mountains, the wafting of ocean air filling their nostrils. The Vestlig Coast was the gateway to lands and sea of the west, undiscovered territory. The Lowland Hills could not have been a better guardian.

As they continued forward, the mountains filled their view. They were smaller than the Crowns to the north, but still a dazzling sight in and of themselves. Resting below them were hills that grew in diameter. Not as jarring as early on, but tiring in scope. Green surrounded them. Small, trickling streams for their steads to refresh poured out from the roots of the mountain chain. It was a beauty Geralt drank in for the first time since his childhood. The last frontier of Islandia. The wild west. As they made their ascent up the last large hill before the base of the mountains, they saw a bustling colony. It seemed to be a mixture of temporary nomadic tents and more permanent structures. Wooden walls had been built around a strategic stream flowing from the base of a mountain. What looked like make-shift watchtowers had been erected, along with some permanent housing.

"Thrumdrin has been busy, I see," Geralt said with a little surprise.

"He's looking to create something permanent to rally all the Hillmen so we can no longer be taken advantage of," Valkin said with an emphasis on the "we".

"The clansmen are willing to surrender their freedom?"

"Times are a changing, Geralt, and we have to change with them. Come on, let's go."

The two men made their final descent down the hill. Scatterings of men could now be seen working on chopping wood and gathering building materials. As they drew closer, stares fell on them, most of them unfriendly.

"Good to be home," muttered Geralt.

"The prodigal son returns," mocked Valkin.

The two of them strolled up to the fortress gate. Valkin let out a peculiar sounding whistle and a cry could be heard ordering the gate to open. As the doors swung wide, Geralt could see a flurry of activity. Men moving this way and that in what seemed like organized chaos. Women were seen sowing and patching tents and preparing the evening meal. Kids played on the dirt path and ran up to them with excited giggles. There weren't many visitors to come to the hills, so any foreigner was attention-grabbing, except, they weren't foreigners. But, as Geralt reminded himself, he would be to them. These people, his people, didn't look like him, talk like him, act like him, or recognize him as their own. No matter the blood in his veins, he was not one of them.

Valkin led them to a building that clearly showed it was the focal point of the small little fort. It was a humble wooden building by many cities' standards, but here it was head and shoulders above the rest. The roof of the hall met at a point and a small window hung above two large wooden doors. To either side sat symmetrical extensions that seemed to house important individuals. Valkin led them to the main doorway. Two guards stood in silence, and with a nod from Valkin, they were let in.

The room was dimly lit by a few candles. Most of the light came shimmering in from the window above. In the room sat a few tables off to the side, nothing elaborate or decorative filled the place. At the far end of the room rested a small throne also made of wood, and beside it a group of men stood conversing. They turned their attention to Valkin and himself. Geralt could now see they were leaders from the clans. One of the men looked a bit taken aback by what he saw, but Thumdrin had a grin across his face that conveyed something more sinister than joy.

"Ahh, the two princes return," he sneered, "I wondered if you'd ever be making your way home, Geralt."

"It seems you have been busy," Geralt replied, motioning around him.

"You like what I've done with the place? You see, I realized something your father, my father, and all the other tribesmen chefs before did not.

"Which is?" Geralt asked, cocking his head a little.

"If we are to survive in this world, we need security. An identity beyond some people who dwell among the hills. We need a base on which we can all rely."

"Ah, so you're the savior of the people, then," smirked Geralt

With one quick flash, Thumdrin grabbed Geralt by his tunic collar. "If you think for a moment that you can come prancing in here after thirty years and act like you know your people's struggles, you're wrong." Thumdrin tightened his grip, "A traitorous Lacka like you is lucky to have breath showing his face here." He let go of Geralt and took a step back, collecting himself.

"So? Why have you come?" the man standing behind Thumdrin asked.

"Gerandir, is that you?" Geralt said with astonishment. Gerandir had been a close friend of his father's. He had to be nearing 75 years old. "I am honored to see you again."

"He asked you a question," came Thumdrin.

"I've come to ask for your help on behalf of Valkara," Geralt stated boldly.

The room erupted with laughter from everyone but Thumdrin.

"I told you this would happen eventually," sighed Valkin.

Geralt turned to his brother quizzically, "You told them?"

"Ahhh yes, little brother here said you had joined the 'mighty' Valkara and you might come demanding something from us someday. He assessed the situation and brought news to us about your wars in the east. He saw the odds, and told us you might come knocking," Thumdrin explained.

"Brother, you knew? Why did you not tell me!" Geralt swirled to face Valkin.

"You're a traitor, brother. You would take our people into a war we don't want, to help a people we hate, and for what? Your own personal gain? I will never let that stand," Valkin drew his sword.

"Your brother came to us with a proposal," Thumdrin was grinning now. "If you were to approach him, he would agree to bring you here and then we, in turn, would allow him to face you in a dual. If he wins, he will become an honored clan leader again in our new realm."

"Always the play-actor," rage burned in Geralt's eyes, "but you would be a fool to take their deal now, knowing what you do."

"It did complicate things, yes. But how about you do one honorable thing in your life and face me as a man," Valkin snarled.

"What do you know of honor…" Geralt's rage settled and in its place, sorrow. It had come to this. His ties, this mission, Valkara, they would all demand his brother's blood. He could see in Valkin's eyes there was no turning back. Ambition and hatred were powerful tools.

"I will say this once more, brother, you don't have to do this," Geralt pleaded.

"I do. For my people and our family's honor."

Geralt had never seen Valkin this way, the hatred that filled his eyes. Had this been there all along? All these years had he really been waiting for this moment?

"We will do this in the ways of our ancestors," declared Thumdrin. "You will have your vengeance before everyone as a mark of legitimacy."

"Come brother, are you ready to meet death?" Valkin smirked.

Geralt turned to see Gerandir's face. It wasn't quite sorrow, but something in his eyes showed a tinge of sadness to see the sons of Hamill slay each other. The old man had to be weary of such tales. Geralt and Valkin were ushered out to the small patch of earth in front of the hall. A horn sounded with four long blasts indicating a trial by dual. Smatterings of people began to form a loose circle around them.

Thumdrin, in a booming voice, proclaimed to the crowd, "Valkin, son of Hamill, challenges Geralt, eldest son of Hamill, for the claim of clan Harnfell. We, the elders of the tribes, have accepted this challenge and will oversee their fate."

The crowd around them was expanding by the minute. Cheers and taunts filled the air. Geralt could feel the situation quickly escalating. Valkin still held his sword in his hand and pointed it at Geralt with his brow furrowed.

"Draw your sword, brother, and let fate rest on your head."

Geralt exhaled a breath and brushed back his cloak to display the sword at his hip. The trusty and faithful steel longsword that had helped him throughout his life. He drew it from its sheath in one swift motion and placed it before him in a defensive stance. It was Valkin's move.

In reply, Valkin sped in his direction pulling something from his pocket? It was a cloud of dust that filled Geralt's eyes and temporarily blinded him. Rubbing his eyes and stumbling back, he caught a glimpse of Valkin bringing his blade downward. At the last possible second, Geralt brought his guard up and absorbed the blow. The strike sent his blade an inch away from his face. He mustered his strength and shrugged Valkin off him.

"What of honor, brother?" Geralt said rubbing his eyes with his free hand.

"A lacka dies like a lacka," Valkin sneered.

"So it's going to be that way," thought Geralt to himself. His mind, for a brief moment, drifting to the blade on his back. "No, if I am to win their respect I need to do this in line with tradition."

Valkin sent a fury of blows. Geralt sidestepped the first and deflected the rest. He sent a countering strike at Valkin's head. He deflected the blow, but a lock of his hair fell to the ground. Quickly, Valkin pushed the blade aside and sent a near-critical blow under Geralt's ribs. He had to throw himself to the ground to evade it, and as a result, the sword in his hand dislodged, landing a few feet away. His still injured shoulder radiated with pain. Valkin, seeing the opportunity, pounced on top of him raising his sword for a devastating blow.

"When did you become such a fighter?" Geralt inquired sending a kick directly into Valkin's knee. He crumbled to the ground, his only reply a howl of pain. Scrambling, Geralt snatched his blade from the grass and turned to face his foe. Valkin stumbled to his feet again, the rage ever growing in his eyes. Geralt sadly recognized that this was his opportunity. If you could enrage an opponent, you had the ability to control them. The blows came, each with a strength that took all his skill to deflect. The opening came. A slightly miscalculated slash caused Valkin's footing to give. Geralt sidestepped the blade and sent a feign at Valkin's legs. He drew his blade to defend, but Geralt pulled his blade back from the blow and sent a thrust directly into Valkin's torso.

A deathly gasp left his lungs. His body slumped, and he dropped his sword. Geralt fought to hold back the tears. He hated this price, the deep heartbreak. That's all "home" had become for him. He withdrew his blade and a flow of blood quickly followed, blanketing Valkin's tunic. His eyes glazed over and his breathing became desperate for his last bit of air.

"I'm sorry, brother," Geralt whispered. "I promise..."

"Don't promise me anything," came a gasping hiss. "Valkara promises are served up in poisoned cups." He coughed profusely.

Geralt cast his blade aside and held his brother, "We could have ruled together as a family again." Tears couldn't help but fill his eyes.

"No..." the words could barely be made out now, "... brother."

Valkin's body went limp in his arms. Geralt became painfully aware of the eyes watching him now, at least twenty men with drawn swords. He gently placed his brother's body to the ground and stood to his feet. A clap came from the crowd. Of course, Thumdrin.

"Congratulations, champion. Unfortunately, our bargain was only for one party involved. I believe the penalty for a traitor is death, as I recall. Valkin just wanted the honor of carrying the sentence out."

The armed men took another step closer.

"You would come to regret that decision, although you won't have much time to do so," Geralt leered.

"HA! Is that a threat? Last I checked even a famed warrior such as yourself couldn't defeat twenty armed men."

Silently, Geralt shrugged his cloak back again to reveal the hilt of the Dawn Blade. Without a word, he pulled it from the sheath. The dark aurora swirling around the blade was stronger than ever. The armed men halted and began to take a step back.

"What, you think we are scared of a magic sword?" mocked Thumdrin.

"You should be. This...magic sword, as you call it, is a Dawn Blade. Made of the most powerful material known to Islandia and crafted by The Founders and their lost arts. It was forged in the fires of the Nawafir's deep caverns and is a blade that subdued our people half a millennium ago. It is the blade that will subdue you now."

With one motion, Thumdrin ordered the armed men to swarm Geralt, sending them to their doom. One by one they fell. It felt like a hazy dream to Geralt. The dark blade sliced through each one as if it had met thin air. Each man collapsing after another in a heap of violence. The blade hummed in his hand. It was made for this, made for destruction, and it rejoiced with each fallen foe. It seemed to pulse with each blow given. When every last man was slain, Geralt's daze faded. All that remained was a dumbstruck Thumdrin and the clan elders.

Geralt glanced around. More than twenty men lay dead or maimed around him. Their groans echoing in the city square. His gaze fell on Thumdrin, the fear now visible in his eyes.

"Are you done sending men to their doom?" Geralt barked. "If so, I have a proposal."

Thumdrin was stricken dumb, visibly shaking. Gerandir came shuffling forward. "On behalf of Harnfell, we will do whatever you ask of us, Geralt, just please put that thing away."

In response Geralt sheathed the blade.

"I came here to take your title, Thumdrin, but I can see now it would only cause these people more pain. This is what I demand of you, Harnfell and all its horsemen and soldiers are mine. When I call for them, you will answer. When I have need of them, you will obey. That is my demand."

Thumdrin just stood gaping, unable to utter a word.

Gerandir spoke once more, "We will honor your order. Harnfell and its men are at your disposal."

"I want him to say it," Geralt pointed his finger at Thumdrin.

This acknowledgment seemed to shake him free of his shock. He blinked, then muttered the words, "Yes...yes... you may call them whenever you have need." He turned, and without another word, entered his hall. The other elders followed after, except for Gerandir.

"That is a foul blade, Geralt, I would warn you to use caution," counseled Gerandir.

Geralt ignored him, "Send word to the clansmen, I have need of them now. How long will it take to muster them all?"

Gerandir pondered this for a moment, "It will take us a day's journey to reach the camp, then maybe another to prepare our riders."

"That will be quick enough. Come, we will go together. I will require your presence to inform them of what's happened here today."

With that, Gerandir bowed in acknowledgment and motioned for Geralt to follow him to a nearby stable. The two men found the quickest mounts available and immediately left for Harnfell.

"I did it," thought Geralt, "We have a chance." But then the guilt rushed over him. At what cost? The life of his brother and the control the dark blade seemed to have over him? Was the price for victory his soul?

7

TITUS

Titus stared at the captives, the two girls. Well, one girl, and the other a young woman with curly hair kissed by fire. The younger of the two seemed anxious about her predicament, but the older looked calm and collected, her sparkling green eyes giving no hint of fear. Titus found her a bit captivating himself. She could not have been much younger than him. He had never had the chance to meet Doran's daughters before. The hostilities between their two kingdoms had kept them apart, but here, now, they were Kingshelm's captives, and it was his decision on what to do with them.

They had been held in the Western Watch's lower holding cells, the most accommodating they could find. It was a small barred room with one tiny window to let in sunlight on a nice day. Today, however, was overcast and the small bits of rain saturated the cell floor under the window. The two princesses were chained to the wall, but given enough slack that they could maneuver around their cell a few feet.

Titus had arrived the evening prior, and after a quick night of rest, rose early the next day to find out just what was going on. He asked that Elorah accompany him to their cell. He needed to piece together what was happening in Valkara.

"So, you're telling me your father was betrayed?" inquired Titus of the two daughters.

The older one, Lydia he thought was her name, spoke up, "Yes, you didn't understand me the first time, did ya? Is it the accent? Too thick for you river folk?"

"No, I understood you fine. I just, well, I didn't see betrayal in the cards is all."

"Ahh, yes, it's that scum that showed up with us, ole one arm. He met up with his goons shortly after we were taken. Seems someone had their way with him, and good riddance."

That was interesting. The man named Jorn, who had shown up with the two daughters, was the instigator of all this? When he'd first arrived at the Western Watch, the story was that he had a peace offering to present. It seems the daughters were that offering. Titus knew what his next question would be.

"Answer honestly, can there be a peace made with your father if we return you or is he bent on war either way?" Titus was curious to see if they would answer truthfully, or try to save themselves.

The younger sister Nara looked to Lydia to answer. Lydia pondered what she would say for a moment. She lifted her head and looked Titus in the eyes.

"I don't know," she said cooly. "My father is a hot-tempered man. War comes easy for men like him. I, too, was eager for battle, but…"

"But what?" pressed Titus.

"Your men, they're nice enough fellows, don't see no reason to fight those who don't deserve it, unlike one arm ya got in yer other room."

"Do you think your father will see it that way?"

"Like I said…no promises."

With that, Titus stood from the stool he was sitting on and nodded to Elorah that he was ready to leave. In turn, he sent an order to the guards outside the cell to open the door. Titus turned to leave and stopped to look back at the girls.

"I promise as long as you are here, you will be treated fairly. I will have you unchained, and you will be given any meal upon your request."

"You're too kind, yer majesty. However could we repay you?" Lydia gave a mock curtsey.

Titus ignored the clear sarcasm and walked out the door with Elorah behind him. The two men made their way to their other guest, the man named Jorn.

"What do you make of their story?" asked Titus.

Elorah mulled this over for a moment. "They spoke the truth of Doran which tells me they're not just saying whatever they can to escape. That much I can tell."

Titus nodded in agreement, "Hopefully this Jorn fellow can give us some more answers."

The two of them reach Jorn's room a level below the princesses' cell. These holdings didn't have a window, and the smell was more potent. It was dark, and the torches lit were just barely sufficient. The guards at the stairs guided them to the proper cell. With a turn of the key, the door swung open. The man named Jorn sat with a blood-stained tunic, his right sleeve wrapped where his arm was missing. Dark bags hung under his eyes, and his face was covered with scruffy hair. His whole demeanor was disheveled.

"Ahh, King Titus, I presume?" Jorn said with a weary smile.

"Jorn," Titus said curtly as a stool was placed for him to sit.

"So tell me, what brings you to my lovely new home?" Jorn said gesturing at his cell.

"Why did you bring Doran's daughters to us? Were you hoping to start a war?" Titus asked.

"I was looking to do the opposite," Jorn replied with a tone of appeasement. "Doran is an ill-tempered king. He was looking for an opportunity to seize freedom from Kingshelm. As one of his head advisors, this was made known to me. Another of my colleagues and I went to Sahra with the desire to gain their help in overthrowing Doran. Together we hoped to bring peace with Kingshelm."

"Seems that plan didn't work out so well," replied Elorah glancing at Jorn's injury.

The sincerity seemed to fade from Jorn for a moment. "No, it did not. My colleague, my friend Lokir, paid with his life. We made an attempt on Doran's life, but we had no idea he had a Dawn Blade in his possession."

"A Dawn Blade?!" both Titus and Elorah blurted in unison.

"Yes, it seems he was given help by a man named Balzara, unknown to Lokir and I."

"This is unsettling. A Dawn Blade appears again after having been missing for 500 years, and who is this Balzara you speak of?" Titus demanded.

"A strange, dark fellow like that strange and dark blade. I'd never met the man, but from the looks of him, he is someone sinister."

Titus mulled this over. It all seemed overwhelming. Being at the brink of war, missing Dawn Blades appearing, and now shadowy figures that stirred up thoughts he'd rather not entertain.

"So how'd you end up here?" Elorah asked.

"When our plans fell apart, as you can see, I escaped to catch up with our 'peace offerings', if you will. I came hoping that your good graces would see we are on the same side."

"Why Fahim?" interjected Titus.

"What?" Jorn asked quizzically. He was obviously thrown off by the abruptness of the question.

"Why would you seek Fahim's help over, let's say, ours? If you truly wanted peace, and not to grab power, why not ask for our help from the beginning?" Titus continued, anger now tainting his voice, "In fact, Fahim would be the one man you'd not seek after if you wanted peace."

Jorn sat quietly for a moment. "Regardless of why we wanted to overthrow Doran, it would seem small in comparison to the idea of us finally having peace, doesn't it? We can use his family, all of them, to keep him in line, and if not, you have others willing to serve you…"

"You would like that, wouldn't you, snake. By your own breath you have admitted the truth. We already had Doran's sons, his heirs, what more could we hold against him? No, I think this is the truth." Titus stood from his stool and lowered himself to look Jorn directly in the eyes. "I think you sent us his daughters for two reasons. The first being, if your plan were to succeed, and you were able to take the throne, you could rally Valkara around your desire to 'rescue' the royal family uniting them behind you. And two, if you didn't succeed, you had the leverage to position yourself with us as an ally."

"That's a lot of assumptions, my king," Jorn replied evenly.

"Time will tell," Titus said as he rose to his feet. "Come, Elorah."

Both men withdrew from the cell. Titus began to make his way to the stairway leading back to Lydia and Nara.

"Where are you going, my king?" inquired Elorah.

"To find out the truth."

Titus hurriedly made his way back to their cell. He nodded for the guard to open the door. The two girls had just recently received a hot meal, so it seemed they did appreciate his hospitality. They looked up at him with a curious expression.

"Why do you think Jorn wanted to kill your father?" he asked without formality.

Lydia stared at him, reading his face. "Because some men just can't help but want power."

Titus nodded his head. "Do you believe he would have continued this conflict with us?"

"I don't know, yer majesty, if he would have gone to war today or tomorrow, but I do know this, men who want power are never satisfied. Do you think a man like that would bow to a king like yerself?"

"A wise answer from what seems a wise princess. You both will be housed with us in the King's Hall. You will eat with us tonight, if you still have room." He glanced down at the meal they had started on. "You will hopefully be returned to your father soon, as well."

"I don't understand?" Nara said with a confused look.

"I have spoken with Jorn, and I believe he is the snake you claim he is. I don't believe you will make any attempt to escape, and my hope is your peaceful return will result in a mending between our lands."

Lydia stood to her feet. "I hope you don't mistake us as weak, Titus, that would be a mistake. But, we will accept your hospitality." She turned to Nara and gave a nod as if to confirm everything was okay.

"Very well. I will have our guard escort you to the Royal Hall. There, you can prep in any way you need. Tonight we will dine together. I will meet you both then."

With that he stepped out of the cell and met back with Elorah. Both men made their way to the Royal Hall, where they would settle any other matters that needed their attention that day.

"Do you believe I made the right judgment?" Titus asked Elorah as they walked through the courtyard.

"Would you like me to speak honestly, my lord?" replied Elorah.

"Of course."

"It is the first time I could see there may be a king in you after all," he said with a slight smile.

These words were like a fresh breath in his lungs. Being king was like painting a portrait without a subject matter. To know that maybe he had painted a correct stroke, was all he needed to keep pushing forward.

"Thank you, Elorah, your words mean more than you know."

***

That evening Titus dressed in his royal garb, a brown and gold tunic woven with two lions facing opposite directions. It was an all too uncomfortable attire, but one a king should wear for a formal gathering. Besides, something inside him had a desire to impress the young Lydia. He quickly pushed that thought aside as absurd, yet it lingered still. A knock came from the door behind him.

"Come in."

Elorah pushed the door open. A slight smile on his face. "Good evening, my lord," he said with formality.

"What can I help you with?"

Elorah shuffled his feet for a moment before he spoke, "I have a proposal for you. One I think could help end this war before it starts."

"Do tell!" eagerness filled Titus' voice.

"We propose a marriage," Elorah said waiting for the shock to settle.

"A...a what?"

"It came to me this evening as I was prepping for dinner. In war, we use every advantage at our disposal to win. You must outmaneuver your opponent. So it dawned on me, what if we send a marriage proposal to King Doran?"

Titus didn't know what to think. It had never crossed his mind that a marriage might be the solution to all this, but it did make sense. Unite the two kingdoms. Doran would feel he had more say in the royal court, and the two kingdoms would be bridged. Besides all that, Lydia was easy on the eyes, but there was one catch.

"I don't think Doran would be too pleased that we hold his daughters hostage, and then propose a marriage as a solution. It's a bit of a loaded offer," Titus said.

"That is a snag, but one that could be played to our advantage. We could release the royal daughters as a goodwill offering along with said proposal. A gesture of good faith."

"What about the sons? We still have them, and there is no way to release them in time. Besides, they very well could be the killers of my father!"

"We use them as leverage still. We can explain that they will undergo a fair trial, and as long as they are cleared of charges, they can be released as well," Elorah suggested.

It was an interesting plan. One that could work. Not perfect, but what plan was? But then the idea of marrying a woman he hardly knew was another unknown he wasn't sure he wanted to face. He felt the drowning of responsibility beginning to grip him again.

"How about we make it through this dinner, then we can talk about a marriage proposal?" Titus suggested with a laugh.

"Again, I would agree on this wise council, my king," Elorah said, smirking himself.

Both men made their way down the royal chambers and into the grand meeting hall. Music filled the air, and many an esteemed commander had taken his place. They all rose as their Steward King entered the room, a moment he wasn't sure he'd ever get used to. Next to his and Elorah's seats sat the two princesses, both arrayed in gowns of green and gold. Something told him the two northern princesses were not the frill and lace kind. He greeted all with a formal and warm gesture, and motioned for them to resume. He and Elorah weaved their way through all the greetings to finally find their seats. His palms began to sweat. What was this strange northern girl doing to him? Her eyes didn't seem to carry the same awestruck feelings he had.

"Greetings, yer majesty, I hope it didn't burden you to allow a shabby pair like us to join your feast," Lydia said in mock greeting.

"Good start," Titus thought to himself.

"I am honored to have you both here," he retorted. "I hope you find your new quarters comfortable."

"Ahh, yes, the plush pillows are much better than a stone floor," she replied.

Titus let out a small sigh.

"Tell me, Lydia, what have I done that has offended you so. I was not the one to capture you, and I have tried to make your stay as comfortable as I can."

A mist began to cover her eyes.

"Yes, yer majesty, you have been kind, and you did not capture us, but you do hold those dear to me, so please do not think I can't see behind your benevolence."

Titus had forgotten her brothers would be weighing on her mind. Of course she would be angry at their capture. Of course she would see behind a kind ruse. It had not even been proven that she did not know about the plot to kill his father. He had been a fool to think a few kind gestures could calm this fire. He shuffled in his chair for a moment. They ate in awkward silence as the meal that evening was laid before them, a roasted boar, which any other time would have aroused Titus' appetite. Tonight, too much weighed on his mind.

"May I speak with you privately?" he asked.

Nara looked at Lydia with eyes that said, 'Please don't leave me'.

"Do I have a choice?" she responded.

"Of course you do. Nara, you may join us as well," his eyes flickering over to her.

Nara gave Lydia her nod of approval.

"Alright, your highness, we will follow you."

"Great. Just one second." Titus stood to address the assembly, "I will be taking our esteemed guests on a tour of the Western Watch. Please, do not stop your merriment for me."

A cheer rang out and the party continued as usual. Elorah stood as if to join them.

"No, I will be fine on my own, Elorah," Titus dismissed him with a hand gesture.

"Sir, if I may, they are still shield-maidens, not to be taken lightly."

"I understand that, but they've promised to behave, haven't you?" Titus said with a wiry smile.

"Of course, yer majesty," Lydia declared with a sarcastic look.

Titus motioned for the two of them to follow him, and they made their way to the back of the royal meeting hall. To the right was a door with a small torch mounted by it. Titus snatched it and again, gestured for them to follow. It was a dark hallway that was only lit by the small fire he carried.

"Where are you taking us?" asked Lydia, clearly confused.

"You'll see in just a moment," a grin stretching across his face.

A few more minutes passed as he weaved down the hall. Finally, he saw it. The faint light from the moon shown through an archway. He lead them out to one of his favorite views. As they passed under the archway, they were greeted by a spectacular sight. They found themselves standing on the city's inner wall. Stretching out before them were the Plains of Terras lit up by a full moon. A flickering of light in the distance revealed that Valkara's army had arrived, a small blight on the otherwise picturesque scene. The River Terras weaved around the city's outer wall shimmering in the cloudless night. Torches lit the city below. Some music and singing could be heard in the streets under them, soldiers soaking in life before it all could be taken away. It was a captivating sight.

"This was one of my favorite places to go when father would bring me here," Titus said after a moment to drink it all in.

"I am sorry about your father," Lydia said in a tone that showed she meant it.

Titus looked at the two girls.

"Was your father behind his murder?"

He said it. Laid it bare. Hoping beyond hope for the truth.

Both of the girls shuffled a bit until finally it was Nara that spoke up.

"No. Father is not always a kind man, nor are his hands clean of blood, but he did not do this. He respected the wishes of Eloy, in his own way."

Lydia sat in silence gazing at the scenic view. Titus turned away from them and gazed out as well.

"It's settled then. You will be released tomorrow."

Both turned and looked at him a bit stunned.

He continued, "I will also release your brothers when I return to Kingshelm, barring your father agrees to terms."

"You believe us?" Lydia said, her jaw slightly dropped.

"I do." He let out a deep sigh. "Maybe I am a fool, but my father was willing to trust others. It's what made him a good king."

"It also made him a dead one," Lydia said pulling no punches.

Titus let the sting subside before replying, "Maybe so, but I would rather be a good king than live as a tyrant." He turned and looked her in the eyes, "Maybe someday you will see me as a good king."

"Why would it matter if I did?" Lydia said, taken aback.

"I think you know why," Titus let a sad smile cross his face. "Maybe it's foolish thinking, but I would like to think that someday we could spend time not in conflict."

A blush crept up on Lydia's face. Titus was unsure if this had taken her completely by surprise or maybe she had thought the same.

"Well…I…"

He cut her off, "No need to worry about any of that now. We have a long road to reconciliation, but just know, I would like to see you at the end of it." He took a step back from the rampart's edge. "I think I will retire for the evening. You ladies have free rein of the Royal Hall. I will inform the guards you may come and go as you please. We will make way to Terras Plains, and Valkara's battle lines, tomorrow."

Titus began to walk back down the hall when he heard Lydia's voice behind him.

"I hope we can see each other at the end of this road as well."

He stopped for a moment, but did not turn around. He held back a smile from reaching ear to ear. After that brief pause, he continued back to the Royal Hall where he would spend the rest of his night rejoicing, or so he thought. He approached Elorah about his new plan.

"There may be hope after all," he said as he neared Elorah.

"Yes, how so?" Elorah asked, eyebrows raised.

Before Titus could reply, a soldier approached them both with a parchment in hand.

"For you, sirs," he said catching his breath. "A message from our spies."

Elorah unrolled it and read it aloud.

Commander,
You should be informed that Valkara has arrived and drawn battle lines. They have a force of 5,000 infantry and some 500 calvary. They will be in a position to siege the Western Watch by sundown tomorrow.

"The time has come," Elorah said to no one in particular. "Good work, soldier, now inform the commanders."

The soldier gave a formal bow and made haste.

"We won't need to fight," stated Titus. "Doran will see reason."

"We can hope. In either case our forces must be ready. You will still ride with me in the calvary?"

"Of course, but I will desire council with Valkara first, where we will free the princesses."

"Let's just hope they are willing to come to peace. Otherwise this gets a lot more complicated," Elorah sighed.

Titus made way to his chambers. The command went out and preparations would be in full swing by the morning. Almost 9,000 men would be counting on him to save their lives. These were the moments that made a king. A memory flooded into his mind of a time with his father.

"Titus, what makes a good king?" quizzed King Richard.

"Uhhhh, someone who is just, fair, and sees after the people."

"Yes, a good king is all these things, but there is more. A good king is a servant. He does not live his life for his own welfare. He gives it for others."

"Gives it? What do you mean?" the ten-year-old prince inquired.

"Well, it may be he gives his time, his resources, his trust, and if called upon, his life."

"Father, surely you dying wouldn't be good for the kingdom."

"It may not be, but when others depend on you to lead, you set the example, the standard. You are the one, no one else. Eloy has trusted me. I am the example to all others. They look to see if we will follow him, son."

Titus mulled this over.

"I'm trying, father," Titus responded to the memory. "I hope to serve Eloy's kingdom as well as you did."

He opened the door to his room carrying the faint hope that peace could win the day. That releasing Lydia and Nara could prove his intentions and at the end of this journey, he would discover he truly was a good king.

***

Lydia awoke with a cold sweat; memories of the evening flooded her mind. How the day had turned. She went from captive, to a guest, to...she wasn't sure. The way Titus had looked at her. What he had said, did he really mean it? Was this just some political cunning on his part, or did he truly feel some sort of affection toward her? The Steward King had been kind to Nara and her. He wasn't the spoiled, greedy, and power-hungry monster she imagined he'd be. He seemed humble, sincere, and a bit unsure of himself. He wasn't difficult on the eyes, either.

"Ah Lydia, you've sure got a right mess now," she muttered to herself. A shadow moved in the corner of the room. Her eyes flickered to the impenetrable dark, then over at her little sister sound asleep next to her. Her chest steadily rising up and down, deep in peaceful sleep. The only light was the moon which shown in from a small window by her bed.

There it was again, barely visible, movement. She reached for the knife she had secretly grabbed from the dinner earlier, hidden under her pillow.

"Ya creep, come on out," she blurted to the darkness.

A face subtly moved into the moonlight. It was Jorn, carrying a haunting smile, a small spatter of blood on his cheek. She let out a startled yelp and jumped to her feet. She had not expected the face of her nightmares to appear.

"Wha…What are you doing here? How are you here?" she said quivering, the adrenaline and fear causing her to shake. She held the knife behind her back.

"Ahh, my little princess. I missed your stupidity," Jorn snarled with eery delight. "I had some 'help' from some guards." The blood was now visible on his hand, which also wielded a large dagger. "You see, my plans have been quite ruined by your family." He began to circle toward the bed, causing Lydia to instinctively circle away from him. He continued, "Titus has not taken to my tale."

"Nor should he, ya snake!" she barked.

"Stupid girl," Jorn said shaking his head.

In an instant, she realized what he'd done. Nara stirred from her sleep as he sent the dagger plunging toward her.

"Nara!!" Lydia screeched. She'd forgotten all about her in her panic! It was too late. The blade plunged into her side and she let out a shriek of pain.

"YOU ANIMAL!" Lydia cried at the top of her lungs. She lashed out at Jorn, now revealing the knife in her hand. The blade lodged itself into his shoulder causing him to release the dagger in his hand. With a howl of pain, they both went crashing to the ground. In the ensuing tumble, Jorn landed on top of her. He yanked the knife from his shoulder and held it to her face.

"Now, as I was saying," he said with a venom filled hiss. "You and your vile little family have ruined Valkara. Doran and all his little spawnlings would be better off dead. I planned to lead Valkara to new heights, but it seems that dream is dead. So I will settle with the second-best option. Killing every single one of you." An evil grin crossed his face as he lifted the knife above his head.

Lydia did not fret. She thrust her hips in the air staggering Jorn forward. With swift reflexes she sent her palm flying into his throat. He let out a gargled croak. In one smooth motion she used Jorn's surprise to turn her torso sending him toppling to the floor and jumped to her feet. Analyzing the room, she noticed Jorn had barred the door so that they could not escape. They.

"That's right! Nara!" Lydia thought to herself. She rushed over to her sister. Nara lay motionless, her eyes glazed over. A bloodstain had perforated the sheets and now was dripping onto the floor. Lydia tried to hold back a sob, but wasn't successful, Nara was gone. She turned in fury to Jorn, except he wasn't on the floor where she'd left him. She scanned the room and saw he was crawling to the knife that had flown across the floor and rested a few inches from a small dresser.

With a heart-wrenching grimace, she clasped the dagger lodged in her sister. With a thrust it came loose. She had to fight back revulsion. Then, it was all fury. The deep fury that was an attribute of her family, filled her to the brim. She yelled at the top of her lungs releasing that rage in a violent torrent. In Jorn's eyes she could see fear, then enlightenment. He took the dresser next to him and threw it at her. She moved at just the right moment to dodge a direct impact, but the dresser caught the blade in her hand. The dagger flew across the room leaving her disarmed.

Now she was on the defense. Jorn strode across the chamber with thunderous steps. She scanned the room for any hope of escape. Her eye caught the window. She sprinted to the frame looking for a way to open it. She found the latch, but could hear Jorn right behind her. He sent a slash at her back, but she sidestepped the blow and sent a kick in return. It caught him in the ribs, staggering him for a few precious seconds. That's all she needed. She threw open the window, and without looking, leaped from its frame. She fell two stories into the mirky mote below that was a buffer around the fortress and its wall.

The water was a freezing embrace. She plunged for what felt like an eternity. With a gasp, she rose to the surface scrambling to the closest escape. A small ladder hung next to the mote's bridge. She hoisted herself up, shivering as she went. She heard a plunge behind her and turned just as Jorn himself began to surface.

"This Valka is insane," she muttered in utter disdain.

She scurried through the early morning streets. Everyone was still asleep except for a garrison of soldiers moving out of the city gate. She saw two men chatting, distracted as they prepped their horses. She snuck behind them and procured one of their cloaks. She wrapped it around her to disguise her face, tucking away the strands of her red curls. She moved from shadow to shadow. Finally, when she knew she had lost Jorn, she stopped.

Catching her breath, she mulled over what he had said. He had help...what did that mean? She didn't believe Titus would do such a thing. If he'd wanted her dead there were a thousand different ways to do so. But others in his company? Sure, why not? The daughter of their greatest irritant in the kingdom. Some might think peace was not ideal, and what better way to start a war then to kill them. Them. She collapsed in an instant. The images of Nara filling her head all over again. She wept and wept. Unable to contain her sobs, she made sure to find a discreet location. She let the flood of emotions envelop her, but only for a short time. She couldn't let the sorrow overtake her, so she took three deep breaths, stood to her feet, and wiped her eyes. Then she saw it. Her ticket out of this city. A chain of wagons, loaded with supplies, were on their way out of the city gate. She crept around to one of the wagons not accompanied by a guard and hopped into the back. Inside, she tucked herself against a storage of grain. The wagon passed under the arch of the gate. She could hear soldiers barking orders to each other. The canvas over her lit by the many torches. She had to hold back a yawn. The adrenaline was leaving her body, but she had to fight sleep. She knew what she must do. The implication came to her of what Nara's death meant. It meant war. The soldiers and commanders of Valkara would shrug her aside. Many of them had wanted this war for many years, "to break free of their bondage," as some would put it. Only her father could bring an end to this, and to her father she would go.

As the caravan of supplies passed beyond the city perimeter, the lights faded. She peaked out the back for any form of steed she could escape on. After a mile or so she saw her opportunity. A cart had become stuck in the mud from the previous rain. They had moved it aside to avoid stalling everyone else. Two horses sat detached as the owners argued on the best course of action. She jumped from the side of the wagon to avoid being seen, and then snuck behind the broken-down cart. Like a bolt, she leaped on a brown and white spotted horse. With a crack of the reigns, the horse reared into action. She could hear the shouts of men behind her, but she was free now. North she would go into the land she knew. She could save her home from destruction. Maybe she could save a king named Titus, too.

***

He was awakened by the urgent voice of Elorah, "My lord, you need to get up."

Titus rubbed the sleep from his eyes and stretched, "What time is it, Elorah?"

"Just at dawn's break, sir, but there is something you need to see now." The urgency in his voice jolted him awake.

"As you say."

Titus quickly scrambled to clothe himself, and without a word, followed Elorah out into the hall. He could barely keep pace as Elorah was just one step slower than a jog.

"Is this necessary?" Titus said with a slight pant.

"I apologize, my lord, but it's best if you see for yourself."

The two rounded the corner to the guest chambers. That's when Titus knew all was not well. It was the same hall that both of Doran's daughters had stayed in, their door broken off its hinges. A knot began to form in his stomach. Without a word Elorah motioned for him to enter the room.

A foul stench of death filled his nostrils. Then he saw it. The gruesome scene. A pool of blood flowed from the bed to the edge of the door. A small body was under the stained sheets, a dagger not far from his feet. Titus lifted his hand to his mouth to cover his shock.

"Is it...?"

"It is Nara, my king. Lydia, we believe, escaped," Elorah said monotone.

Titus approached the corpse, the glossy eyes, the haunting eyes of life drained from a body. He grasped her hand, tears filling his eyes. He grit his teeth in anguish.

"Who?" he said through his gritted teeth. "Who did this?"

"We believe it was the captive Jorn, sir. We found two guards slain near his cell with the keys left in the lock," Elorah explained.

Titus silently shook his head.

"We need to find Lydia, she can explain.."

Elorah cut him off, "Excuse me, my lord, but some men running supplies described a girl who stole one of their horses earlier this morning and took off toward Valkara. I believe Lydia is long gone by now."

Titus' shoulders dropped. A thousand thoughts rushed through his mind.

"So war it must be," he finally said.

"I fear so. What should I do about the council with Valkara, my lord?" asked Elorah.

"Forget it. We cannot explain our way out of this. It seems blood is the only answer today," bemoaned Titus. "But, do give one command to the men for me, Elorah."

"Of course."

"Have Jorn found."

Elorah began to walk away when Titus followed up with another question.

"Elorah?"

"Yes, my lord?"

"Has there been any word from Lancelin?"

Elorah seemed hesitant to answer.

"Yes, but it seems his father will not send help. We are alone in this fight, my king."

"Lancelin, I needed you, friend," Titus thought to himself.

"The blows just keep coming. When will they stop, Elorah?"

"When we begin to punch back, my lord," was his reply.

"Very well then, I guess we have no choice but to start punching. Prepare my armor."

8

IMARI

The Endless Wastes. There is a reason it is called that. Imari had never traveled through them, and now he knew why, mile after mile of bone dry rocks and dirt. The wind was another issue. Winds coming off the Southern Sea had molded and formed the wastes. Those same gusts created blinding sandstorms. On top of it all, The Wastes were the hottest terrain in all of Isandia. He took his Shama and wrapped it tighter around his face.

"It won't get any better," came the voice of Khaleena.

"You didn't have to say it," Imari grumbled in return.

A smirk could be seen beneath Khaleena's covering.

They had escaped the massacre in Wahah, and sure enough, the Bomani and Masisi had met them at the edge of The Wastes. Time had not been on their side. Scouts from their small army had informed them that the Sycar were close behind. It lead to a less than prepared journey through the most inhospitable territory in all Islandia. Death seemed to mark every step of the way. Imari knew that their journey through The Wastes was only the beginning. At the end awaited The Grand Wall. No enemy had ever overthrown it.

The company had been traveling for four days now. Water was being rationed, but would only last them to the very edge of their journey.

"Brother," Imbaku strode up next to him, "we need to talk."

"Speak," Imari said giving him a welcoming gesture.

Imbaku moved in close. "What is our plan? I mean, for The Grand Wall."

"I...I don't know Imbaku. It feels as if we stumble from one disaster into the next at every step," he lamented.

Imbaku took a deep breath. "Yes, it does seem that way."

They rode for a moment, the voice of the howling wind filled the void.

"I'm sorry, brother," blurted Imbaku.

Imari was taken aback.

"For what, brother?"

"Since our escape all those years ago, I've blamed you for our parents' murder, for our misfortunes. I thought you marrying that shuka Nabila was the problem, but now I see we are all cursed."

A slight smile crept on his face. Imari punched him in the arm.

"Ah, here I thought you were serious!" Imari gave a teasing laugh.

"I am, brother," Imbaku said. "This journey has shown me something. We may not agree, we may see the world differently, but you are no coward. You have believed in Khaleena when I have not. Besides, it is likely when we reach the wall we will die. I don't want animosity between us."

Imari fought back tears. "Brother...I," he paused, "thank you."

Imbaku gave him a nod and slowed his mount to give Imari space. It was what he needed to keep going forward. A family united despite his failings. Forgiveness. Maybe he could be a worthy Khosi. The sacrifices of James, Impatu, and so many others depended on it.

It was evening when they decided to make camp. Unfortunately, the winds did not die down. They had traveled next to the curve of the Sahra mountain chain all day.

Near their base they were able to take shelter from the gusts. Henry and a few others made a fire for them to prepare dinner, a small amount of game found before they had entered The Endless Waste. Imari was sore from endless riding. To recline near a fire was like a dream.

"Khosi, it should be three more days, and we will arrive at the wall," conferred Henry.

"Three more days?" thought Imari "I see why they call it a waste. I feel a waste myself."

"When we arrive we will need to have a plan, otherwise it will be over before we even begin," Henry counseled.

"Has anyone been to the wall?" Imari inquired of the group.

Khaleena shook her head no as did Imbaku.

"Those of Khala don't typically choose to go this far west," she said.

"I have seen it from a distance, but we always traveled to Sahra via the port," Henry confessed.

"I have been," came the gravelly voice of Lombaku.

All of them looked up. The rugged man who could be mistaken for a dark-skinned barbarian from the Lowland Hills stepped forward. His arms were scared with tribal markings and his face an array of piercings.

"Many years ago my clan traveled to the west to raid a special caravan. The finest steel one could find," he mused. "We reached the caravan under the shadow of The Grand Wall. Couldn't have been less than 200 feet tall. The sun had cast its shadow on us. I remember the arrows that rained down. They alone killed half of us."

"Did you see any way in?" Imari asked.

"Hmmm," Lombaku scratched his scraggly beard. "There were several small gates at the base large enough to let a small cart through. If I remember they were evenly spaced out. None without a watchtower."

Gloom's shadow fell on them all. A company of a few hundred had no hope of overpowering even a weakly armed tower.

"What if it could be climbed?" Imbaku asked.

They turned in disbelief.

"You want to scale a 200-foot wall with winds as strong as these?" Henry responded dumbfounded. "There is no chance we'd make it."

"Then not we, how about I? We only need one, or maybe a handful, to make it. The Wall is huge, at least 50 miles long. Each tower can't possibly be manned by that many guards."

"So you volunteer then, huh brother? And who else would join your suicidal campaign?" scolded Khaleena.

"I will," Imari replied. He looked Imbaku's way, "We have no choice. We cannot take the wall with a frontal assault. We must climb it, and then dispatch the gate's guards from within. We can't allow fear to stop us now."

"I don't see many options," Henry sighed. "But Khosi, I am not so sure you should accompany the decided party. If you die this whole mission fails."

"I will not let other men die for me," Imari said turning to look at Imbaku, "I am not a coward."

"So you two will take on a whole squad of guards by yourself?" Khaleena asked.

"We've done it before," smirked Imbaku.

"I will go, too," said Lombaku.

"Me as well," echoed Boani who had remained silent up until now.

"So now you two want to throw your lives away?" Khaleena said placing her hands on her hips.

"With your permission, I want to avenge the men that died that day," Lombaku said.

"I just like the thrill of a fight," Boani said with a childish grin.

With a sigh of exasperation Khaleena threw her hands up.

"Fine, go die, big bad heroes. See if I care."

"So this is the plan?" Henry asked.

"This is the plan," Imari confirmed.

"Now, to find some rope," Imbaku said with a smile.

Imari slept well that night. Maybe it was because having a shuka plan, as Imbaku would say, is better than no plan at all, or maybe it was because for the first time he felt he really was a Khosi.

The dawn came too quickly for his liking. The next day was full of the same things, wind, dirt, and exhaustion. It wasn't until the next day that The Wastes showed their hidden beauty. The road began to incline. Higher and higher it began to ascend. They reached a bend in the road that took their breath away. To the right was a sheared cliff's edge, and below, a drop that had no visible bottom. All around down below were Mesas, many blasted by untold years of wind, some with gaping holes, and others were whittled down to sandstone arches. In the middle of all that was a chasm deeper than the eye could see. It was a beauty formed from danger. They began to decline shortly after, a path winding down into the Mesa filled valley below. Night would soon be upon them, and this elevation was not ideal to make camp.

"What do we do!?" shouted Imari over the wind which had increased dramatically.

"I don't know," shouted Henry. "It looks as if a storm is coming through."

Sure enough a crack of thunder roared above them.

"Run!" Imari ordered.

The whole company made their descent as fast as they could. The wind threatened to sweep them off the edge. The sun now fully set, presented even more peril. Imari could hear faint cries that trailed off in the distance. He shuddered at what had caused them. The wind yanked at his tunic whirling and whipping it across his face. A flash of lightning struck not far above him sending his camel into a panic. It set off in a rush down the path in blind terror. He yanked and pulled at the reigns in a vain attempt to stop it.

His heart was bursting in his chest just waiting for the feeling of weightless free fall. He felt a hand grip his back, and in a flash he was thrown off his camel and onto his back. Moments later he heard the shriek of his camel. He looked up to see the extended hand of Lombaku. Speechless, he reached to take it, his mind whirling over his near death.

The rest of the evening continued as a living nightmare. Countless times he had felt they would find themselves crashing down into oblivion. Imari prayed for the morning light, but it felt as though it would never come. Finally, as if some force had been satisfied, the darkness lifted. It started with a bleak colorless grey, but a faint ray of light flickered behind an array of storm clouds. In this new light, Imari could see they had at last reached the valley floor.

They took an assessment of those remaining. To their astonishment no more than ten had perished the evening before. For those who did, a moment of silence was given, then they turned their attention to the next great obstacle, The Grand Wall.

Soaked to the bone, they made camp at the base of The Wall where it connected to the Sahra Mountains. No sentries or towers were in sight. A tent was quickly erected for shelter as a light rain continued to fall. Khaleena, Imari, Imbaku, Henry, Lombaku, and Boani all gathered to finalize their plan. In exhaustion, the small party sat in silence for a moment, none of them knew how they survived the night before. Finally, Henry spoke up.

"Are you still up for scaling the wall, gentlemen?"

The four of them looked to each other.

"Do we have any other option?" Imbaku asked.

"This is it," Lombaku replied soberly.

"Then it's what we must do." Imari turned to Henry, "After we scale the wall, you and Khaleena will lead the men through the first gate west of here. We will kill the guards and open it for you. From there we make for Sahra as fast as we can before we are discovered."

"What about when we do make it to Sahra? Surely we will be recognized," Imbaku added.

"Henry?" Imari looked to him.

"Yes, there is a large warehouse used as a hideout that Nabila has secured. That will be our best bet. From there we will make contact with her and see how we should proceed."

"But how do we sneak a small army in?" Imbaku asked.

"A caravan," Khaleena stated to no one in particular. "We can raid a caravan on the open plains to Sahra."

"Could that work?" Imari inquired.

Henry rubbed his chin for a moment.

"All of this hinges on us moving quickly. We will be discovered, that is just a matter of time. What counts is that we take Fahim out beforehand." He paused a moment.

"This is what we should do." Henry stood to his feet. "When you open the gate, I will go ahead of us and make contact with Nabila. I will tell her it's now or never that we must strike. In the meantime, you prepare the caravan disguise. They travel daily to the port a few miles from the city. When you arrive, we shall all gather together to make a push to the palace."

"A lot of ifs," Imbaku stated.

"We don't have many options here, and we can't go back now," Khaleena said.

Imari stood to his feet.

"It's the best plan we have. Have the men rest for an hour, then we move. We should rest as well. We have quite the climb ahead."

He turned his vision to the three others. They all gave a nod of agreement.

"Eloy help us," whispered Henry.

***

Imari stood looking up at the wall, a towering presence looming over him. This was an undertaking that did more than
raise his pulse.

Imbaku came and put a hand on his shoulder and with a
sheepish grin said, "At least it stopped raining."

The wall was still slick from the rain. Finding a grip would
prove to be even more difficult. What came to their aid was
the structure of the wall itself. It was built in three tiers, each
having a protruding lip onto which they could hook a rope.
The only issue was that one of them had to get up there first.
Boani had offered to go, claiming to be the most skilled climber
of the four of them although Imari assumed the man was a
suicidal thrill-seeker. Each of them grasped a small wicker
shield and a rungu for their assault. Imari stared on as Boani
took two deep breaths and began his climb. Hand over hand
with careful, but surprising, speed, he made his way up. The
blocks that created the wall didn't offer much in the way of
grip before being wet, so Boani used a small pick to dig into
the creases of the wall. The mudbrick gave way to the small
pick allowing him to make his ascent. Close to the first tier a
gust of wind blew over him. In a blink the mission looked as
if it would fail. The wind caught Boani's shield mounted on
his back. It was like a falcon's talons had dug into him and
were desiring to carry him away. He held on for dear life to
the small hooks in the wall. When the wind let up, he slowly
unstrapped the shield from his back and let it cascade to the
ground below. After a few more heart-stopping minutes, he
reached the first tier. He let down a shout to those observing
below.

"Lose the shields."

No one complained as they all handed them to a few
warriors watching the spectacle. Shortly after, a rope came
tumbling down about ten feet above them.

"Looks like we will still have to climb a little," jested
Imbaku.

One by one, Lombaku, Imbaku, and then Imari started their climb. Several times Imari felt his footing give way. The other three stood making fun of him from the top. When all of them reached the first tier, Boani began again.

Slowly he edged his way up again making sure not to look down. At this height even the thin lip they stood on brought no comfort. Every gust of wind created a moment of desperation and fear. Imari could only imagine what Boani was feeling. After what felt like an eternity, he reached the next tier. The same sequence ensued. Only this time the height was dizzying. Imari mustered everything within him just to put one hand and foot in front of the other. Finally, after another hour, all four of them reach the second tier. All that was left was the top of the wall.

"We almost did it, brother," a slight smile crossed Imbaku's face.

"We are not there yet," Imari said panting.

"Don't tell me, brother, you have a fear of heights? Maybe I need to take back my "not a coward" statement," a grin from ear to ear stretched across his face.

"Eiisshhh, I am not a coward brother, but this, this is another thing entirely." He would have mustered a laugh if he didn't think it would send him toppling over the edge.

They watched as Boani was only ten feet from the edge of the wall. That's when disaster struck. A guard became visible as he was patrolling down the wall. All of them pressed against the wall as closely as they could, the slick mudbrick clinging to their clothes. Imari could feel his heart pounding against the cold stone.

Boani, doing all he could to remain hidden, was visibly shaking to hold himself up. The long climb was taking its toll. The guard was humming a tune as he patrolled, oblivious of the invaders below. He reached the end of the wall that attached to the mountain and turned to make his way back. Boani was now shaking violently doing everything he could not to be seen.

The guard passed a few yards beyond them. That's when Boani allowed himself to move forward. When he went to stab the pic in again, his foot slipped. The pic came screeching down the wall to a halt near his abdomen. He froze gritting his teeth. The guard stopped in his tracks and turned to look over the wall's edge. His eyes became saucers as he saw what was transpiring. He let out a yell and turned to run back to the nearest tower. In a lightning fast move, Boani grabbed the rope at his hip and swung it on to the parapet of the wall. With all his remaining strength, he pulled himself up to the top, his hand moving to his rungu. With a swift thrust of his arm he sent the rungu flying into the back of the guard. The Sahra soldier collapsed to the ground. Boani, seeing the opportunity, swiped his rungu from the ground and moved to pound him to death.

He leaned over and whistled to the rest of the group. As quickly as they could, they made their way up. Just as Lombaku was crawling over the parapet, Imari heard shouts. A squad of guards on patrol had spotted them. He could hear the clanging of weapons and cries of men. Imbaku was now making his way into the fray. Imari saw Lombaku pick up a man and toss him over the edge of the wall. His shriek echoed as he fell, followed by a sickly thud.

Imbaku leaped into the fight. Now it was Imari's turn. With sore muscles and depleted strength he climbed the final stretch. When he was close to reaching the top, he noticed the sounds of fighting had died down. Before he could pull himself up a hand was there to greet him. The childish grin on Boani followed.

"What took you so long? Afraid of a little fighting?"

With one strong yank that Imari could hardly believe Boani could still have, he was on top of the wall. On the other side lay the vast expanse of Sahra. A flat, arid, and lifeless plain, but now was not the time to dwell on the landscape.

He turned his attention down the rampart. It was likely half a mile to the first tower, as well as where a small entrance gate would be. They caught their breath for only a moment. Imari observed the damage. Fifteen guards laid strewn out before him.

"You made quick work of them," he quipped.

"Lightly armed, green recruits," spat Lombaku. "I'm waiting for the real challenge."

"Don't worry, I think you'll get it sooner or later," Imbaku replied.

The four of them made their way to the tower. They needed to move quickly if they were going to reach it before their forces below could be spotted. It would not take long for a whole squad of missing guards to go unnoticed. After several minutes the tower came into view. It was made of the same red, mudbrick as the wall. It had a capped dome at the top, and two guards could be seen through the windows. The party entered a dead sprint to the tower entrance. Bursting through the door, Lombaku let out a roar slamming his rungu down onto the skull of the first guard he saw. Following him, Boani flung his rungu into the face of a guard just sitting down for a meal. Imbaku and Imari followed countering strikes sent their way and sending their weapons into the chest of their foes. The guards collapsed, and they finished them off with one last strike.

"Boani, come with me. We will take care of the tower guards above. Imari and Imbaku, you take care of the gate?" They nodded in agreement.

They all sprinted into action. Imari and Imbaku flew down the stairs that lead to the bottom of the tower. Around and around they went. When they reached the bottom, they observed several more guards standing completely unaware of what awaited them.

"How do you want to take them?" asked Imbaku.

"Let's see, five of them? I'll take the three to the right cleaning their gear. You take the two guarding the door," Imari posed.

"Why do I only get the two?" asked Imbaku feigning insult.

"Because, brother, we both know I'm the better warrior," Imari teased.

With that, he rushed the guards sending his rungu crashing down on an unsuspecting man. With a follow-up blow, he sent a crushing strike to the face of the guard caught in surprise. The final guard had enough time to process what was taking place. He sent a slash with his scimitar at Imari's head. He ducked out of the way at the last second and threw the rungu into his ribs. The soldier dropped his sword and crumpled to the ground. Imari picked up the scimitar and sent a decisive blow. He looked over to see that Imbaku was already searching on how to open the gate, two guards dead at his feet. He moved over to help him.

"You couldn't help me back there?" Imari asked.

"You are the better warrior, I figured you wouldn't need any help," sarcasm thick in his tone.

They quickly found a key on one of the guards to open the small gate. Shortly after this Lombaku and Boani arrived down the stairs.

"Glad to see you made it," Imbaku said.

Both men snorted in reply.

"There!" Imari turned the key and the small gate opened. He turned to the rest of the group, "I guess we wait now."

They didn't have to wait long. Henry was the first to arrive, breaking off from the group to get a head start.

"Good work, gentlemen," he said leading his camel through the doorway. "You made quick work of them."

Lombaku and Boani snorted a thanks. Imbaku gave his signature grin, and Imari could only help but think of the next step.

"Henry, if I may, I would like to alter our plan," Imari said.

"Okay? What is it Khosi?"

"I want to go with you."

The group all looked at each other.

"Imbaku, you can lead the men as well as I can. You take them and meet us at the designated spot in Sahra. Henry, I need to come with you. To see if the one I have placed all this trust in will come through."

"A little late for that isn't it?" spouted Boani.

"Maybe so, but I need this for myself. Besides, you three seem to be able to handle yourselves just fine."

"So be it, if that's what you desire," replied Henry.

Imari turned to Imbaku, "Brother, you have placed your trust in me, now I am placing it in you. You can do this. You have proven to be a capable warrior and a trustworthy ally."

Imbaku was silent for a moment. "Thank you, brother. I won't let you down." Imbaku then turned to Henry, "Where should we regroup in Sahra?"

"Ah yes, when you reach the eastern gate you will need to show the proper certificates that authenticate your merchandise. You should find that on the caravan leader. After that, you will need to look for the palace street. Just before you reach the ancient tombs you will see a red banner above a large warehouse. That is where you'll find us."

"Alright, certificate, palace street, red banner, warehouse. Shouldn't be too difficult, huh?" he said letting out a self-assuring laugh.

"Let's hope. Now come, Imari, we should hurry," Henry said.

Imari gave an agreeing nod and the two opened the southern gate to the tower. Before them lay the ten-mile stretch to Sahra. Imari hopped on the camel behind Henry and they were off. Henry rode with a swiftness that made Imari more than a little nervous, the red dust below a blur. It was only an hour before the looming wall of Sahra was in view.

The city was carved into the Nawafir Mountains named after the only source of water in all of the Sahra. It was these mountains that allowed for a thriving city in the middle of a wasteland. The city's palace was unmatched in its craftsmanship. Magnificent arches and designs were etched into the heart of the Nawafir Mountain chain expanding upwards of fifty feet. Next to the palace lay the ancient tombs of old where many of Sahra's rulers slept, including Yeshu. Another day perhaps Imari could visit such an amazing site.

The two of them approached the gate and were greeted by two Sycar. They were ordered to halt with a motion of the hand.

"What kind of business does a Northerner and a Khalan have in Sahra?" interrogated the man.

"Here we go again…" thought Imari.

"Official business with Princess Nabila. I am a royal emissary of King Richard, and now King Titus. I have news to deliver. This man with me is my friend Imbatu, chieftain of clan Khalad. He brings with him the monthly tribute to the Sulta." Henry pulled out a letter with some sort of royal seal.

The Sycar looked it over, and then waved them on with disinterest.

When they were a safe enough distance away Imari asked, "What was that all about?"

"I told you I was a spy for King Richard in the South. I didn't tell you I was sent as an official ambassador of the North. It just so happens official duties and unofficial work often go hand in hand."

"Eiisshh, politics," muttered Imari.

"The games we play," Henry smirked.

As they entered the city it was like entering Wahah, but at a scale amplified by ten. Vibrant color, sights, and sounds filled the air. Shouts and laughter were around every corner. A buzz of people wherever you turned. Only it felt slightly different. As if under the mask of joy and energy there was fear. A cloud that, if lifted, would show a darker truth beneath.

Henry turned sporadically through side streets and alleyways. Imari assumed that it was a precaution to uncover anyone who might be trailing them. After some time Henry felt they were all clear. He finally entered the palace street and made way for the visible warehouse he had described. The two of them dismounted and Henry lead the way to a back door. He gave a knock in a specific sequence and a small window in the door slid open.

"Here to see her," said Henry lifting a small ring on his finger to show the door guard.

A few seconds later the door opened.

"You're four days late," said the guard.

"We had some…complications," Henry replied.

"Where is James?" the guard asked.

Henry's silence was all that was needed. The door flung open with a masked figure standing to the side. The two of them were ushered into a vast open warehouse where barrels of what had to be grain and urns of water were being stockpiled.

"What is this place?" asked Imari.

"The city storehouse," answered Henry, "for times of famine. The royal court stores up grain and water for the people and keeps it here. No one without official approval can enter, hence the privacy."

"But how can you trust you won't be sold out?" Imari asked.

"Let's just say the rule of Fahim has gotten on the wrong side of many people."

The two of them followed their masked escort up into a room that overlooked the storehouse. It had a small stairway that lead up to it. The escort opened the door and ushered them inside. Henry entered first, with Imari just behind him. As Imari looked into the room his heart stopped.

There she was. The slender form with dark olive skin in a red silk sari. Her back was turned from him. As he stepped fully into the room, she turned to greet them. Her dark brown eyes locking with his. In that moment he was raptured again into the moment of their wedding. Her lips parted in a smile.

"Hello, Imari."

9

TITUS

He could feel the uneasiness of his horse beneath him. The mount anxiously dug at the earth below. Beyond him lay the vast plains of Terras, a lush, green array of windswept grass. On Titus' left, the forces of Valkara gathered in formation. Their banners were fluttering in the wind with the field of postal blue and the midnight black ram head of their realm. Each man in dark steel, their faces covered by a mask that resembled the ancient Valkaran warrior king Odain.

To his right, the armies of the Riverland were at the ready, each man in the lion crested armor. A tint of gold and dark silver was shining in the sun, the banner of the young lion cub on a purple field. Each of them a man under his charge. Standing at their head was Dios in the king's armor, his armor. The lion's mane splayed behind a golden helm shaped like a roaring lion. He would be the object of all Valkara's wrath.

Titus glimpsed around him. Elorah was to his flank, giving commands to his captains. Close to 1,500 horsemen were at their backs hiding just behind a hill's crest ready to flank Valkara when the battle ensued, a gleaming display of thunderous death. Titus could feel his heart thumping in his chest. Battle was never something he craved. He saw no glory in the death of men, especially by his own hands. For many years he believed this made him weak. It wasn't until his mother's words, that he believed differently.

He was raptured back to Kingshelm's gardens for a moment, his mother carefully trimming a bed of roses. Her hair was pulled back, hands and clothes caked in dirt. She turned to greet her young prince. He came to her crying, tears streaming at the hurtful words of his stupid friends. She held him for a moment before looking him over.

"Titus, what do you think brings a man glory?" she asked examining him.

"To win honor in battle, I suppose, to prove your strength. At least that's what the others say," Titus recited.

"Ahh, so strength comes from a bloody battle, does it?" she asked.

He stood, shuffling his feet. "I mean…it's how all men gain fame, mother."

"So is fame strength? To be known? To be the hero?" she pressed.

This time he gave no reply.

"My young Titus. Glory is not found in taking life. It is not found in achievements or being the hero."

"Then where to do you find it, mother?"

"Glory is found in being a faithful steward to what you are given. All of us, one day, will stand account, love. What will be to our credit is what we build up, not what we destroy." She turned to her garden. "Now, are you going to help me with these flowers?" she asked, grinning at him.

"I miss you, mother." Titus thought as he clutched the pendant under his breastplate. "There is no real glory won today, only death."

Titus was rushed back to the present. He observed as Valkara sent out an emissary to make terms. No one was sent in reply. Valkara made short work of this response with a horn blow, signaling a call to action.

"It seems we will have a battle," Elorah muttered. "A shame we couldn't find Jorn."

"It would have brought me some solace to an otherwise miserable day," Titus said shaking his head.

"Come now, don't let the men hear you," scolded Elorah.

Ahh the men. Yes, he would need to perform for their sake at least. He tapped Morning's Dawn hanging at his side. "At least I have you, you'll make up for the warrior I am not."

The horn blew out from Kingshelm's forces followed shortly by the cry:

"A lion's roar they hear. They fear his cry. They fear to die. They know the men of Eloy are here."

In an instant a flash of swords were drawn, and a shield wall erected. The two forces began to move slowly toward each other in an inevitable collision.

Elorah cried out beside him, "Get ready men!"

Titus watched as the front lines drew nearer. When they reached about 200 yards, the arrows began to fly. The waves of whistling bolts filled the air, followed by the thud of contact. Some into flesh, some into steel. Corpses from both sides began to litter the ground. The earth beneath would not be satisfied yet. Shouts were heard as the forces continued to move closer and closer. Now javelins were thrown, more men collapsing to an early grave. Titus fought back the tears he could feel welling up.

"It's for the men, you must show no frailty for them," he told himself.

Then the real horror began. The two battle lines, some twenty yards away, erupted. Men, in an all-out sprint, crashed into each other like waves onto a rock. The utter chaos of battle. Steel flashed in the air, the baying of horses rang out. Cries of agony, despair, fear, and blind rage. This was what war made of men.

"Men of Kingshelm at the ready," barked Elorah.

Now it was his turn. Titus moved to put on his helmet which he had tied to his saddle. The sharp sound of swords being drawn clanged around him. He performed his part to the symphony, now to dance to the tune. The horn blew.

"Men of Kingshelm, charge!!" Elorah ordered.

The rush began. In a blaze of emotion and thunder, the calvary streamed forward. Titus rode as hard as he could, not thinking of anything other than moving forward. Forward, to the ever-growing madness before him. He could hear nothing but the deafening clamor of hooves. It was a blink when they had reached the 200-yard mark. That's when the arrows came followed by a shriek of terror. He brought his shield up with a blind guess, and received a sickly thud as a greeting. He thought he could hear the faint choke and collapse of the man next to him, but the thundering hooves could not be overcome, and he dare not look back.

He kept his shield raised, and again another greeting from Valkara came his way.

"Fifty yards!" came the cry.

He looked beyond his shield to see the terrified flank of the Valkaran army. Men trampling over each other to escape the coming onslaught. The onslaught he was bringing. A few more endless seconds and it would be time to shed blood. The fear now visible to him in the whites of their eyes over the exchange they both recognized was about to happen. Then it came.

He, without thinking, without hesitating, lowered his blade at an angle to receive its offering. Then came the crash. He felt his horse give for a moment as it collided with the bodies below. Then he felt Morning's Dawn catch its target. It sliced with ease through the man's shoulder, rendering his arm off. The next victim was caught on the collarbone slicing clean through. Another was relieved of his head. Warrior after warrior met a swift end as the calvary continued their charge.

A tide of death washing over their foes. The men before them fleeing now to the open field.

Then Titus remembered. The orders! They were to ride to meet Dios, the decoy king's aid. He caught his bearings as the organized line shattered before them. He looked around to see where the front lines would be. He scanned to see the king's armor cutting down foe after foe some hundred yards to his right, between them a sea of men.

"Titus! Look out!" came a voice.

He turned in bewilderment to where the warning came from and felt his mount give beneath him hearing the shriek of pain it exhaled. He collapsed to the ground, pinned beneath its weight. He could just make out an arrow that had pierced its side as he tried to squirm free. He heard a roar and a clanging of steel behind him. He twisted to see what was happening.

Elorah was engaged with two men who had been making their way toward him. Elorah, from his mount, sent a spear through one of the men's chests. He deflected a blow with the sword in his left hand then maneuvered his horse to collide into his enemy sending the soldier reeling. With the opening, he sent a fatal slash across his body. His enemies vanquished, he strode over and dismounted to help Titus. The two men gave their full effort to push the horse off of him. In his peripherals, Titus could see a cluster of horseman encircling them like a protective wall.

"You need to pay attention to your surroundings," complained Elorah.

"Yea, I'll quit horsing around," Titus said with a dry cough.

The look on Elorah's face was pure disgust.

"Come, my jester king. We need to save Dios before he dies on your behalf," a coolness in his tone.

Titus winced at his failed attempt to deflect the horror he was experiencing. With the horse removed Elorah motioned for Titus to join him on his horse. Titus followed the order and hopped onto the back of the mount. Elorah, without a sparing second, darted toward the fray, barking for the calvary to fall in line. They entered a wedge formation as they plowed through the hordes of Valkaran soldiers. Titus hacked at a soldier to his right, cutting him down where he stood. Elorah sent a spear through a man trying to grab the reins of his mount. Carnage surrounded them, man after man being slain, senseless and unforgiving. Titus paused only briefly to see the blood-stained gauntlets covering his hands. His mind shuttered, but he was shaken from his thoughts when a Valkaran came rushing at them. The blade gleaming over the warriors head. The soldier brought it down in a swift blow. Titus' deflection sent the blade shattering in two. The Valkaran stood dumbfounded. Titus stood staring into the eyes of a man terrified of what was to come next. Titus lowered his blade in a gesture of peace, the fear in the man's eyes morphing into confusion. Before Titus could motion for the man to run, a spear came piercing through the Valkaran's chest. The soldier dropped to his knees, eyes fixed on the protruding spear point. Titus let out a cry.

"NO!" he yelled reaching down for the man.

It was too late. Another swift blow sent him collapsing to his side, eyes empty of life. Elorah turned his attention to the scene.

"Pull it together, my lord," he said yanking Titus' shoulder. "We have a battle to win, plenty more Valkarans will die."

Titus knew that would be true, yet the haunting image wouldn't leave him, a man with hope cut down. They continued their fight toward the front lines. Dios was now only a small distance away, the Battle the thickest around him. The cavalry charge had created a wedge, dividing Valkara's forces nearly in two. The tide of battle was almost reaching the tipping point of victory. One need not be a tactician to see victory was close at hand. That's when he heard it. The strange sound of an unfamiliar horn rang out from behind him. The entire battlefield paused and turned toward the strange sound.

From the west he could see a whole host of half-naked men painted with a strange blue paste. A barbaric cry rang out as they rushed toward them.

"Reinforcements!!" Elorah shouted. "Calvary form up to engage."

With a sudden turn, Titus and all the rest of the mounted men left the rest of the army to charge the incoming force. There were not nearly as many sallying forth with them this time. As they came nearer to the new opposition, Titus jaw dropped. It was not a mere hundred men they were rushing to engage, but rather several thousand stood to greet them. Titus could sense the panic in Elorah as he, too, recognized what they were about to rush into. Regardless, he felt him stir their horse onward ever faster. The new wave of men charged to meet them, and meet them they did. The two forces crashed into each other like two tidal waves sending out a ripple of steel, blood, and death. Elorah and Titus managed to cut down several men. Momentum began to stall, however, and soon their horse was halted. Countless arms and weapons came pulling at them threatening to drag them down into the raging ocean of violence beneath. Titus swung with all his might slicing off weapon and limb alike that reached for him, but they just kept coming. It was madness. These men were different. They carried no fear, no regard for safety, just wave after wave of pulling, reaching, and attacking. Titus felt his arm strength waning. "How long could he keep this up?" he wondered to himself.

Then, another blade came swinging down toward him. He went to deflect it as he had done a hundred times now. This time something different happened. Unlike before, Morning's Dawn did not shred the weapon to pieces. It sliced a deep wound into the incoming sword, but caught toward the middle of the blade. Titus yanked it free and looked at the sword in bewilderment. This was just the opening the enemy needed. One of the wild men took the opportunity and yanked on his leg. Another grabbed his shield arm, and using the momentum, flung him off his horse. Titus came crashing to the ground in the midst of the madness. He felt suffocated. Angry faces, flying limbs, blood, and mud flooded his vision. He swung Morning's Dawn blindly feeling it catch here and there, but unaware of any damage he might be inflicting. After a few moments, he stopped his wild swinging and realized a small circle had cleared around him. He caught his bearings and looked about. He saw Elorah, forced to a kneeling position next to a lightly armored man. This man distinguished himself among all the others by wearing a Valkaran tunic over his chainmail. He stood a little over six feet tall and looked as if he knew the ways of war. Titus slowly rose to his feet, now realizing how heavy his armor felt.

The man in the Valkaran tunic spoke. "King Titus, a pleasure to finely make your acquaintance."

Titus brought Morning's Dawn in front of him, looking around at all who surrounded him. Some of the blue barbarians began to chuckle.

"That isn't necessary. You can see, can't you, that this fight is over," said the man.

Titus assessed the situation. With Morning's Dawn he may be able to cut them free, but what happened a moment ago shook his confidence.

"My name is Geralt," said the Valkaran man. "I represent King Doran and the men of The Lowland Hills."

The Hillmen? That's who these men where. Titus was putting it together now.

"Why would the Hillmen help Valkara?" Titus demanded. "They hate each other."

"New management, besides, they owed me a debt. But that's not what matters now," replied Geralt.

"Then what matters now?"

"What we do from here," said Geralt. "You have a choice, King Titus. Will you surrender this fight, so I don't have to kill any more of your men today?"

Titus' eyes flickered over to Elorah.

"Yes, today, but what about tomorrow, or the days after that?" Elorah spat.

"No promises, but I am sure Doran will be more understanding if you surrender now. If you kill more of those dear to him…well, I can't say it will go well for you."

"And the realm. What is to happen to Islandia?" Titus asked.

"It will belong to us. Doran will take control until something can be sorted out in this mess."

"What about when Eloy returns? Will he surrender the kingdom back to him?"

"Ha, I think you have bigger worries than a dead king's return, my lord. No, there is to be a new realm. One of our own making, I do believe."

"We will not, then," Titus replied defiantly.

"You will not what? Surrender? Surely you are joking. It's over, and if you are banking on a false hope that…"

Titus interrupted him, "I would surrender this kingdom from my control, I would spare the life of each of my men, but I was entrusted as Steward King for one task, to safeguard the realm till Eloy's return. If you will not return it to him, I, and every man in my army, will fight to the last. That is my solemn pledge to you."

Elorah had a faint smile creep across his face.

Geralt let out a sigh. "So be it."

He flung his sword's sheath to the side, revealing to Titus what could only be a Dawn Blade, but no, something darker? A black aurora swirled around it, a sickly green glow on its edges.

"Come, foolish King, if you wish to be remembered a martyr, let's make you one," Geralt motioned with his hand.

Titus took one hesitating step forward. Two men rushed from the circle. One sent an axe flying at Titus. He deflected it and sent a thrust into the man's torso. He quickly removed his blade to block the next blow. This time Morning's Dawn did its job and sent the sword flying in two. He flowed with a fatal stroke.

"Enough!" Geralt ordered. "He has a Dawn Blade. Don't throw your lives away. I will handle him."

He stepped toward Titus. In a moment of surprise, he sent a flurry of blows. Titus barely dodged the first, and only partially deflected the next. He could feel the raw, untamed energy radiating from this fell blade. With all his strength he managed to shrug Geralt off.

"What is that foul thing?" Titus asked.

"A blade much the same as yours, only it feeds off its foes," Geralt replied as he sent another staggering strike.

It was as if the blade gave him some supernatural strength, enhancing his own strength as his foes diminished. Titus knew he was outmatched. Even without a Dawn Blade this Geralt was a seasoned warrior. Blow after blow sent Titus retreating. He was running out of steam and Geralt could sense it. He sent feigning strikes that Titus could barely counter from. He fought back the panic beginning to well up in him. Something had to change, and quickly. He looked to Elorah who was motioning with his eyes for Titus to look beyond Geralt. In the small circle was a patch of mud that had been stirred up from their horse. Then it clicked. Titus dodged a blow sent toward his head then sprinted toward the mud pit. Lying close by was their slain horse. He rushed near it and pulled a small dagger hidden in a supply bag.

"You think that tiny thing is going to help when your Dawn Blade won't do the trick?" Geralt said mockingly.

Titus waited for him to draw near. Geralt sent a strike that he deflected. It was enough to bring him down to one knee. He rolled and as he stood up he threw the knife. Geralt deflected it with ease slicing it in two.

"That's what all your effort was for?"

"No, it was for this."

Titus now had Geralt's back to the mud. He mustered all his remaining strength and sent a flurry of offensive strikes. Geralt easily blocked them all, but it did put him on the retreat for a moment, just enough that suddenly his footing gave way. He lost his balance and was sent crashing into the thick ooze. Mud engulfing him. Titus leaped into action raising his blade for a finishing strike when two more men came charging at him. Titus turned, exhausted, and like before, destroyed their weapon with Morning's Dawn. He sent one man hurling to the mud missing a leg, and thrust the blade into the abdomen of the other. Without missing a beat, he sent one final slash with all his remaining strength down onto Geralt who, partially blinded by the mud, lifted his sword in a faint attempt to block the blow. Titus knew it wouldn't be enough. He had done it, he'd won. Morning's Dawn crashed into Geralt's sword, and then the inexplicable happened. Titus' sword rendered in two, the hilt flying from his hand and the top half of the sword crashing some few feet away. The light faded from the blade until it looked like any other sword.

Titus sat atop Geralt, mouth open in utter shock. It wasn't long until two Hillmen came behind him and thrust him off Geralt by his arms. He came crashing back, half covered in mud himself. Another man came to the aid of Geralt, but he pushed him away. Clumsily he rose to his feet, mud-caked head to toe, and trudged over to the kneeling Titus.

"About that surrender," he said.

Titus looked away in absolute shame. He had failed. Failed in protecting his men, failed in keeping the peace, and worst of all, he had failed Eloy.

Indistinguishable orders were given by Geralt to his men who began to move toward the battle. Titus didn't hear it, though. He was back in Kingshelm as a boy sitting on his father's lap.

"Dad? Why is it so important that we keep the realm for Eloy? Aren't you as good a king as him?"

Richard shuffled in his seat. "My son, there is no one fit to truly be a perfect king, but the king who rules well does so as the servant of others."

"Yes, dad, you've said that before...but if Eloy is such a servant, why did he leave us? Wasn't that a selfish reason?"

Richard closed his eyes for a moment. "Someday, son, you will understand. Eloy confided in me before he left. There is more to his journey than knowledge, my son. He has been called to a task I don't know if any man can accomplish."

"Tell me, father, I can keep a secret!" Titus said with delight.

"I am sorry, my son, but it is not for us to discuss. But, can you give me a promise?" Richard said with a faint smile.

"Of course, father."

"No matter how bleak it becomes, no matter how dark the night seems, trust Eloy will return. Keep the realm safe if for some reason I am unable. He brings back a greater gift than any king has given before and, I believe, ever will. Can you promise me that you will stay loyal to the true king?"

"Yes, father, no matter what. It is our duty, right!?" replied Titus eager for approval.

Richard let out a chuckle. "Yes, my boy, and no greater joy does a father have, than seeing his son faithful to walk on the path of a good man."

"Just like you! Right, dad?" Titus grinned looking up at his father.

Richard let out a slight sigh. "I hope so, my son, I hope so."

"Chain them up and bring them with me," came the order from Geralt.

Titus was brought back to reality.

"Ferir will finish the job. I want to bring them before Doran. Let him know, and I will meet them after I deliver our captives."

A Valkaran soldier bowed and headed off toward the Valkaran army. Titus dared not look at the still ensuing conflict. He knew the result was now determined. He couldn't bear to see any more needless loss of life, lives that were fighting for him. Geralt grabbed him by the shoulder.

"Stand up. You're going to need to walk so we can find you a horse."

Titus obeyed without defiance. What good would it have done? He was a defeated man. He had failed, and now he would receive the consequences without complaint. Elorah stood next to him. He leaned over to Titus.

"What is your order now, my lord?" he asked.

Titus looked him in the eyes, unsure of what to say. He looked over at Geralt who was gathering together a group of men to help him find a horse.

"We accept our failure," Titus replied. "It's the least that we can do."

Some time had passed before several men came striding over with a horse, Geralt following close behind. He turned to Titus and Elorah and motioned for them to shuffle over to him.

"Come on, you two. Time to meet your new king."

10

GERALT

The carnage was over. Geralt looked over the gruesome scene. Shredded banners flapped in the wind over a field of corpses, weapons scattered and plunged into victims. What was a beautiful meadow field, was now transformed into a wretched, muddy, graveyard. The carrion birds were already circling in the air. He weaved his way through the wreck of battle in hopes of finding Ferir still alive. As fortune would have it, he was. He was standing amongst some soldiers issuing orders on what to do with the wounded. Geralt approached in silence, waiting for Ferir to finish.

"And for Lackas sake, do not forget to tell them to prep the siege," Ferir barked to his men.

He turned to acknowledge Geralt.

"I see you convinced the barbarians to help us. I have to say, I had my doubts. The timing of your arrival was impeccable, as well."

"Good to see you're alive too, Ferir," Geralt said a bit annoyed. "What does the situation look like?"

Ferir seemed cautious for a moment.

"What do you plan to do with that new army of yours, Geralt?"

Geralt squinted his eyes, then his face filled with rage.

"Really?! I come to your rescue and now you think I will use these men against you? Is your prejudice that deep, Ferir? These men died for you! Or wait, is it because you think I'm one of them?"

Geralt had to restrain himself from socking the man in the face. After all he'd done for Valkara, this was his reward, mistrust?

"You seem to hold all the cards in your favor. With your own words, they are 'your' people. They followed you, didn't they?" Ferir replied.

Geralt composed himself before responding.

"Ferir, you're lucky you're a good general, otherwise I would show you just how 'barbaric' I could be. No, my promise to them was this battle and any other we may have need of, and in return, Valkara would leave them be."

"That's worked so well in the past," Ferir said with a sigh.

"We don't have time for this, Ferir!" Geralt barked. "We won a battle, but the war isn't over. What did I count, maybe half of Valkara's men remain? At least 3,000 of those Riverland men retreated into The Watch. So I would best watch your words to the 'barbarians' if you'd still like their help," he finished in a mocking tone.

A faint light lit up in Ferir's eyes.

"I do have a use for them, if they are willing to fight with us still, that is."

"They'll fight if I give the order. Now get on with it."

"We need to move onto Kingshelm quickly if we are to make a swift end of this. I can't do that if all our forces are tied down sieging the army in the Western Watch. I don't even know if I could maintain a siege with the forces I have now, but with the number of hillmen...they do know how to siege don't they?"

Geralt ignored the jab at the end.

"That could work. I need to return to Valkara, so I will leave them in your capable hands," he smirked.

"For what reason?" complained Ferir. "We need our greatest warriors in the fight!"

"I have a special kingly package to deliver that I don't trust with any of my men or yours. I will join you after, that is if you haven't won by then."

"One can hope, can't he? Fine, just make sure they know they will be answering to me."

"I have no worries that will be made plain to them. Just try not to insult them so greatly that you have a whole army at your back as well."

Geralt extended his hand and Ferir took it in agreement. Geralt turned when Ferir spoke behind him.

"Thank you, Geralt, you saved our lives today. I do believe you may have won us this war."

He turned, in shock of the actual thanks.

"You're welcome. Now finish the job."

He searched the indistinguishable faces of the battlefield looking for anyone he might know. The only face that he could see was that of his brother. Valkin's face haunted him wherever he went. Geralt resolved not to continue his search, once again burying the deep sorrow that lurked just around the corner. It wasn't long before he saw Gerandir and Fairand, the army captain, standing by his captives. Both men greeted him with formal courtesy. Geralt acknowledged them in kind.

"New marching orders," he informed them.

"Where's too?" asked Fairand.

"You'll be under the command of Ferir. Your assignment is to keep The Western Watch under siege while Valkara's army marches on Kingshelm."

"So we get the babysitting duty, huh?" Fairand said unamused.

"Just think, a shorter ride home when all this is over," Geralt said.

Fairand didn't find it as amusing. He let out an annoyed snort and walked away to give the command.

"Give him time. They still aren't so fond of a new chieftain giving orders, especially one considered an outsider," consoled Gerandir.

"I know this," snapped Geralt. "Keep your pity for someone else."

Geralt could see the instant coolness settle over what had been true concern in Gerandir. Geralt again felt the pain of what he'd done, but instead of saying something, he just let it go. It was what seemed to be his way as of late. Gerandir didn't stick around and went to join the rest of the clansmen.

Geralt turned his attention to his kneeling captives, the defeated Steward King and his commander. He motioned with his hand to have his guards stand them up. Both men rose without a word and were guided onto some horses the guards had found.

"Come on, you two. Time to meet your new king," Geralt said with a bravado he didn't feel.

In fact, all that he had said to Titus before felt fraudulent. He truly did not know Doran's plan beyond rescue or vengeance. He had hoped to stir the king into submission, and if he was even more honest, he was saying and doing a lot of things lately he hardly recognized. A darkness was over him. Whether it was that wretched blade, or this wretched war, he could not tell.

Both the men complied without complaint. Geralt could see the defeated spirit in them, especially Titus. He looked like a man broken, much like his blade. Geralt had taken the broken sword as a token to Doran. Maybe he would hang it as a trophy or throw the thing away. Geralt made his way onto the mount next to Titus and Elorah. He motioned for two other men to follow them and lead the reigns of their captive's horses. He hoped to reach Valkara within three days. The small party made their way back to the northbound King's Path leaving the stench of the battlefield behind them. It was a beautiful cloudless day. Nothing more juxtapose to what any of them must have been feeling, their own storms swirling as a turmoil beneath the surface. The first day's journey was uneventful. They had passed Rodenhill on their left some hours back. Geralt would normally have stayed the night there rather than in the open country, but he desired to return to Valkara as soon as possible. They reached the beginnings of the Northern Pass as night began to fall.

"Alright, time to make camp. Roland, Valmir, go find us some firewood."

Both the men that accompanied them nodded and began to scour the area. Geralt moved to help Titus and Elorah dismount. Both men's legs and arms were chained together. They slumped off their mounts in a weary depression.

He kept an eye on them as he set up the tents for that evening. When Roland and Valmir returned he had a fire made. It wasn't long before they were all sitting around the fire eating a small rabbit that Valmir was able to catch while fetching wood. The small circle sat in awkward silence. Geralt's stomach grumbled with discontent from the small amount of meat.

"What else we got for supplies?" he grumbled.

"We have some potatoes, but that's about it. I was hoping to pick up some supplies from Rodenhill." Roland confessed.

"Yes, I heard it three times as we passed it earlier. Now go get the potatoes," Geralt groaned.

He turned his gaze on Titus, who sat eyes fixed on the fire.

"I've got a question for you that's been burning in my mind this whole time."

He got nothing from the young king. He had been silent since his defeat.

"Why was it so important for you to keep Doran's children? I assume that's why this fight even began. I don't see it as unreasonable terms to stop a war, or were you just looking to make a name for yourself in the histories? It would seem you've got one now, though I don't know if it was what you were looking for."

Nothing. Titus just sat there, gazing into the fire as if he had said nothing to him.

"You alright, lad?" he asked.

"She died," Elorah replied.

"Who died?" Geralt asked hiding the panic that fell over him.

"The girl named Nara. We believe a man called Jorn killed her in her sleep. We don't know what happened with Lydia. She wasn't there, but we assumed the worst seeing as Jorn was nowhere to be found."

A fit of anger welled up in Geralt. The two girls he had spent the last 20 years protecting, dead? He wasn't there for them...

"You Lackan idiots! How could you let him kill them! You give him a key to the room?" he raged at the two men.

"He broke free," Titus said distantly as he didn't remove his eyes from the fire.

Geralt settled back down.

"Tell me how he came to be in your possession."

Titus lifted his eyes.

"He arrived with the two princesses at The Western Watch. He used the girls as leverage, hoping to barter his freedom, but I saw through his facade. He was just another man hungry for power and willing to pay any price to get it."

Geralt chewed on this for a moment turning over the events of Jorn's betrayal in his head, the moment he'd removed Jorn's arm from his body. How he'd like to do that a thousand times over again.

"So what of the princesses? What was your plan for them?" he asked.

Titus turned again to the fire, a clear signal he didn't want to talk about them.

Elorah answered on his behalf. "We had planned to release the two daughters the next day, the sons as soon as possible, on the condition that peace could be had, of course."

"Kind words in hindsight, but I don't see a lot of action in the direction of peace."

"It's the truth," Titus turned his eyes to stare at Geralt, the campfire reflecting in his gaze, "but I don't think Doran or Valkara would have taken too kindly to his youngest child dying in our care. You tell me could we have had peace?"

Geralt knew that answer. No, there would have been no peace. Nara's death left a gash in his heart, Doran would have been cut to the core. There would have been no peace, and now there was no chance for its resurrection. Without any more questions, he stood to his feet.

"Goodnight, gentlemen, we have a long journey ahead of us. I suggest you get your rest soon."

He made his way into his tent finally allowing the tears to stream down his face. That night he did not rest so much as weep for Nara.

He arose just before sunrise. Its shimmering rays were just peeking above the pine treetops making a canvas of orange, yellow, and purple, the light breaking on another night of darkness. How he wished his internal world could reset so easily. He went to awake Titus and Elorah and found them already awake and packed for the journey. It took only a few minutes before the small gloomy band started on their way.

It was another uneventful day. The clouds hung overcast, but it didn't stop nature's chorus. Birds chirped, the wind swayed the pine branches, and every so often a territorial squirrel made its cry. It had been a while since he could drink it all in with no rushing about. There was much still to be decided and very likely more battles to be fought, but for now, on this dusty road, he could just rest in the moment.

Evening fell again, this time he did not ask any questions. "What good would it do anyway?" he thought. Only more details that wouldn't be his job to sort and very likely more pain, and he wasn't in the market for any more. Besides, he doubted his prisoners wished to relive any of the horrors either. The same pattern ensued, he awoke and they set off. It was about midday when the dreary peaks of Valkara rose ahead of them, the snow on the crowns behind now receding near the top. The dark stone walls loomed over them as they made their way under the gate. The large doors creaked open with a quick signal from Roland.

Geralt turned to him and Valmir, "Get whatever supplies you may need, then return to Ferir. They're going to need all the help they can get. Make sure not to delay."

Both men let out a sigh, but gave an acknowledging nod. They broke off from the small party and went down a side road. Valkara seemed more dreary than when he had left. It had always been a bit rundown, but women could still be heard singing while washing clothes, children would be laughing and playing with wooden swords, and old men would share wise tales on the street corners. Now upon his return no one was out on the streets. No songs could be heard. No children were seen playing. No old men sharing the same old tale on the corners.

They soon reached the markets outside the fortress where King Doran made his dwelling. Some vendors could still be seen, the booths fluttering with their blue and black canvas, but business, which had always been steady, was almost non-existent. Geralt let out the horn blow to be let in. The gate door crackled as it engulfed them.

Now Geralt was truly concerned. What should have been a lush and tranquil courtyard, now had dry and drooping plants. Doran had always enjoyed this as a peaceful place to think. He would never in his right mind let his garden go to decay. His eyes followed to the centerpiece of the courtyard. The ram fountain no longer flowed with water and moss was beginning to sprout. On its edge a young redheaded princess sat, clearly distraught.

Geralt's heart leaped.

"Lydia!" he cried, suddenly realizing he'd shown more emotion than he desired.

She looked up and grinned from ear to ear. She ran, tears already streaming, into his embrace.

"Geralt, you don't know how glad I am to see you. So much is happening," she sobbed into his chest.

He let her cry for a moment before he pried her away to look her over.

"How are you? Are you hurt? King Titus and Elorah told me what had happened."

He gestured over at the two captives. Lydia's face shifted to shock, then a slight blush, not a look he'd seen her have before.

"King Titus, Elorah. That means. Oh my…" her voice trailing off.

"You're alive! Thank Eloy! I had feared the worst with that animal still on the loose!" cried Titus behind him.

"Is that so?" asked Geralt now with a raised eyebrow.

Titus stepped back, now realizing others were present to hear his outburst.

"Uh, yes, I mean I told you the truth, Geralt. We planned to let her go, all of them," his voice now shrinking as he said it.

A brief silence fell over the group. Lydia then spoke up.

"It seems we must now prove our hospitality to our captives," she said smiling at Titus and Elorah. "Sadly, I don't know if I can promise the same kindness," her voice sorrowful as she shifted to look at Geralt. "Something is happening with father. I don't understand, but maybe you can."

Geralt cut her off. "Lydia not in front of them." He gestured with his head at the two captives.

"Yes, right. I promise you both, as long as I have a say, you will be treated as well as you treated me. I swear to you," she said with a slightly sorrowful smile.

"Lydia…I am so sorry," Titus said with genuine anguish.

"Me too," she mumbled.

Geralt wasn't sure what was happening between them, but he could discover more later when he could talk to Lydia alone.

"Alright, Lydia, I need to take them to the holding cells. Afterward I will speak to your father. Will you join me?" he asked.

"Of course. And please, Geralt, place our guests in the nicest cells we have. They deserve that much."

"Yes, my lady," he bowed. "Come, gentlemen."

He led them to the right of the palace where a barred door was located. A guard opened it from within and ushered them down a dim hallway. Small rays of light shown through the cell windows creating the only source of light. They walked several paces until they reached an unoccupied cell.

"Will this do for you?" Geralt asked.

It was a simple cell. A small latrine was built into the outer wall. A small luxury to be sure. Other than that there was an old wooden cot to be used for sleep.

Elorah was about to speak when Titus spoke up, "It will do just fine."

Both men shuffled into their new home, their shackles finally being unlocked from their wrist and ankles revealing skin worn raw.

"I'll send in someone with ointment to treat those," he said after removing the shackles.

They thanked him. He moved to the door of the cell and took one last look at them. They both stretched out with their newfound freedom.

"The princess has taken a liking to you?"

It was more a statement than a question.

Titus looked up with a look of hurt he was not expecting.

"Lydia is a good woman. I think highly of her, but her sister died under my watch. What can I say to her now?"

Geralt gave him a nod of acknowledgment. What else needed to be said? He shut the cell door behind him and

motioned for the jailer to lock the cell. It was time he found
out exactly what was happening here.

He first made a trip to his chambers. The hallway was dark,
but mostly kept up compared to the rest of Doran's fortress.
He opened his door. His room stood relatively untouched from
his last night there. He drew himself a bath to clean off the
rest of the mud that he was unable to remove from bathing in
the river earlier on their journey. He paid careful attention to
clean off his armor and sword as well. He left the dark blade
untouched, however, desiring to be rid of the thing. After an
hour or so he was finished and presentable to the king. "The
Steward King or Islandia's new High King?" he pondered.

It felt somewhat wrong knowing the Steward King was
in a cell not far from him now. In any case, he made his way
through the halls, making small observations of the state of
things. He soon entered the throne room. It was not so much
in disrepair, but unattended. Cobwebs filled the vaulted rafters
and a musty smell permeated the air. It looked uneasy, much
like he was beginning to feel. Doran's door was slightly parted,
and he could hear the king's booming voice.

He opened the door further to reveal the king speaking
with a few attendants and Lydia sitting in the corner half listening. The king immediately turned his face to see who had
arrived, but in his recognition there was no smile. The King's
face seemed shrunken, as if the life in his bones was drying
out. His hair was disheveled, and the faint smell spoke of a
few days without bathing.

"My lord," Geralt said as he entered.

Doran grunted. "What have you come to disturb me with
now, Geralt."

He was a bit taken aback by the sting in his voice.

"I bring good news, my King. Our enemies have been
routed and I have delivered to you the Steward King and his
general as captives."

"Good news, huh? Was it not my order to bring my daughters and sons back? I receive one daughter and a corpse all thanks to my 'great' army!" He said, anger flooding his voice.

"My lord, it was the snake Jorn that..."

Doran burst in, interrupting him, "You think I don't know who did it!" he shouted at the top of his lungs. The attendants stepped back from him in fear. "That Shuka will pay with his life! But who was to take care of my children? Who was their trusted guardian?" his eyes burned an inferno.

"My lord, I assure you I did all that I could to save them. I.." Geralt wasn't sure what to say.

"Ohhh yes, you did all you could. You cared so deeply as to raise your own private army to 'save' us. How noble of you! What will you do next? Bring your barbarian horde at our gates and come to 'rescue' us?" Doran shouted.

"My king, I assure you I raised no army against you. It was the only way I saw a victorious outcome. I did all I could, I gave all I could to save you!" Geralt was now raising his voice.

"Well you couldn't. With all your cunning and strength, you couldn't save me. Nara, my sweet Nara, lies dead despite your salvation. My sons I am sure to follow," his voice now tainted with sorrow.

Geralt was piecing it together now. His heartbreak and rage had to go somewhere. Why not him? The guardian of his children, the outsider, the pet barbarian. His sacrifices meaningless to a disinterested king. He fought back the anger welling up in him, the deep betrayal he felt.

"What would you have of me, my king?" he asked with a coolness he did not feel.

"I have been made to look weak, needing the aid of your barbarians. I want you to send them home. We must win this victory on our own to show our strength to the rest of Islandia."

"My king, that would be unwise. Those 'barbarians' are all that hold Kingshelm's army from flanking our own. If you have them withdraw it would be to your own demise," Geralt insisted.

"When did a servant give orders to their king?" Doran said venom in his voice. "You have my orders, now will you obey them?"

Geralt looked over at a distraught Lydia mortified by the man she called her father.

"I am loyal to you, my king, I will serve as you see best," bowed Geralt biting back the pain of that answer.

Valkin was right all along. A dog on a leash.

"We shall see," Doran said in a dismissive tone. "Also, one other thing before you go, Geralt. I would like my sword back."

For some reason, this hurt the most. It was a sign of loyalty broken, of mistrust and rejection. It wasn't the sword, it was Geralt that Doran had thrown out, uninterested in him as a pet any longer. All that Geralt had given, now ashes blown in the wind. He unbuckled the sword and threw it on the ground, the clattering of metal echoing in the room as he walked out in silence. He could faintly hear the sobbing pleads of Lydia on his behalf only to be followed by the growl of an unapologetic father. His heart broke knowing there was nothing he could do. He drearily made his way into the courtyard, the dead and drying plants revealed in a new light. They were only a reflection of the brokenness of this place, of its ruler. Doran would not be the king Islandia needed, and for the first time in his life, he hoped a man named Eloy was really coming back.

He found a mount in the royal stables and began the journey back to where he had come. Hopefully he could catch up with Roland and Valmir. As he passed through the haunted city streets, the sense of fear was all around him, a dark presence taking hold. Every one of these people would suffer by the end, and he could do nothing to stop it. Never had he felt a pawn more than on his return journey.

He never did catch Roland and Valmir who had likely followed his order to hurry. It was all fine and well. Geralt wasn't sure he wanted to spend the next few days with them. As the hours rolled by, they blended with the days. His thoughts were a whirlpool of unease, dread, and unknown. What was next? What would he do? For the first time there was no clear order or direction to follow. How would he reconcile the mess before him? Surely he could not just let Doran rule as a mad king? But what would he do? He would not march his own army to Valkara only proving Doran's words. No, there had to be another way. Maybe…just maybe, Ferir could see the folly of this king. Maybe, if they could free Doran's sons, he could see reason. If not, maybe one of them could rule in his stead. Whatever the case, he must get to Kingshelm.

He rushed onward making it to The Watch in record time. The battlefield of days earlier was now a scattered ruin of history. The scavenger birds had picked clean the dead. Tattered banners still flapped in the wind, like a desperate last breath. Most of the weapons had been gathered already, but here and there you can still see a weapon protruding from its victim. It was a field of dead dreams, dead hopes, and ended futures. Of that he could take solace for he still had all of those, if he could somehow muster up the courage. That he was less sure he could do.

He saw off in the distance the battle lines that had been drawn. His clansmen had set up a perimeter around The Western Watch cutting them off from all access of escape besides the river. Even there, they had archers at the ready. Large wooden spikes were laid out sporadically to prevent a sally from any remaining calvary tucked away in their keep. It was a well-organized siege, as sieges go. Geralt was impressed. He was sure the news of withdrawal would leave a bitter taste in his clan's mouth, but this order was to serve a greater purpose. Hopefully one that could usher in peace.

Geralt entered the camp of Harnfell's warriors. The Hillmen he found had a bored disinterest masking their face. They restlessly meandered the camp waiting for the call to action. He asked a group for directions to find Gerandir and Fairand. They directed him east of the camp. Up close, the camp was a simple one. Nomadic tents and campfires were sprawled across an open field, men singing and dancing in the traditional tribal fashion. Geralt felt his shame in not knowing the traditions of his people like he should. He remembered some of them from his childhood, but the steps to become a warrior were robbed from him. In many of these men's eyes he would never be one of them.

It wasn't long before he found Gerandir and Fairand's command tent. Armed guards stood posted at its opening allowing him entry with a quick nod of the head. As he stepped in he could see Fairand, Gerandir, and a few other captains scouring over a map.

"We could potentially use the river to find access to the city. Then, we could send a group of scouts to open the gates," Fairand suggested.

"But what if there is no clear way from the river? We would send some of our best men to die. We must be sure first," Gerandir counseled.

"There is no way to know unless we scout!" Fairand countered, growing in agitation, not something that was hard for a Hillmen to do.

"Excuse me," Geralt said to grab their attention. "Planning aggressive action on what is supposed to be a siege?" he asked eyebrows raised.

"The men are restless. I can't just have them sitting here. We will have a revolt if we don't do something. We aren't used to 'sieging'," Fairand said defensively.

"I have new orders. You are to break off the siege and go home."

Everyone in the tent looked dumbfounded.

"What do you mean?" asked Gerandir.

"Exactly what I said. Break off the siege. Your part in this war is over. You can go home. Doran no longer has need of you."

"Does he want his army to be crushed?!" Fairand exclaimed. "You told me he was a great commander of his day, but this? This is madness."

"That's exactly what it is," Geralt thought to himself.

"He desires to win this war, just not with our aid."

"Ahhh, so he's just a racist shuka!" spat Fairand. "I will take pleasure in watching his army burn, then."

"So will you still follow him?" Gerandir asked Geralt.

Geralt wasn't sure how to answer that in a way that would make sense.

He finally replied, "Unto a point. I have my own plans made. I need to reach the Valkaran army at Kingshelm as soon as possible. Can I trust you both to follow this order?"

Gerandir and Fairand looked at each other.

"Of course, it's no pain to us to see Valkara slide into the gutter. The men won't be happy, but I am sure there are ways to change that," Fairand replied.

"Very good. Do what you must, but give me enough time to reach Kingshelm."

"They won't be going anywhere soon," Fairand snorted.

Geralt noticed Gerandir giving him a curious look. It made him feel uneasy. He shook it off and nodded to them both.

"Safe travels. I will return to the Hills when this is all over and reward you for your work here."

"We will see, you shuka," Fairand chuckled.

"Travel well," Gerandir said still staring intently.

Geralt made haste to find his mount again. This time taking special care to notice his token he would offer to Kingshelm. The hilt of the Dawn Blade protruded from underneath a bag on his saddle. He mounted his horse and was off. He debated on which route to take to Kingshelm, but eventually settled on the Riverland Road. Traveling alone, it would take him a day and a half to reach the army.

The road was one of ease. The Riverlands, the flattest territory in all of Islandia, made for quick travel. As he traveled he found the road was almost completely abandoned. Travelers were now aware that an enemy army was treading on their land. Occasionally, Geralt would see the result of those who had the misfortune of running into the Valkaran army. Picked clean and destroyed caravans littered parts of the road, the bodies strewn in the fields. The bloody misfortunes of war. "Wrong time and place," he muttered to himself. He couldn't help feel something was deeply broken at the sight of families slaughtered by this needless war, one he intended to end quickly. He made camp at a small outlet from the road just past the pathway leading to the city of Des Rivera, the great trading city of the Riverlands. The nights alone on the road left him to reflect on all the dreary moments of the past few weeks, the monster he felt he was becoming, and how he intended to put it to rights.

The next morning he arose making rapid pace to reach Kingshelm. It was just past midday when he saw the flapping banners of Valkara's army surrounding the western edge of the city. It pleased him to see no conflict had yet ensued. He rushed through the camp paying no mind to the hoots and jeers of the soldiers. He was in an urgent need to find Ferir.

He finally saw the large canvas tent with the black ram plastered onto the side. He hopped from his horse pulling the Dawn Blade from hiding. He burst through the tent without so much as an acknowledgment to the posted guard. Ferir was reclining in a chair talking over battle strategies, a reoccurring sight not unnoticed to Geralt.

"Ferir, I bring urgent news," he blurted out.

Ferir stared up at him with a puzzled look mixed with annoyance. This was going to be the difficult part.

"Hello, Geralt, why do you come to me with so much haste?"

"I need to speak to you alone," he said, looking at the surrounding council.

"So be it," Ferir motioned with his hand for them to leave. When all had exited the tent Ferir spoke again, "Now, what is it?"

"Doran has lost his mind. He has ordered me to dismiss the siege surrounding The Western Watch. All the Hillmen have left."

"What!?" Ferir shot up out of his seat. "All of them?!"

Geralt smiled internally, he had him now.

"Yes, he told me we must win this on our own if we are to gain respect from the rest of the kingdoms."

"Shuka..." Ferir muttered under his breath. "How much time do we have?"

"I told the Hillmen to give me enough time to reach you here, but listen, Ferir, I have a plan."

"Go on," he said nodding.

"What I am about to say will sound like treason. I know you think less of me because of where I come from, but I am for Valkara. I have given more than you can imagine to this cause."

"Just say it," Ferir snorted.

"Doran is not fit to be king right now. He has lost his mind. I have learned the reason Kingshelm did not take council with us was due to the death of Nara, the royal daughter. He is lost in his grief and believes his sons to be lost as well."

"So what is it you are suggesting?" Ferir pressed.

"We need to free the royal sons. If Doran will not compose himself after that, then we need to crown one of them. This is bigger than honor, Ferir. If Doran rules in this state he will destroy Islandia."

"A royal son would still sit on the throne either way?" probed Ferir.

"Yes, a royal son will rule and this war can end without any more conflict."

"How's that? As I see it, Kingshelm is still alive and well, and now we have an army at our back that matches us, if not outnumbers us."

"We make a trade," Geralt said revealing the hilt of Morning's Dawn. "We will approach the advisors of Kingshelm and inform them that we hold the Steward King prisoner. We will tell them we are willing to trade him and not destroy the city in exchange for the two sons and our entry into the city."

Ferir mulled this over.

"They hold the leverage with the sons and the army at our back. Why would they agree with anything we say?"

"This is where the deceit comes in," Geralt smirked. "They do not know they still have an army. For all intents and purposes you showing up at their doorstep means their army is dead. If we act quickly, we can pressure them to open the gates. In doing so we have enhanced our position and claimed the sons back. We would hold a defensible position that Kingshelm could not hope to conquer."

"This could work…there are a lot of 'if's' though," Ferir sighed.

"There always is in war. If we can get in the city we have a chance," Geralt exhorted.

"We don't have much choice do we? We have what, maybe three days?" Ferir replied, a bit exasperated.

"We can do this, and we must call for a council right now with the leaders of the city."

"Alright," Ferir sighed. "We will go now."

He grabbed a few parchments and organized them, then threw on a light cloak. He walked past Geralt toward the entrance and turned to look at him.

"What is it you plan to get out of all this, Geralt?" he asked.

"Hopefully, a new kingdom," he said putting his hand on Ferir's shoulder motioning for them to go.

The two men convened with the rest of the captains to tell them the plan. The same party of delegates, Geralt included, moved up to within shouting distance of the city gate. A towering ash grey wall surrounded the city. At the center, a dark wooden gate with iron bars held it in place. At the parapet stood a battalion of city watchmen. Ferir shouted up to them.

"We wish to speak with the city delegate."

No answer was given. The watchmen disappeared behind the wall. Some time passed with no reply.

"Well that plan ended quickly," mocked one of the captains in their delegation.

Not a minute later the gate swung open. A small group of finely dressed men made their way toward them. A man at their head greeted them.

"Hello, Valkarans, my name is Eli. I am the standing leader of the city. By your arrival I can only assume the worst. What is it you wish to say to us?"

Ferir spoke up. "Greetings Eli, I am Ferir general of this army. We wish to deliver terms for the surrender of the city and the sons of Doran."

"Those are high demands, general. What makes you think we will listen?" Eli asked.

Geralt could see through all his politician's veneer. He was bluffing.

Ferir spoke again. "For the safety of your citizens, and your king, I would counsel you to listen to our terms."

Eli turned to the others in his group for a private conference.

"We don't have much choice now do we, general?" Eli frowned.

"No, Eli, you do not."

11

IMARI

"Nabila" is all he could say. His mind raced for another sentence, even another word, but nothing came.

"After all these years that's all you can say?" her red lips parted into a smile.

He scrambled for anything. What was there to say? It's good to see you? Are you truly rebelling? Did you murder my family? I love you! All valid choices, but none chose to be the frontrunner.

She continued to speak after he didn't respond, "I am glad you came." She paused with that brilliant smile again. "I had hoped Khaleena could find you out in the desert. I began to give up hope, although it's probably for the best." She rested her hand on a chair next to her. "If I could find you, so could my father."

Henry, thankfully, said something next. "My queen, Khaleena, Imbaku, and the rest are on their way. They took, how would you say it, an alternative route. They will be arriving disguised as a large caravan coming from the port."

Nabila turned to one of her associates in the room. "Make sure we have one of our men stationed at the east gate tomorrow."

Without a word the man nodded and left the room, Imari assumed to carry out the order immediately. Nabila turned her attention again to Imari, those dark brown eyes burning a hole into his soul.

"So you really have nothing to say, Imari? I don't remember you being so quiet," a teasing look passing over her face.

Finally some words came, "Nabila, you don't know how long I have waited for this moment. Dreamt of it, in fact. I just never believed it would be a reality let alone like this."

"You mean on the same side?" she cocked an eyebrow.

"Yes, I imagined if I ever saw you again it would be in chains."

"I had nothing to do with that evening, Imari. My father used our wedding for his own gain like he does with everything else he touches," a bit of venom in her words.

She turned to the rest of her associates in the room, "I would like a word with Imari alone."

They bowed respectfully and found their nearest exit from the room. Henry took this as his cue to leave as well. They now stood all alone in the small room. Imari's heart was pounding.

"I hope you know," he said fumbling for the words, "I truly did love you."

"Did love me?" she asked.

He searched his heart for the truth he had suppressed all these years thinking if he said it out loud to anyone he would be scorned and mocked.

"I still do love you," he said drawing out the words, "though I feared ever saying it."

Tears welled up in her eyes. She covered her face with her hand. Imari stood frozen, unsure of what to do. Her shoulders began to heave as she let out a sob, raw emotion bubbling to the surface likely suppressed as long as his own. He moved, and in a moment he was holding her in his arms allowing himself to weep alongside her. He didn't know how long they stood there sharing their grief over all they had suffered, the years taken from them, and the horrors they both witnessed. A time came when the tears stopped flowing for a moment and he pushed her away, just enough to look into her eyes. A smile overcame her grief. She grabbed his neck and pulled him in, embracing him with a kiss. A passion overcame him from the long years apart, a love they had been robbed of sharing. They were lost in a moment, a moment Imari had no desire to leave anytime soon, but, like all moments, it came to an end.

Several hours had passed by his reckoning. The sun was beginning to set. Imari turned to see Nabila wrapping her red sari around herself. He rose himself, putting his arm around her waist. She returned the gesture.

"What's next?" Imari wondered aloud.

She turned and smiled at him. "Now that is the Imari I remember, always thinking of the future."

Imari returned a smile of his own, " 'The kingdom never sleeps and neither does the Khosi' as the saying goes."

Nabila dropped her arm from his waist.

"I must get going. If I don't return soon, Father will suspect something. You can stay here, it will be safe. I will have my men bring you a mattress to sleep on. I will return to you as soon as I can in the morning."

Without waiting for a reply she leaped up and gave him one last kiss. She quickly ushered herself out of the room taking the opportunity to turn toward him one last time with that captivating smile. As she left the room, he caught his breath. For a moment, as fleeting as it might be, all was right in the world.

He awoke the next morning with the faint light of the sun creeping into the small window of his quarters. He stretched out trying to work the stiff muscles that were the side effect of the weeks-long journey he had just finished. He rubbed his face and slowly rose to his feet. It wasn't a minute later that he heard a knock at the door of the room. He scrambled to finish dressing before opening the door. A small woman with a black face wrap stood to greet him.

"They're here, downstairs," she stated.

Imari quickly followed her and was greeted by the whole assembly of Masisi and Bomani warriors.

"Sleeping in, brother, when there's work to do?" Khaleena said as he approached.

"Eiishh, I am sorry, sister. The first bed in weeks caught me off guard." He rubbed his head sheepishly.

"While you were snoozing we had our own bit of a journey," said Imbaku as he joined the them.

"Yes, what happened? I am so glad to see you are well!" Imari exclaimed.

"It's a long tale Imbaku, please keep it short," Khaleena begged.

"Yes, yes, sister. Well, we were chased down by a battalion of guards from the wall. We struck them down, only losing a few men. From there we went as fast as we could. Sure enough, a large caravan was coming in from the harbor. We waited till they left the port and sprung on them at an abandoned part of the road."

"It was quite the tale!" interrupted Khaleena. "Imbaku was almost killed!"

"I was going to leave that part out sister..." frowned Imbaku. "Yes, a disguised soldier in the caravan almost caught me off guard."

"Till his baby sister came to the rescue," Khaleena said with a smile.

"Anyway, we captured the caravan losing maybe ten men. We made our way to the city and camped outside Sahra last night. We arrived early this morning not sure what to expect, but when we reached the gate the head guard didn't ask any questions."

Khaleena chimed in. "We didn't know until we got into the city and were greeted by the woman who woke you, that Nabila had stationed her men to let us in."

"So, she is not a traitor after all," Imbaku pondered aloud.

"No, I met her yesterday," replied Imari. "She was not behind Father or Mother's death. She was as shocked and broken-hearted as us. Fahim used her."

"What a shuka," spat Imbaku.

"His reign ends today, brother," encouraged Imari.

"It starts now," said the face wrapped woman.

The trio turned to look at her.

"Nabila cannot leave the palace today. She has a few other things that call for her attention. She has informed us that today we move. I have a key to the palace's private entry. We will sneak in and let your men inside."

"And what of Nabila's men? Will we be doing all the work for her?" Imbaku asked.

"They will lock down the city. No one in or out. Those who belong to her in the palace will join you."

"Very well, then. We are ready at your command. Also, do you know of Henry's whereabouts?" Imari asked.

"He will join us in the palace. He wished to speak to Fahim as a delegate of the North. So which of you will lead your men?" she asked.

The three of them looked at each other.

"I will stay to lead the Masisi. I doubt they'd listen to either of you," winked Khaleena.

"Eiishhh, you save my life one time and you think I am incapable," said Imbaku exasperated. "Fine, Imari and I will do the dirty work once again."

Imari smirked at his siblings. It felt right, them all being together as a family once again united to restore Khala's freedom.

"It's settled then. Bring the main forces down to the palace gate as soon as you can. Our men are creating a 'distraction' on the other side of town. It will take the focus off of your men, at least for a short time. Imari, Imbaku, come with me," the masked woman ordered.

They did as she said and followed her to the side door in which Imari had entered the day before. Following her through what, only yesterday, had been bustling streets but now sat hauntingly empty. Imari could hear a faint cry in the distance followed by a loud crash.

"What is happening?" he asked.

"Our distraction," the woman said.

"Sounds more like a riot," commented Imbaku.

"You're not far off," the woman murmured.

It was only a few side streets later that they appeared before the large white quartz wall surrounding the palace. The inner workings behind carved into the Nawafir Mountains. A small wooden door in the wall was their entry point. The woman guiding them casually approached the door unlocking it with a key in her possession. Imari and Imbaku followed her into a torchlit guard room where two men sat casually in chairs talking with each other. They both stood to attention as the three of them entered.

"How did you?" But that was all the guard got out before their mysterious guide sent a dagger flying into his throat making the rest of his sentence a gurgle. The other man stood, immediately pulling out his sword. Imbaku pulled out his dagger, but before he could reach the man their companion slammed her foot into his knee. He convulsed to the ground in pain dropping his sword. The finishing blow shortly followed.

"Next time maybe warn us?" Imbaku scolded as he put his dagger away.

"We need to go this way," she said ignoring him.

She lead them through a door that lead to a tunnel within the palace wall. No one was present which struck Imari as strange. It wasn't a minute more until they reached a door at the end of the narrow passageway. She flung it open with surprising force. Two more guards stood at attention before the main gate of the palace. With unparalleled swiftness she disposed of them both as quickly as before. She motioned in silence for Imbaku and Imari to open the palace gate. They rushed over to the door and unhitched the wooden plank barring it shut. They proceeded to pull the large doors open, exposing the empty main street of the city.

"They are not here yet? I told them to hurry," muttered the woman.

"I see them!" Imbaku said pointing.

Khaleena and the men were just visible over the horizon of the street. In a matter of moments the small army was at the palace doorstep.

"That was quicker than expected!" Khaleena said with genuine shock.

Both men turned to look at their mysterious guide.

"Who are you?" prodded Khaleena.

The woman began to unwrap her face, revealing someone almost identical to Nabila.

"Who?"

The woman interrupted Imari, "I am Amira, daughter of the Sulta Fahim, younger sister of Nabila."

The three of them stood shocked.

"I did not know Nabila had a sister," Imari said not a little confused.

"Our father would like to feel the same. I am the outcast of our family, shipped off to train for the Sycar as soon as I was able. He likely didn't want me as the reminder of his wife's death."

"So you're a Sycar?" Imbaku asked.

"Yes, but it should not concern you. I am on Nabila's side. I am, in fact, one of her most trusted allies. I'm the reason you haven't been killed in this city already. We don't really have time to answer these questions. We need to keep moving!"

Without waiting for a response she started making her way toward the palace complex.

"Come, we need to keep up," ordered Imari as he followed suit, the whole of their forces trailing after.

They quickly climbed the palace steps leading up to the grand entryway. All of a sudden men in black robes and silver masks began to appear from the many entrances of the palace. Silently, they descended upon the steps creating a barrier between them and the palace. At their head stood the golden masked man that had slain James that night in Wahah, and the one who had stopped them on the road.

"It seems we have a traitor," the golden masked man's eyes fixing on Amira. "Men, exterminate our pest problem."

With that order he calmly turned his back and made his way toward the palace complex. The Sycar, however, descended upon them with a unified shout. The black plague of at least two hundred of Sahra's best swept down on them. The Masisi and Bomani let out their cry in response, Imari a roaring lion at its head.

The two forces crashed like two wild beasts into each other. Chaos erupted on the palace steps. Imari lost sight of Khaleena, Imbaku, and Amira. He did his best to keep the Sycar in front of him at bay. These men lived up to their reputation, soldiers of ferocity and skill. Imari found the rungu in his hand dislodged from a countered slash. He quickly adjusted to block with the shaft of his spear, splintering it in two. With the metal point he deflected the next blow, countering with the splintered wooden end sending it flying into the torso of his foe. The blow stunned the Sycar just enough for him to send a devastating strike with the point of his spear. The Sycar collapsed in a heap. He rushed up the steps and saw Imbaku engaged with his opponent dodging and deflecting each strike sent his way. He was unaware of the enemy just behind him. Imari sent a saving blow just before the deadly slash could hit its mark. Imbaku ended the foe in front of him and turned to Imari.

"Now neither Khaleena or you will ever let me hear the end of it," he sighed with exaggeration.

The two brothers stood back to back, fending for their lives. Imari could see Amari a few stairs up slaying a foe and then turning to them.

"Imari, Imbaku! Up here!" she shouted, motioning with her arm toward the palace.

Imari scanned the battle and found Khaleena only ten or so stairs below them. Lombaku and Boani were fighting at her side. Imari shouted down to her.

"Khaleena, follow us!"

Her gaze shifted up to them. In that moment of distraction a spear came hurling behind her. Imari's heart sank as he saw the scene unfold. A flash crossed his vision and in a moment a spear came thrusting through flesh, the victim dropping to his knees. It was the face of Boani, blood splashed across his face the life fading from his eyes. He had stepped between Khaleena and the incoming blow saving her life. She let out a cry of grief.

"GO!" barked Lombaku. "We will hold them off, you end this," he said giving her a nod to move.

Without any time to mourn, she scrambled to Imari and Imbaku dodging stray strikes at her. The three fought their way to the top of the stairs where Amari awaited them, fending off any who dared to approach her. They made a break from the battle to the palace door.

"Locked, of course," complained Amari. "Come, I know a different way."

Under the shadow of the palace entrance looming over them, they arrived at a small door off to the side, a servants entrance, the battle still raging below some twenty feet away.

"So was this part of the plan, an ambush?" Imbaku snarled.

"No, somehow...somehow they found out..." Amari's voice deep in thought.

"Can we still win this?" desperation filled Imari's eyes.

"Yes," Amari's gaze breaking from thought, "if we can get to him."

The key she had used to unlock the small wall entry worked for the servant's door. It swung open to an empty, humble quarters, a small kitchen and dining hall used by the palace servants. Amari lead them swiftly through the room to another door which lead to the main hall, her knowledge of the palace workings backing up her claim of royalty. The main hall was empty. At its peak sat a dark ebony throne. Because the palace was built into the mountains, the only light that came in was through the front windows of the room which was a mosaic display of history on stained glass, the dazing colors splayed out in the room. Imari would have enjoyed staring at the story they told, if it weren't for the urgency of their mission. Amira lead them to a stairway behind the throne that spiraled upward. Imari felt as if they had gone around enough times that they should be at the peak of the mountains by now. The stairs finally stopped at a long hallway lit only by torchlight. At the end of the hall stood a single doorway.

"That's it. The Sulta's room," Amari said in a hushed tone.

The four of them paused briefly to collect themselves. This was the moment that Imari, Khaleena, and Imbaku had been waiting for. The moment to set their records straight, to free their kingdom from oppression, and to be made a true Khosi once again. They slowly moved down the hall with weapons drawn ready for any more surprises that might be waiting, but none came. Amari was the one to slowly open the door. As it opened, Imari was taken aback by the view.

Carved out of the mountain, not far from the peak, a large open space was dug. So large and high one could see the land of Sahra all the way to The Grand Wall. The city below was a dizzying sight that made Imari's hands go numb. A large clear barrier made of glass prevented the wind and elements from crashing in and from anyone having an unfortunate mishap. Divided in the room itself were walled off rooms to both left and right. In the middle sat a large stone table carved from the mountain itself filled with official documents and maps. Behind the stone table was a regal wooden chair decorated with red cushions and embroidered with gold. It sat turned to look out over Sahra.

The voice of an older man in a thick Sahra accent rung out from the chair, "So you have finally come, Khosi?"

A man, who looked to be in his early sixties, stood up. His wrinkled face weary. He had a thick black beard peppered with grey that hung to his chest. A red turban was wrapped around his head matching the red and gray robes he wore. He moved like a man who had received an injury. His dark brown eyes, the same as Nabila and Amira, shifted from guest to guest. He rubbed a ruby ring on his ring finger. An eerie silence filled the room.

"Father," Amira started.

"Enough." Fahim's voice echoed throughout the room. "Amira, you have never ceased to disappoint. No need to explain yourself now." His gaze turned to Imari.

"So, young Khosi, why have you come?"

Imari stepped forward, "I think you know why."

"For revenge? A long journey for such a petty thing. I would be disappointed if that was all." He let out a tired sigh.

Imari contemplated his words then spoke, "I am not here for revenge of my parents, Fahim. You will answer for their blood someday. No, I have come to break Khala from your chains and to unite our people with the marriage given to me from you. I have come to end my life on the run. I have come so that the name Khosi might mean something again, but most of all, I have come so that there can be a new day over these lands!" Imari took a step forward.

"Very noble of you, but let me explain why you're wrong. Bring them in," commanded Fahim.

The door from the room to Imari's left swung open. To his dismay he saw Nabila and Henry marched out, but then, to his dread, more followed. Behind them came Impatu, Moheem, and Riah. They were all marched out into a row and made to kneel before them. Lastly, the golden masked Sycar came out wielding a sinister-looking spear. It swirled with a dark aurora and glowed a sickly green color. The four of them stood stunned and waited for Fahim to speak again.

"You see, Khosi," a smirk now on his face, "your plan was never going to succeed. I know what is happening in my kingdom. It is the only way to maintain control. So I used Nabila hoping she would draw you here unbeknownst to her."

"You're a monster, you shuka," spat Khaleena.

"No need for that kind of speech here, my little Khalan princess." Fahim now moved toward Nabila. "But even if you would succeed in ridding the world of me, I don't think you know all of my daughter's intentions. Nabila, would you care to explain to your husband your ambitious schemes?"

Her only response was silence.

"Very well I will explain them to you, Imari." He began pacing behind his captives.

"You see, after disposing of me, she would begin to rule in my stead. I am sure there were some vague promises that you would get to return to Khala, lead the city, and be Khosi again. Sounds great, I am sure. What she seems to have hidden from you is her desire to create her own little kingdom. She planned to break the South away from the rule of Kingshelm entirely. She would be the queen of the South and you her client king. Not so different from me, really."

"Except the part where you would put our corpses in an unmarked grave out in the Wastes," retorted Imbaku. "I see no problem with her plan."

"Ahh, you might not, Imbaku, but I think your Khosi feels differently." Fahim's gaze fixed on him. "He is too much like his father."

It was true, Imari would never go with such a plan. From the time he was a child, until his father's murder, he had been instructed in the story of their freedom. How the line of Eloy had freed them from Sahra, those who'd wish to enslave them again. Loyalty to the king and his kingdom was paramount. It was the oath his father had made him swear. He would not break it.

"Fahim is right, Imbaku. We owe our lives to Eloy's family. To betray them now would be a most sinister betrayal."

He could see Henry visibly relax as all this must have come as a revelation to him as well. Imari turned his eyes to Nabila whose head was facing down and covered by her hair.

"Is this true, Nabila? Was this your intention all along? To use us to build your own kingdom?"

She didn't reply. Imari's heart sank. So it was true.

"So what do we do now?" Imari asked turning his gaze back to Fahim.

"I will present to you two options. Option one is this, you slay my daughters with your own hands, killing off these rebel leaders. In return, I will grant you a vassal kingship over Khala. You will independently rule, but you will answer at my call whenever that need may arise. Tribute will be extracted from your people like what is being done already. I will also require your brother to live here in Sahra as insurance that you will obey me."

"And the other option?" Khaleena snarled.

"Not a pleasant one, I am afraid. Asad, take off that mask."

The Sycar warrior did not move for a moment.

"Alleana, boy! There is no need for ceremony in my chambers. You are the Sulta's son, are you not?!"

The masked warrior hesitantly removed his mask revealing beneath the face of a younger Fahim. Handsome, with jet black hair and dark olive skin. He carried the signature brown eyes that belonged to their family. A bit of dark stubble peppered his face. His gaze was cold and unyielding.

"Thank you, son. Now, where was I? Ahh yes, Asad here is wielding what we in Islandia call a Dawn Blade. It is the only one of the five in spear form, I believe. It belonged to you, Imari, yet you did not know it. Asad procured the weapon from you on your way to Wahah. The spear has been robbed of its true power for centuries now."

Imari fixed his eyes on the spear. Sure enough, under the swirling darkness he could make out the distinguishable markings of his spear.

Fahim continued, "I have a certain ally who has the power to revive such ancient weapons, but with a power they did not previously possess, but I digress. If you do not take option one, then Asad will drive that spear through each and every one of you. Then, he will throw your bodies off this mountain and leave them to be eaten by dogs in the street. Nabila will be spared, mind you. But she will be made to suffer."

It was a trap and Imari knew it. He was playing him to see what mattered most. He would either lose the woman he loved and the loyalty he honored, or it would be the death of himself and everyone he cared for. He looked around the room for any sort of hope when Imbaku spoke up.

"What makes you think one spear can take all four of us?"

"Young, foolish boy. Do you not know what a Dawn Blade is capable of? They must not teach proper history in Khala. Asad, give us a demonstration."

Before Imari could move the spear flashed into the torso of Moheem. He let out a cry of anguish as the spear pierced him with ease. His body collapsed to the floor in a heap.

"Father! You are a raving monster!" cried Nabila tears streaming from her eyes. She then turned to face Imari fighting back tears as she began to speak, "It is true Imari. What my father says is true. I deeply care about you and your people.

I believed a united southern kingdom would be what was best for its people, but I cannot see this monster live. He will destroy everything beautiful about our land." Her eyes were ablaze as she turned to Fahim, "I have seen who you're colluding with, father. That is why I know there is no hope for you. You have given yourself over to the darkest depths, and for what? More power? More land? Is what we have not enough? Are we not enough?"

Fahim approached her lifting her chin to look in her eyes. "Silly, silly girl." His backhand came like a flash across her cheek. "It was very unwise of you to tell me that you know about my...associate."

He turned to look at Imari, "I am afraid option one is off the table."

He slowly moved to his chair reaching to grab something. In his hand was a red and gold scabbard. He pulled a scimitar from it, revealing a sinister blade with the same dark aurora.

"Another one!" exclaimed Imbaku, exasperated.

"Asad, kill them," ordered Fahim.

"My pleasure, father," Asad replied as he made his way toward Imari and Imbaku.

"Khaleena, Amira, save the others! We will take Asad," commanded Imari.

They nodded in reply. The dark spear was sent in a whirling thrust that Imari went to deflect with his shield. To his horror the spear burst through his wicker shield as if it were parchment. Asad pulled it back taking even more of Imari's shield with it.

He could hear Henry cry out, "It's useless, Imari. It can pierce anything!"

A weapon he couldn't deflect. This would not end well. Imari tossed his shield aside and drew out his rungu wielding his spear in his right hand and it in his left. Asad moved to send his next strike, but before he could, Imbaku leaped onto the scene. He sent his spear flying at Asad's chest. Asad swatted it away with the shaft of his spear.

"At least we know that the entire thing doesn't destroy whatever it touches," jested Imbaku.

In a roar, Asad sent another flurry of blows that Imbaku dodged like a nimble cat. He was living up to the leopard symbol of their kingdom. Imari joined in the fray sending a strike from his spear while Asad was distracted. He turned to see the blow coming at the last second, stepping out of the way. Imari's spear screeched against the stone floor. Before he could recover, Asad sent a thrust that grazed his shoulder tearing through flesh with ease. His arm felt like it had been lit aflame. He let out a shriek of pain, his spear clattering to the ground. Asad's eyes grew large as he saw the finishing blow at hand. Imari braced himself. Instead of the cold grip of death, he heard Imbaku shout with all his might as he leaped over him. Using his spear, he knocked Asad's dark weapon away paying careful attention to avoid contact with the sinister metal. In a follow-up move, he thrust with all his might sending his spear hurdling at Asad. The joy of victory now swallowed up by desperation in Asad's eyes. At the last possible moment he was able to bring his spearhead to block and then shatter the incoming strike. Imbaku would not be deterred. In an act of pure, self-sacrifice, he rushed at Asad grabbing the top of his now shattered spear. Asad moved to a defensive posture lining Imbaku up for a defensive blow. Imbaku, with reckless abandon, continued his charge. The spear came, and Imbaku only made a half-hearted attempt to avoid it. He allowed the spear to pierce his side, but kept up his momentum. Asad, terrified, tried to drop the spear and retreat, but it was too late. Imbaku grabbed his arm stopping him in his tracks. With one last effort of will he sent the tip of his spear into Asad's ribs. A faint gasp of air left his lips as he dropped limply to his knees. Imbaku, now spent and critically wounded, collapsed to the floor. Imari rushed to his side flinging his rungu away.

"I told you, brother, that I was the better fighter," Imbaku coughed. Blood began pooling beneath him.

"No, Imbaku, please. Why! Why were you so foolish!" Imari began to sob.

"You know why, Imari. You are going to be a good Khosi. I am just sad I won't get to see it."

"Don't talk like this, Imbaku." Imari went to grip his hand, but Imbaku pushed it away.

"You need to help them," he struggled to point at Khaleena and Amari who were doing everything they could to defend against Fahim.

Imari turned his gaze just for a moment more at his brother.

"I love you, brother. You truly have made me proud. Now go. Save our sister, and remember to tell her who the hero was today," Imbaku choked out a laugh.

"I love you, too, brother."

Fighting the tears, he searched to find his spear. The king's rightful spear. It sat a few feet away from the collapsed Asad. He bolted for the weapon. Reaching down he hesitated for a moment wondering what would happen if he touched such a foul thing. Sweeping that thought aside, he picked it up. Standing to his feet he saw Fahim now cornering the two women. He took a deep breath. One…Two…his eyes shot open and with every fiber left in his good arm he hurled the spear across the room the shaft whistling as it went.

It was as if time had stopped, the spear stuck in the air, Imari's heart pounding. Fahim's back was partially turned. He wouldn't see it coming. The spear found its mark. A sickening thud rang out as Fahim's body collided into the glass overlooking Sahra. The spear pinned his chest, the glass behind him a spider's web. Imari and the two women moved to free their friends. As the last one was being untied, they heard a voice croak out.

"Nabila..Imari..you want to..know why..?"

They all turned. With each breath Fahim's chest rose and fell like a crashing wave. Nabila approached him.

"Know why?" Nabila asked.

"Why I..did..what I..did? Not for power…land..I did." A cough caught in his throat, "I did it…to live forever."

As the words left his mouth, he vanished, a cloud of swirling dark vapor in his place. It dissipated, leaving nothing behind but a spear wedged into the glass.

12

TITUS

The door closed behind the man named Geralt leaving Elorah and himself sitting in the dim cell. Silence was the hole that he wished to climb into forever, and yet he knew if he stayed it would turn into his tomb.

"You can have the bed, Elorah, I will take the floor," Titus said as he slumped to the ground ignoring the grimy sensation flooding his palms.

Elorah looked at him in confusion. "You are the king, why would I?"

Titus cut him off. "I am the king of nothing now, Elorah. You and I are both the same. Why should I force you down in the dirt when I am the one who brought ruin on us."

Elorah didn't answer right away. "My lord, when you were first announced king I thought it would all come to ruin."

Titus looked at him a little wounded. "Well, it seems you were correct."

"No, sorry, that's not what I meant." He shook his head. "I thought you would be a young, naive, and power-hungry child. But I was wrong. Every turn, every decision, whether I agreed or not, you truly did it to serve others whether it be Eloy, our kingdom, or Lydia and her sister. That is what has proven to me that you are a good king."

Titus let out a sigh. "What difference do my intentions make, Elorah? Kingshelm is still doomed, I still failed, and we have ended up in chains regardless."

"It makes all the difference, my lord. To do the right thing at any cost, men will follow someone like that. A tyrant may have his day, but when disaster befalls him he has no friends." Elorah looked up at the window. "I do not think our tale has ended. Even if it has, we can say we did all we could to stand for the rightful king."

"You really believe that?" asked Titus.

"I do. I think you do, too. Just sometimes we need others to remind us. Besides, you're the one that told me hope is what we must cling to in times like these."

The two men let the stillness hang in the air for awhile. The sun was now beginning to set as evening made her appearance. The sky was a work of majesty even in a cage. Titus reflected on that for a moment, the perspective of it all. Here and now he felt trapped in his failings, but outside his cage, out in the world, the display of beauty remained the same. He yearned to break free to join in its grandeur once again, to be a part of the grand story being written. But maybe this was part of the tale even if he didn't understand his role. Maybe in the midst of all this suffering something or someone could bring sense to it all.

He had to believe that darkness would not win the day. That even if he failed, there was a victory that could still be won. What it looked like, how it would happen, he could not say, but he clung to it, for it was the only hope he had right now.

"Thank you, Elorah," he said breaking the silence.

"For what, sir?" Elorah asked as he rose from the bed.

"For hope."

Elorah smiled, "We all need it sometimes, sir. You gave it to me when you proved to be a king worth following. It is the least I could do for you now." He laid his head back down.

That night was the first night Titus could remember having a peaceful sleep.

The morning's light was barely peeking through the window when a voice woke them both.

"The king will see you in an hour, prepare yourselves."

The footsteps trailed away down the hall.

"I don't suppose they have a hidden bath in here for us to prepare for his highness," Elorah jested.

A slight grin cracked on Titus' face. "We will catch his attention without one, I can promise you that."

Both men waited patiently for the hour to pass. They had been stripped of their armor when they had been captured, leaving only a dark grey tunic for Elorah and a beige one for Titus. They had successfully rinsed off the gore of the days before in the river along the Northern pass, but even still the smell had lingered. Their cell had also seen better days adding to the aroma. Both of them had thick stubble now growing in. They could easily be mistaken for men of the wild.

Footsteps soon were heard echoing down the hallway.

"Well, I suppose this is our moment to meet with royalty," mocked Elorah.

"Come now, Elorah, we may receive mercy as you suggested."

"One can hope," his tone not enthusiastic. "I find our hope not so much in Doran, but the mercy of a fiery redhead princess."

Lydia's image was an easy memory flooding Titus' mind. One he found himself thinking about more and more. "Would she say something on their behalf?" he thought. It was a hope, a faint one, but one he deeply wanted to believe.

The two of them were escorted out of the cell into the blinding light of day. Titus blinked trying to make any sense of his surroundings. When he regained his vision, he recognized the courtyard from the day before. What looked to have once been a lush and fertile garden, now lay a decaying and rotting scene. The large fountain of a ram was crusted over by crude minerals, empty of any flowing water. Statues of ancient figures were now covered in grime.

They passed under a large oak tree, the only healthy vegetation left. The doors to the throne room stood open letting the early summer air fill its halls. Two men stood posted allowing only those invited to come in. Titus was unsure if it was a desired invitation.

The room was brightly lit by the sunlight shining in from mirroring windows on each side. Only a few had gathered for the occasion. The most important caught Titus' eye. Lydia was standing next to the throne, her hair a golden red swaying gently with the summer breeze and her eyes a piercing emerald. His heart stopped for a moment, not a feeling he was accustomed to. Time slowed until a booming voice broke him from his trance.

"Welcome to my court, King Titus." The voice belonged to King Doran.

Titus' eyes shifted to look up at him sitting on his throne. He was not what Titus was expecting. He looked like a man who had the life slowly drained from him. Just a hint of former strength remained. What truly revealed this, were his eyes with dark rings around them. They spoke of a tired soul. What were shining emeralds in Lydia's gaze, were cloudy gems hidden under mirky water in Doran's.

"Hello, King Doran," Titus said with cold formality.

"No warm welcomes for a fellow king?" Doran asked with a tint of annoyance.

"Sadly, I cannot say there has been anything of warmth between Kingshelm and Valkara for some time," retorted Titus.

"Taking the loss hard are we, lad? Well, I suppose so."

Doran stood to his feet stepping down the few stairs from his throne to stand before them. Titus wondered if this was a gesture of intimidation. Just then he noticed someone he had not seen before. Standing in the shadows behind the throne was a hooded figure in all black. Titus squinted, but couldn't make out a face, only the faintest reflection of light in a pair of silver eyes. He turned back to Doran.

"Why have you brought us here?" asked Titus. "What is it you desire from me?"

"I wanted to see the boy king for myself. To see the man who refused peace and allowed the murder of my daughter," Doran snorted.

Titus dropped his head slightly. "Not for peace," he muttered to himself. "King Doran, I cannot express how deeply distraught you must be at Nara's death but…"

Doran cut him off, "Don't you ever say her name aloud again." The threat echoed from a deep wound.

Titus saw Lydia's eyes grow misty. Had he hurt her too, by bringing up that name?

"I apologize…but you must know I had no desire for anyone to be harmed. My aim is peace!" he pleaded to Doran.

"Desire. Where does that bring us? Me, a dead daughter and my sons still captive. Your desire seems lacking in my book."

"Lydia," Titus turned his eyes to her, "Please, you know the truth. Our desire was your freedom and peace. I know your heart must be aching, but you know this is true."

"Silence, boy. She has told me the tale already. If it wasn't for her you would be dead already."

Joy sprung up inside. "So she does believe us."

Doran continued, "It does not change the fact that I have lost all that matters to me!" His voice roared. "Besides the fact, the lacka snake Jorn is still out there. So what am I to do?" his eyes flickered to the sword hanging around his waist.

Titus knew there was only one plea left.

"Remain true to your oath, to Eloy. We can be reconciled back to peace. Violence and death don't have to have the last say in this. I understand your claims against me, I have failed you as Steward King. Eloy has not. Kingshelm belongs to him. Call off this war. Create terms, but I beg of you do not betray the true King."

Doran let out a sigh. "Betray, huh." He followed with a tired chuckle, "Yes, I've been disloyal. Disloyal to the ohh so gracious king who abandoned us all after his mind had cracked from studying ancient scrolls. Yes, betrayed the king who in my hour of need was nowhere to be found, the king who chased a fantasy over the sea while my wife and child were slain by the barbarians with whom he wanted peace. Yes, I would say I have betrayed that king."

Titus was silent for a moment.

"He is returning, Doran. You know it's true. You know he wouldn't have left if it wasn't of the greatest importance."

"I hear your father speaking. Richard was a good man, but he was an idealist. A king who saw the world for what it should be, not for what it is. Boy, you best learn now, Eloy is not returning, and he will not rescue you."

"Are these your words or another who has spoken them to you?" Titus asked, his eyes flickering to the hooded man in the shadows.

"Whether they came from me or not, they are what I have come to believe," Doran snorted.

"So, what are we to do now?" Titus said staring at the withering Doran.

"That is the question indeed," he replied pacing before them his arms drawn behind his back. "My forces are already on their way to Kingshelm. We will give them a chance to surrender of course, but if they resist? Well, then things will look far different."

"You will destroy Kingshelm?" pain and anger filled Titus' voice.

"If I must," Doran said cooly. "In the meantime, you will be held in the prison, till I decide what is the best thing to do with a potential imposter king."

179

"We can still have peace!" yelled Titus. "You don't have to do this, Doran."

But it was too late. The king ignored his plea. With one swift motion he ordered for Titus and Elorah to be taken away. Doran's eyes were careful not to look as they were dragged off. Titus could hear just faintly the voice of Lydia sounding as if she was pleading on their behalf, but his hearing was impaired as the throne room's doors slammed shut.

They were dragged through the courtyard, this time with no feigned courtesy. When they reached the holding cells, they were escorted to a new room. This room was without a window or any bed to rest on with a single bucket sat in the corner. A wretched box to hold men in. The door slammed behind them.

"It seems this may be the end," Titus said as he took a deep breath regretting that decision immediately.

"It may be," Elorah replied a bit absent-minded. He looked over at Titus, "But we still have to hold on to hope that maybe Doran will see reason."

"I believe Doran could, but did you see that hooded figure behind the throne?" Titus asked.

"I did," there was concern on his face, "A hidden counselor?"

"Something more sinister, I fear. Dark blades appearing, shadowy figures, plots of betrayal," Titus mused.

"You think it could be them?" fear entering Elorah's voice.

"I do not know. But this kind of darkness has not been seen for many years. I can't help but think this could be their return," Titus said in a hushed tone.

It was The Felled Ones he was speaking of, the incredibly dark forces that had once threatened Islandia. It had been foretold that they might come again.

"If that were the case, what can we do?" Elorah asked.

"We can hope whatever Eloy was looking for he found, and that he is returning soon."

The rest of that day Titus tried not to dwell on the dark truth that grew ever-present in his mind. Could such a foul time really take place in his life? But did anyone ever expect their time would be the one to sink into the black night?

The day was uneventful besides the lack of a provided meal. Not a good sign, both of them had determined. It was beginning to look more and more like a claim to the throne was going to be a death sentence for them both. Titus could not see that night had fallen, but by the extra torch light creeping under their door, and with the time that had passed, he assumed it was. That was when they heard a rattling of keys outside their door. Both men sat up. The light from the hall blinding to their darkened eyes. A hooded figure stood in the doorway wearing a thick cloak, their face was hidden in shadows but for a small red curl peeking out from the hood.

"Lydia?!" Titus said in an excited hush.

"Shhh, keep yer voice down," she scolded.

She pulled her hood back to reveal that it truly was her, those emerald eyes gleaming from the torch in her hand.

"What are you doing here?" probed Elorah.

"I have come to help you escape," she whispered. "Now show me yer chains."

Titus presented his shackled wrists to her. She knelt and began fiddling with the keys in her hand.

"Now, which one was it," she muttered to herself.

"Why are you doing this?" inquired Titus.

"It's too long a story to share, but the simple bit of it is," her eyes looking up into his for a moment, "I believe yer truly a good man, and," a small tear rolled down her cheek, "something is wrong with my father…He's…he's not the same man I once knew."

She finally found the right key and there was a satisfying click of freedom as the shackles fell to the ground. She quickly moved to do the same for Elorah. In a moment, both of them were free of their restraints.

"Now you'll need to move quickly. I've told the guard I needed to speak with you alone, but he will come to check on you soon enough." She reached into her cloak and pulled out two standard broadswords. "These should at least give you something to help you defend yerself with."

They took the swords from her weighing them out in their hands.

"I have prepared two horses with food, water, and some supplies for yer journey. It's not much, but enough to get you to the Western Watch."

"But The Watch should either be destroyed or under siege at this point," protested Elorah. "It won't do us any good to go there."

"In that regard, yer in luck. In my father's state, he has told Geralt to withdraw the siege at The Watch. He has sent all his men to capture Kingshelm."

"When was the order given!?" both men asked in surprise.

"Could not have been later than yesterday that Geralt left with the order. If you leave tonight you will reach The Watch in time. As for Kingshelm…I cannot say."

"It's a chance, at least," Titus said.

Elorah gave a nod of agreement. He turned his attention to Lydia. "Come with us. If what you say is true, when your father finds out what you've done…" His voice trailed off not wanting to finish the thought.

A small bit of fire filled her eyes. "My father is not that far gone. He will be upset yes, but he will see reason from me. I must stay to make sure this spell on him is broken."

"You cannot be convinced?" Elorah asked.

"No, I cannot." Her eyes turned to look at Titus. "But you can do this for me." She paused a moment searching his gaze. "You can keep your promise."

"What promise is that?" Titus asked.

"That you'll see me at the end of this road. I am counting on it." She gave him a quick kiss on his lips. "Now get going. This kingdom needs you both."

Titus sat in utter shock, his face growing red, unsure of what to say in response when Elorah's voice broke in.

"Come my king. We should listen to her." He placed his hand on his shoulder.

Titus nodded half-heartedly following him from pure instinct. Just before leaving the cell he turned and looked at her.

"I promise."

They carefully crept through the halls dodging any flickering torches. They soon found themselves at the entrance where two guards were posted, one leaning in a chair enjoying a mug, the other cleaning his armor. They moved quietly, motioning to each other which one they would incapacitate. Titus chose the man enjoying his beverage. Like a cat, he pounced taking the mug from his hand and slamming it into his face. This stunned the man just in time to grab him by the collar and throw him to the ground with a thud. When Titus could see he was unconscious, he turned to see Elorah choking his own man. The guard slumped to the ground in a heap.

"No need to take a life when it's not needed," Titus thought to himself.

They found a key on the armor cleaner and used it to unlock the entrance door. They scurried across the dark courtyard looking out for any guards that might be posted. To their complete surprise no one was around. It felt too easy. They saw the stable with two horses prepped for their escape, just as Lydia had said.

When they were mounted and ready Elorah spoke up, "Now, how to get out of here unnoticed?"

But again, fate had smiled on them. No one was posted at the fortress gate, and it was unlocked.

"Lydia did all this?" Titus asked out loud.

"I am uncertain, but this seems eerier than that. I suggest we not stick around to find out."

Alongside the swords, Lydia had slipped them a note that spoke of a small escape door that royalty could use to leave the city. They weaved throughout the empty moonlit streets the eerie feeling growing in them both. Whatever was going on it could not be good. Titus felt a tinge of regret leaving Lydia knowing something strange was taking place. He would keep his promise, but in order for him to do anything he had to win at Kingshelm first. Besides, he told himself, this was her home.

After a few minutes of scanning the wall toward the mountain's roots they found a small escape hatch just big enough for their horses. They slipped through the opening single file and, after a moment, they were free. They rode as swiftly as they could through the night not wasting any precious seconds knowing the fate of so many hung on their timing.

The next day and a half of travel was one long sequence of riding, stopping for a quick meal, and continuing on. Titus could think of nothing but arriving at The Watch. Elorah was of the same mind. The summer weather stirred them on even more. Lydia had not cheated them on horses, either. The two stallions rode on tirelessly, as if they, too, understood the importance of their task. It was late morning when they could just make out The Western Watch over the King's Cross Bridge, but there was some trouble. A siege looked to be in place over the city by the wild men of the Lowland Hills. They must have been charged with keeping Kingshelm's men at bay. The beautiful summer day by the mighty Terras River was marred by the scene of war. Campfire smoke was billowing up into the sky. The landscape, normally a picturesque scene of small grassy hills and flatlands, was now turned into a muddy and fortified encampment around the city. Wooden spikes were spread all around, small channels were created sinking into the ground, and the leftover waste from a large gathering of people littered the landscape. In the mess of it all something caught Titus' eye. It looked abandoned. In fact, it was. He could now see, just beyond the siege, a group of men numbering in the thousands moving their direction. He could hear the faint sounding of horns and beating of drums.

Elorah spoke up, "It seems we've arrived just in time."

"It looks that way," Titus said gazing off into the distance at the retreating army. "I can't imagine what the men in The Watch are thinking."

"They are bloody well amazed, I can imagine," Elorah said with a chuckle. "I know I would be."

They sat back and watched as the Hillmen slowly crossed over the King's Cross back toward The Lowland Hills. It was like watching an army of ants marching in a row back to their colony. It took the better half of the morning and afternoon before they deemed it safe to cross themselves.

As they approached, the carnage of their fight from days earlier came into view. Much of the battlefield had been picked over, but corpses still littered the ground without a proper grave, their resting place an open field.

"This place will be a haunt for the history books I am afraid to say," Elorah commented as they strode through the field.

"We cannot let this violence be a waste. Too many men died needlessly if so." Titus replied.

They rode in stillness for the remainder of that trek allowing the wind's howls be the sorrowful cry for words they couldn't express. The King's Cross, the bridge that connected the Terras Plains to the Riverlands, was just before them, The Western Watch not far behind.

As they approached the mote leading to the city gate they could see a squadron of soldiers on top of the wall.

"King Titus!? Is that you?" cried one of the guards in shock.

"It is," a smile crossed his face.

"Open the gate!" rang out the order. The large wooden door creaked open to receive them. The two of them were greeted by Dios who had miraculously survived the battle on the Terras Plains. He held his arms out wide with a grin on his face.

"King Titus, Elorah, now this is a strange day. How did you survive? How did you get here?"

"I am sure it has been for you," chuckled Elorah, both he and Titus barely containing the delight of their return.

Titus began to explain to Dios and the men around them what had transpired, how Doran desired to call off the siege, and how Lydia set them free.

"So what is our next move, my lord?" Dios inquired.

"Valkara has marched to Kingshelm. We must stop them and liberate the city," commanded Titus.

"How many men remain?" asked Elorah.

"Some 3,000, sir. I believe we still outnumber the Valkaran army. We devastated their forces until the Hillmen arrived."

"That's good to hear," Titus said. "When can we march?"

"I can have the men ready by tomorrow morning, sir, if full preparations are to be made," Dios responded confidently.

"Very good. Yes, I would counsel that we not rush into this, my king, without our forces fully equipped," Elorah advised.

"Tomorrow morning it is, then," Titus said.

"I have to ask, Dios, how did you survive?" Elorah asked.

"Ahh sir, it's nothing glorious. As you began to break through with the calvary charge, Valkara's forces stopped their press against us. This gave our forces enough time, when the battle swung in their favor, to retreat. I saw that, without returning to The Watch, this war would be over. I am sorry we didn't press for your rescue."

"No apology needed, Dios. You may have saved the kingdom," praised Titus.

"I believe there is one more battle to fight, sir, before we can make that claim."

"Very true." Titus turned his attention to the royal quarters, "I think I will retire for the evening. We have a journey ahead and a fight to win, and I haven't had a proper sleep in a week."

Dios nodded and Titus could see that Elorah was not far behind him.

"It's good to be back," he thought to himself.

***

LYDIA:

She hoped what she'd done was the right thing. It was a betrayal to her father, she knew it, but what her father was doing and saying...they were not his words, at least not the father she knew. Quick to anger, brash, loud, fiery, yes, he was those things, but he was also hesitant to inflict punishment, not known for injustice, and had a tender heart when it was all said and done. But he was operating from a deep pain, one she had not seen in a long time. She would confront him and bring an end to this madness, to this senseless war. As she made her way out of the prison she took note of Titus and Elorah's handy work with the guards. She was both pleased and impressed at their disarming them without lethality. She walked right past them as they moaned, half-waking from their wounds.

She entered the courtyard, aware of the eerie silence that hung in the air. Even moments before she made her visit to the prison a few guards had patrolled the area. She had no time to ponder its meaning as she made her way into the royal hall. Now real concern gripped her. Every torch and light was extinguished. Only the moonlight shown through the windows. At the end of the great hall sat her father's door wide open. She crept carefully toward his room when she heard the slithering voice that could only belong to one person, Balzara.

"You see, king Doran, you must kill this would be king. Otherwise there will always be one to oppose you."

"There is always someone. It doesn't mean I lop their head off anytime I see a threat! How can you rule in constant paranoia?" Doran protested.

"I have seen many a king rule ruthlessly...but I do not see the others protesting, only one other perhaps, but the rest will submit to the kingslayer," retorted Balzara.

"I..I..cannot do it. Yes, he is a young fool. He let my Nara die, but Lydia speaks to his character. That counts for something, and if he truly would set my sons free."

"You already have your sons in hand!" Balzara blurted. "Kingshelm will soon fall. There is no need to go licking his boots, begging for your sons."

"What if Kingshelm gets word? What if they are able to hold out and as retaliation they decide to kill them? He has already promised me the kingship, why shed more blood?" rationed Doran.

"Yes, father, you are still there," Lydia said smiling to herself.

"Then Kingshelm will come and smash you in short time rallied under some other would-be king," Balzara's voice dropping into a low annoyance.

"I would rather error on sparing my men and sons then spill more of their blood. I know you have helped fund this campaign, but we have the victory and for the price of no more bloodshed. If you're afraid of retaliation we hold the young king hostage as leverage."

"So you will spare him?" Balzara seethed.

"Yes, I see no reason to kill him now. That would side on error."

"I see...come in Jorn," ordered Balzara.

"Jorn!?" Lydia's skin crawled at the mention of that name. She could hear the rage in her father's voice.

"You brought that snake here!?" Doran roared. "I hope so that I could end his life myself!"

"So quick to deal death now are we?" hissed Balzara. "No, I am afraid that is not why he is here. He is my assurance of success."

"Your what?" snarled Doran behind clenched teeth.

Jorn stepped from the shadows. Lydia could barely make him out from where she was eavesdropping. What she could see of him was not good. His skin was an ash grey as if he had walked out of the grave. That was the best description for him. His eyes were missing their light, his hair and clothes dulled and disheveled.

"I found him on my way to you," said Balzara. "He was on the edge of death, much like the day I found you grieving over your loss. Do you remember that?" Balzara's smile turned Lydia's stomach in disgust.

Doran didn't answer, but the look of pain in his eyes was all the answer needed. Balzara went on.

"I made him a similar offer. In exchange for my gift, he would serve me. So, I brought him here as assurance that Valkara would serve my purposes. Seeing that you no longer will accept my counsel, there needs to be a new ruler on the throne," Balzara said with a venomous hiss.

"I see." Doran silently pulled out the dark blade from its sheath. "Your gift is ash in my mouth, and you're a dubious snake, Balzara. Do you know what we do with snakes in Valkara?" Doran sneered, "We cut them to pieces!"

Lydia watched as her father swung with all of his might at Balzara. She stared in amazement as the blade in his hand froze inches from Balzara's face.

"You really believe the blade I have gifted you would bite its master?" mocked Balzara.

Lydia could see the fear fill her father's eyes. She fought back the lump in her throat and the tears burning her eyes. She knew what would happen next. It seemed like it was the only thing that could happen to her family.

"Jorn!" barked Balzara.

Jorn moved toward her father pulling a small dagger from his belt. On his face was the nasty grin he always carried. He licked his lips as he approached Doran.

With a desperate croak Doran cried out, "Guards!"

Both Jorn and Balzara gave a disgusting laugh at her father's plea. "Oh Doran, you know that no one is coming. Men are easy to buy off, especially if they are afraid," reprimanded Balzara. Jorn moved to place the knife at Doran's throat.

"I will give you my offer one last time. You can keep your life forever, but you will serve a new king." Balzara extended an open hand for Doran to take.

"Shuka, on your life, I see the corpse you are caring around," his eyes flickered toward Jorn, "I have enough respect for my life not to place it in your hands. Besides, I think Eloy, even as a dead king, is more worthy to follow then the likes of you!" Doran spat as he finished.

A rage like Lydia had never seen began to rise up in Balzara at her father's response.

"Fine, go meet death, he's always hunger for fools like you!" Balzara said.

With that Jorn grinned and slide the knife. Doran's body collapsed to the ground, the fell blade spilling from his grip ringing as it hit the ground.

"The blade is yours, Jorn, pick it up. Now hurry we have a kingdom to build."

Lydia gripped her fists into a ball and bit her lip as hard as she could. It took everything within her not to scream out her pain, to scream at the evils of this world, to scream at the nightmare that she wanted to wake up from. But that would not do. Evil doesn't lie down and die. She would live to see this evil rot. She composed herself and fled out the hall resisting the urge to look back. Her home was gone, swallowed by these evil men. No, not men, monsters. Where could she go? There was only one place she felt remotely safe, and he was miles ahead of her.

***

TITUS:

He awoke that morning to news that shocked him, Lydia was waiting to speak with him. He got dressed and hurried down to the council chambers where she was waiting. She was a mess. Mud was caked to her boots and cloak, her red hair knotted and tangled. Even still, it could hardly disguise her beauty.

"Lydia, what happened?" he asked immediately after seeing her.

"Jorn and a man, no a monster, named Balzara have killed my father."

The small group of men in the room, including Dios and Elorah, stopped what they were doing and looked at her.

"Say that again," Elorah said.

"A man named Balzara, who had disguised himself as an advisor to my father, betrayed him. He is the one who gave my father that foul blade used against you. He is the one who brokered our army, and now he is the one who has enthroned my sister and father's murderer as king of Valkara."

"Lydia, I don't know what to say." Titus wanted to hold her in his arms, but knew that he couldn't, not now at least.

"This is what we do," she ordered, "I ride with you to Kingshelm and explain to the army, to Geralt, what has transpired. Then we all march together to end this madness."

"Seems reasonable," agreed Elorah.

"It will be done, Lydia. We are with you till the end of this road, wherever that may lead us," Titus said nodding with affirmation.

"Are we ready to march?" Elorah asked.

"Yes sir, on your order, my king," Dios answered.

"Then prepare to march," Titus said.

It was within the hour that they were moving toward Kingshelm. It would take them two days to reach their goal.

"Two days too long," thought Titus. He was unsure of what to say to Lydia. He wanted to say something, anything at all. He understood loss, pain, loneliness. He wanted to comfort her, but knew she would not find comfort in his words so he didn't say anything. Instead, he steered his horse next to hers at the front of the caravan and, looking her in the eyes, gave a reassuring nod. He then rode by her side in silence. She grabbed his hand, saying, without words, not to leave. They rode like this for some time. It was the peace and mourning he had not been afforded since this all started. They wept together in their silent companionship each with the pain, loss, and devastation they carried, unspoken, but understood. This was the moment he knew his heart would forever be hers. She could see him in a way others would not.

The sun was setting when they broke apart for the first time, Titus to his duties as king, Lydia to her own dwelling. He went through the routine he was all too used to by now, strategies for how to take Kingshelm if needed, flanking maneuvers, tactical advantages, and all the military jargon that went with it. He nodded his head in agreement to the commanders and their consensus. It was later than he would have liked before he arrived at the tent prepared for him. "Another night on the road," he sighed as he entered. His sleep was the kind that follows a letting out of deep sorrow.

Bright and early the next morning he arose. They began the day on the road once more. It was a beautiful sunny afternoon which led to another evening, another talk of strategy. This night was different, however. Tomorrow they would arrive at Kingshelm. His adrenaline keeping him from a restful sleep.

The morning seemed to fight its own arrival. When the sun finally began to rise he went to personally see that the marching horn was blown, anxious for the day to begin. He searched and found Lydia packing up her small tent. He moved to help her. She didn't say a word, but moved to the side to let him join her. They worked for a moment without speaking, then he reached for her hand. As he touched her, she looked up into his eyes.

"Lydia, I have something I want to say to you."

Without letting him speak, she kissed him. Not like the kiss in Valkara. This one was full of passion, a lover's kiss. He was shocked, but only momentarily. He embraced her and the kiss. After a moment he gently pushed her away.

"I truly do need to say this, in case…well, in case this does not go how we plan."

"Shut up, Titus," she said pushing back a loose lock of hair. "I know what you want to say. Save it for after."

"After? But why?" he protested.

Her eyes glazed over.

"Save it for the moment you can follow up with those words. I won't hear them then lose you, too."

He shook his head in agreement and rose to his feet a smile crossing his face.

"I better stay alive then, huh."

She smiled back at him, then threw a strap she had previously been rolling up, hitting him in the chest.

"You better. I don't have any more room for mourning." A joke dipped in truth.

He knelt one last time kissing her on the cheek.

"See you at the front of the caravan."

"You best hope yer that lucky!" she teased as he playfully tossed the rope back at her.

Within the hour the army was on the move not far now from reaching Kingshelm. It was another sunny day, the heat radiated off the armor plating of any who bore it. Lydia and a few others called out a strange sight. Just down the road, in the direction of Kingshelm, a pillar of smoke was rising into the air. With alarm Elorah called out.

"Is that from Kingshelm?!"

"It looks to be," said Dios.

Titus turned to the small company with him, "Lydia, Elorah, and Dios we will ride ahead. The rest of you keep the men at a steady pace. We may be fighting sooner than we'd like!"

The four of them shot off in a whirlwind, dust from the road kicking up in trail behind them. Within the hour they could just make out Kingshelm, several towers of smoke rising from the city.

"This cannot be good," Elorah muttered.

"Are we too late?" Dios asked.

"We don't know anything yet," Titus said fighting back the fear welling up within him.

He looked over to Lydia who looked just as concerned as the rest of them. They rode on as fast as their horses would carry them. As Kingshelm came into view, the scene was grim. A large cloud of black smoke blanketed the sky, darkening the sun above. As they approached the walls, their greatest fears were realized. Kingshelm was gone. Bodies were strewn all along the ground, most of them civilians. The gates hung loose and broken on their hinges. Screams and cries of agony could still be heard ringing out from within the walls. The city was a pile of ashes, only a few buildings remained. The four of them stood stunned and unable to speak. The great and ancient city of Kingshelm had been destroyed.

13

GERALT

Eli led them through the grand halls of Kingshelm's palace. He had agreed to allow Geralt, Ferir, and a few other leading men into the city to discuss its surrender. Unlike the others, Geralt did not gawk at the grandiose displays of craftsmanship or the ancient historical pieces on display. He had a mission and that was it. Besides, to him splendid palaces meant nothing if the king who dwelt in them was an ugly tyrant. More often than not, it was they who cared deeply about reputation and appearances, the core purpose of these magnificent displays.

As they reached the end of the main hallway into the center of the palace, two guards stood welcoming them through towering doors, their cold looks fixated on their captors. Behind the doors stood a vast lobby made of white marble and covered with fine tapestries. In the center, two huge stairways converged welcoming guests into the famous throne room of Kingshelm. Underneath these stairs sat a smaller set of doors. This was where Eli was directing them.

As he opened the doors to usher them in, they were greeted with a large table, likely used for councils. A small meal had been prepared for them. Each man took his seat around the table. An awkward silence hung in the air, no one sure what to say first. That's when Ferir cleared his throat.

"Gentlemen, we appreciate the hospitality, we really do, but we have certain clear demands and we don't care to waste much time on pleasantries."

"Just like a skulking Valkaran…" muttered one of the councilmen.

"What was that!?" clamored one of the commanders slamming his axe into the table and sending splinters flying.

"Now, now sir, put that foul thing away," said Eli. "We have come to hear your terms, at least show us the dignity of an official convening."

Ferir motioned for his commander to sit down and put away the weapon.

"As I said, our terms are simple. Surrender the city and the two sons, and no one will be harmed."

"Simple, yes, realistic…I am not as sure," chimed in a skinny man with a long black beard. He stroked it as he thought.

"We do have some concerns," said Eli. "How can we know once we open the gates your army won't simply sack the city? Valkarans and Riverland men have never been too keen to live in each other's territories."

"A legitimate king must sit on the throne in Kingshelm. We know how this works. Why would we wish to destroy the city?" countered Ferir.

"No throne, no need for legitimacy," Eli said candidly. "We see no need for loyalty unto death."

He panned his arm out to the other council members, all of them nodding in agreement.

"We just want to come to a conclusion where certain properties and persons can be guaranteed safety."

Geralt was disgusted at these men. They simply cared for themselves and their wealth. What does it matter if a few peasants die as long as those with influence can keep it. "Were there any men of honor anymore?" he thought to himself.

"That can be arranged." Ferir answered picking up on the hint. "How can we put your mind at ease?"

"We would like certain securities," proposed one of the councilmen wearing a purple tunic with golden fringes, his hair a greying brown.

"What counselor Jorath means is we want our personal properties throughout the Riverlands to remain ours. We also want to make sure that any of our families in the city will remain safe from your army if we are to let them into the city."

"Of course, we don't come as savages," Ferir said. "We plan to harm no one during our stay. We only wish to free Doran's sons and restock our supplies. A small force will remain here, and we will return bringing Doran back to be crowned king."

At this some of them muttered.

"I see, so he intends to rule as Steward King?" inquired Eli.

"No, he intends to be the High King of Islandia," Ferir stated. "The Steward King is no more, as is this Eloy that no one has heard from for who knows how long."

"I see. May I speak with you privately?" requested Eli.

He looked at the other members, giving them a look to leave. They stood at once and began filing out of the room. The Valkaran commanders followed suit from a similar look given by Ferir. Geralt however, stayed. Eli, a bit puzzled, turned his gaze to him.

"Did you not hear me?" he asked.

"Oh I heard you. Ferir and I are sharing this position. I just don't like talking as much as him."

Eli squirmed a little in his seat.

"Very well."

He waited a moment till the door had closed behind them before he spoke again.

"There are a few things you should know," he stood to his feet, "I received a letter from The Western Watch this last evening."

Geralt and Ferir glanced at each other.

"This won't be good," thought Geralt.

"They have informed me of their return to Kingshelm and that they should be arriving any day now." He moved to pluck a grape from the table. "I haven't shared this bit of news with the other council members, they are such small thinking little men. But, I assume your stay at Kingshelm will not be the short little visit you have proposed."

"Our plan is..." Ferir started before Eli cut him off.

"I know what your plan is, or at least I can assume. I think it is time you've heard my proposal."

Both men sat up.

"Go on," growled Geralt.

"You see, I do not serve Kingshelm or the Riverlands, not in the way that you may assume. I have...another who has promised me quite the bargain if I help carry out his plans."

"Who would this friend of yours happen to be?" Ferir asked.

"I am getting there, don't you worry," Eli responded plopping another grape into his mouth. "This associate had a much larger future in store, it even involved your small kingdom for a time. Sadly, that plan was ruined, but it seems fate has given us a new opportunity."

"You can stop with the theatrics, just speak plainly of what you want," snarled Ferir.

"The theatrics are so much more fun," sneered Eli, "but I digress. I was the one who planted the poisoned robe on king Richard, but it was not my plan in full. My associate was the one who pulled it all together. He knew tensions between Sahra and Valkara had grown over the years toward the rule of a Steward King in Kingshelm. I imagine they felt quite snuffed from the honor." He grabbed another grape savoring it for a moment. "So he reached out and found they, too, would like to be free from a united rule. The plan was put in motion. He knew Doran was a traditionalist, so he promised two men eager for power the thing they craved. In exchange for Valkara's throne, they would take care of Doran and secure the poison only found in the deep south. This is where Sahra comes in. They promised to manufacture the poison in exchange for independence in the new order of things. My associate agreed, thus the poison was delivered to him from the two Valkarans." Eli stopped to pause and smile for a moment. "It was rather brilliant. No one would expect the grand advisor of treason. Who, with such an illustrious position, would complain. So it was set. Richard would die, and amid that chaos a new freedom would arise. Independent rule for the kingdoms of Islandia. Of course, some blood would need to be shed. It always does. Sahra would come to the aid of Valkara in its fight against Kingshelm seeing as they were always going to take the fall. The young, boy king Titus would feel the pressure to go to war with a bit of council in that direction," Eli stopped to gesture at himself. "There he would meet his untimely end. Then, and only then, could a new era begin."

Both Ferir and Geralt sat in silent shock. Never in Geralt's wildest dreams did he imagine this sinister of a scheme was behind it all. How could he? To anyone it would easily pass as another conflict in the building tensions of past and present.

"I still don't understand," stated Ferir.

"What is there not to comprehend?" Eli said a bit exasperated.

"You still haven't explained what is in it for you."

"Ahhh yes, why risk all that I had? That is what you want to know. Because, there is always more," his voiced deepening, "You see, most men would be content to live with a prestigious position, but there are born some who should, no who deserve, to have a larger voice. Why do you think we crown descendants of kings? But for a man like me? My voice was never the final word in the room. I grew tired of my advice falling on deaf ears when I knew my council would serve best.

So, with Richard gone and the boy king removed from the picture, The Riverlands would need a new king."

"You selfish shuka," mumbled Geralt.

"Ahh, so high and mighty, are we? I do recall your betrayal of your own people for certain interests," sneered Eli. "No one's hands are clean."

Geralt brooded in silence at the searing remark.

"So who is your associate?" pried Ferir.

"Not till we make a deal. No one gets to know unless they want to be a part of the new way of things. That's how this is going to go."

It dawned on Geralt that this is why Eli had brought them in the city. He had flipped the tables. They had come in as the proud conquers, now, if they were to escape with their lives, they must submit to him. He could see the same conclusion beginning to dawn on Ferir's face as well.

"Lacka," Ferir muttered.

"So? Would you like to hear the proposal?" Eli asked with a smile that said, "Yes, I do own you now."

"What choice do we have," said Ferir, fire in his eyes.

"Not much at all," Eli said with a smirk.

"Lets hear it," Geralt snarled.

"You will take your army to gather with my associate. I know you don't have the forces to take on Kingshelm alone, and I'd rather not have my new kingdom destroyed in a siege. There, you will wipe out Titus and his forces. After, you are free to take Doran's sons to rule your little kingdom up north and do whatever you Valkarans do. Maybe raid some Hillmen villages?"

"May we speak alone for a moment?" requested Ferir.

"Sure, just don't take too long."

Eli moved out of the room closing the door behind him.

"It's not a bad proposal," Ferir suggested.

"Hmph." Was Geralt's only response.

"That response again? Not very helpful," sighed Ferir.

"I don't trust men who manipulate their way to power. Who's to say they will keep their promise at the end of this?" he asked.

"The alternative is he has at least twenty guards waiting to kill us before we can take a step out of this palace. Our men, leaderless, maybe wait till tomorrow before making a move. By then the city is sealed and they are trapped in-between a wall and an army. Valkara loses. That's the end of it."

"Well, we don't have an option then," Geralt replied.

"I need you to agree with me," Ferir growled in frustration.

"Why? You have clearly laid it out that we are at their mercy."

"So we take the deal?"

Geralt sighed, "We take the deal."

Ferir nodded and stood to his feet. He tapped at the door signaling for Eli to come in. Several seconds later he opened the door with a smile.

"Ahh gentlemen, do we have a decision?"

"We will join you and your...associate."

"Excellent! I knew you would see reason. Now, would you like to see your two princes to inform them of the news?"

"Who is he?" pressed Geralt.

Eli stopped, giving him a somber look.

"You really are no fun are you?"

"Can't say I've been described that way."

"Come, let's go speak to the princes, and then I'll tell you."

He led them through the door and into a side passageway out of the main lobby. It was a pattern of confusing halls that crossed and turned and descended. They reached a door some three levels below where they had started. There, they went down a spiral staircase. It felt an eternity until they reached the bottom. Their descent grew darker and darker as they went. The few top stairs were surrounded by windows, but as they descended below ground a torch was needed to light their way.

As they reached the last of the stairs, they were greeted by a warden that opened a door to a single, long hallway.

"We don't have many prisoners kept in the palace these days," explained Eli as he lead them down the hall.

They passed empty cell after empty cell until they reached the final door. Inside, two young men in ratty tunics sat chained to the walls their hair matted and covered in dried blood. A grotesque odor filled Geralt's nostrils. He shuddered to think what might be its source.

"Shuka! This is how you treat royal prisoners?!" Ferir exclaimed in disgust.

"Ahhh no, not normally, but you see, I planned on killing the princes when this was all said and done. No need for rivals on the throne. But when things went off script, well, I improvised. I needed them as security in case of any measures taken against us. I figured the poorer their condition, the more pressure would fall on Doran to cooperate. But now that you're here, that is all water under the bridge."

The warden unlocked the door for them. The clanking of the keys stirred the princes awake. They sluggishly raised their heads to greet their visitors. Both of their eyes shot open at the sight of familiar faces.

"Ger...alt?" moaned Aiden. "Is that you?"

Brayan started to weep.

"Does...does this mean we can go free?" he said quivering.

Geralt did all he could not to cut Eli down where he stood.

Ferir answered for them. "Yes, my princes, it does."

The warden moved to unlock them from their shackles. Both slumped to the ground unable to hold themselves up.

"How long has it been like this?" interrogated Geralt.

"I..I can't say. Some time, but I am sure they both will recover," Eli stuttered.

Geralt bent down to help the younger Brayan to his feet.

"Come, lad, we're getting you out of here." He turned his gaze to Eli. "Provide us a place to clean them up and get them fed, then we can move forward."

"Of course, of course, but please do remember time is of the essence," Eli replied a bit concerned. "Kingshelm could arrive soon."

Geralt stared at him.

"Once they are taken care of then we will talk about this associate of yours and his plans."

Geralt and the warden carried the two princes up the ascending stairs. They had become too weak to make the small journey up. Geralt could feel Brayan's bones through his filthy tunic. The once strong and eager prince was now a hollow starving shell.

"What did these children do to deserve such a fate?" he thought to himself.

They were quickly ushered into a private room reserved for royal guests who would come to visit. Some servants came, stripping the young men down and bathing them. Tunics removed, Geralt could see the horrendous torture that had been inflicted on them. Scars that would last forever, and not all of them visible. The two young men were quickly clothed again in soft robes befitting royalty. A hot meal was presented quickly after. Geralt watched as they eyed the food fearful it might be taken away at any moment, that the dream would end and the nightmare would start all over. They scarfed the food down which resulted in them vomiting it up. Geralt counseled them to take it slow, reminding them several times to take a break. He looked at Ferir whose unease was visible. He moved to speak with him out of earshot.

"These are the men you want to be in bed with? The same ones that did this to them?!" he raged in a hushed tone.

"What choice do we have? He said it himself, he didn't plan on them living before. Things have changed."

"So he tortures them and takes them to an inch of their life instead! What makes you think that won't happen again?"

"I can't say," Ferir turned away. "But if we want to survive, if we want Valkara as we know it to survive, we should stick to the plan."

"When Doran sees this he will absolutely lose it," Geralt protested.

"I thought the plan was a world without him," Ferir said suddenly growing cold. "Seems it is only wrong when it's inconvenient?"

"You know that's not what this is about, Ferir," Geralt's voice raised a little higher than he would have liked.

They both turned to see if the princes had noticed, but they had collapsed into a deep sleep on the bed.

"Fine, have it your way. We stick with the plan," Geralt turned and stomped off toward the princes.

They allowed them to rest for an hour before waking them. Neither of them wanted to be the one to explain what was going to happen next. Finally, Geralt explained it to them and how all this madness had taken place. The two princes sat on the bed in silence. Geralt was unsure what they thought of it all. He could see Aiden gripping the covers of the bed and Brayan shaking ever so slightly.

"No," Aiden finally said. "No! No! No! No! No! No!" He was screaming now, "NO!!!!!!"

Brayan began twisting, clawing, and violently convulsing. Both Geralt and Ferir stepped back, unsure of what to do. Finally, after some time, they both stopped. An eerie quiet filling the room.

Ferir took a step forward, but Geralt placed his hand on his chest to stop him. Aiden looked up at them an animal rage in his eyes.

"I will never be chained to these monsters again. You don't know. You don't know! Get out! Get out now!" He took a pillow and flung it at them. Then, scrambling across the room, he began picking up various items and throwing it at their heads.

"We should leave," Geralt said.

Both men scrambled out of the room as Aiden rained down curses on them. Geralt shut the door to the room with a deep sigh of anguish.

"What are we going to do, Geralt? We can't crown one of them. They are completely insane! And if what you tell me is true, Doran is not much better off."

"We failed them, Ferir. We can't just abandon them now," Geralt barked.

"Let's go find Eli and get this name. We can worry about what to do with them after all this is done."

Ferir stomped off not waiting for a reply. Geralt followed knowing Ferir was right, even if he wished he wasn't.

Ferir fumed down the palace hallways entering into the royal courts' housing where Eli stayed. A large open courtyard was in the center of the various living quarters with a small white fountain with a roaring lion spewing water from its mouth. Eli sat on the edge of the fountain feeding some fish that swam in the pool. It was a calm and serene scene, the opposite of the two men invading it.

"Ahh, gentlemen, have you settled in well?" inquired Eli as he stroked his hand in the water.

"Enough! We want the name, now," ordered Ferir.

"Valkarans, always the impatient ones," Eli said standing to his feet. He dusted off his cloak and reached inside, pulling out a small letter. "Here," he said handing it to Ferir.

"What's this?" snarled Ferir. "I said a name, not a piece of parchment!"

Eli rolled his eyes. "Read the parchment."

With one eye on Eli, Ferir broke open the small seal. Unfolding the letter he began to read. After completing it, he slowly lowered his arm.

"It is truly him?" shock clearly on his face.

"Yes, I know. I was doubtful myself at first. It seems ancient loyalties don't always come with the bloodline."

Geralt motioned for Ferir to hand him the letter. Ferir still in shock handed it to him absent-mindedly. Geralt unfolded the parchment and read the words himself.

E,

When Valkaran forces arrive at Kingshelm, inform them to meet me in Leviatanas. There we may end this feud once and for all. My army is ready. I will inform Titus that I have tricked Valkara into siding with me so that we may defeat them together. In reality I hope that, with Valkara's help, we might wipe any remaining forces from the Riverlands off Islandia. We may rule in independent peace when this is done. Make whatever concessions needed to bring them here. I will be waiting.

L.

"Leviantanas is behind this," Geralt said aloud lowering the letter.

"Please. No word aloud!" scolded Eli. "Now give it here."

Geralt handed the letter to Eli, who moved toward a lit torch in the courtyard. He proceeded to set the letter ablaze. He turned to the two of them.

"You're in it now. I suggest you get moving before the day is over. I will give you access to the port so that you may get to Jezero quickly."

Both Ferir and Geralt stood in silence.

"Well! You know, now it's time for you to hold up your end of the bargain!" Eli said.

Before they could reply they saw smoke rising in the sky above them. Eli's anger turned to confusion.

"What? What is that?" he said.

He rushed out of the courtyard toward the smoke. Both Geralt and Ferir followed behind him. They rounded hall after hall following the smell of smoke and burning reaching the grand lobby they had been in earlier. Thick black smoke was billowing from the throne room doors half open, two guards laid slain on the floor.

"What is going on?" Eli cried.

That's when they heard a crazed laugh. Above them on the balcony stood Brayan, lit torch in one hand, a bloody dagger in the other.

"Burn! Burn! Burn!" he cried in a maniacal screech.

Like a madman, he began running across the balcony lighting banner, tapestry, and any other object he could find. The entire lobby was beginning to be engulfed with flame.

"What have you done you, shuka!?" screamed Eli pulling a dagger from his belt.

Ferir went to grab his arm. Eli shrugged it free from his grip.

"You want to stop me? Then the deal is off and you will die in this flaming hell," he snapped.

Ferir hesitated and took a step back.

"You are the cause of his madness," roared Geralt over the cracking of wooden beams caught ablaze just above them.

"Silence, little Valkaran pet," sneered Eli, "or you, too, will see Valkara ablaze."

With that he rushed after the boy who had made his way down the stairs. Ferir, in panic, fled through the doorway that led out of the palace. Geralt settled in his mind that he had to save the boy, his madness the result of all of their failings. He chased after them down an offshoot hall.

It was a few moments before he caught up to them. Brayan had lit anything and everything he could as he ran down the halls, creating a small inferno in his wake. Eli leaped at him in a fit of rage. His sparkling kingdom was now afire by the madman he'd created. He slammed into the boy throwing them both to the ground. They wrestled. Brayan sprawling like a trapped animal, clawing and biting at anything he could get ahold of. Eli, clearly untrained in combat, was struggling to pull his dagger hand free.

It happened in a blink. Geralt was only a second or two away when he saw the flash of a dagger. It plunged into the young prince's chest. He squirmed for a moment, but his body eventually became very still. Eli stumbled to his feet panting heavily and turned to face Geralt, his face ghostly white. Geralt looked down to see a small dagger plunged into his side. The young prince paid with his life, but he had got his revenge.

Eli dropped to his knees and muttered, "Shukan madman, I...it can't end like this..."

Geralt stepped toward the kneeling fiend.

"Oh, it can. Sometimes justice does win."

He pushed Eli to the ground with his boot. He fell, letting out a gasp of air, his last breath. Geralt took notice of the growing flames around him. He, too, would need to find an escape, or he would be joining them very soon. He hastily knelt beside Brayan placing his hand on the young man's forehead.

"I am so sorry it has come to this. Please forgive me."

He rose to his feet, knowing he could spend no more of his time in mourning. He scanned the hallway to find a door at the end of the hall. He ran as quick as he could. It was locked. Nothing a boot couldn't fix. With all his might he sent his foot crashing into the door, breaking it free. Inside was a small room connected to a stairway. Just what he needed. A small window overlooked a part of the city below. It was worse than he could have imagined. The wind had begun to carry the fire from the palace into the city below. Small shops were beginning to catch ablaze. With no way of stopping it, Kingshelm could very well burn to the ground. He put his hand to the glass.

"What have we done," he whispered to himself.

The sentiment couldn't last long. He turned to the small stairway that led out into an open garden in front of the palace complex. All that stood between him and the city was the wall surrounding the palace. He could see guards abandoning their posts in terror as the fire continued to rage. The palace gates were flung open so they could escape. Geralt followed suit. He joined the small crowd of those fleeing from the palace. Cries of terror rang out as women and children searched for their way of escape. Geralt could see that the others fleeing the city from the main road were being crushed by a growing stampede. He made sure to avoid that way. Swerving in and out of side streets, he forced his way through the mass of humanity in fear for their lives. Smoke filled the air and the smell of burning houses, food, and flesh made him want to vomit. He pulled a small piece of cloth from under his tunic and covered his nose and mouth. The scene before him was a nightmare, the sky above black as night, only to be lit by the hell behind him. More and more began to fill the streets in an attempt to escape, some taking the opportunity to try and rob others. "Even with an inferno just behind them, they'd still try to rob the poor," Geralt thought to himself as he saw the horrors take place. He was almost there. The city wall loomed above him, but no one was moving. That's when he noticed the city gate was shut. A group of soldiers standing before the crowd.

"Now listen, citizens, we have been given orders not to open the gates from Grand Advisor Eli. Even in crisis we will not allow an invading army to enter the city."

"Who would want a chard corpse of a city?!" cried one citizen.

"They can have it! Let us go!" another cried.

The men around their commander stood unsure of what to do when suddenly everything broke loose. A group of young men with swords charged the officer and his men. The crowd soon followed. It became a blood bath. Citizens being cut down by their own soldiers. The tide of humanity pressed the small guard against the gate eventually crushing them. In a matter of moments the crowd burst like a dam out of the gates, flooding the bridge out of the city. Seeing a small opening, Geralt joined the tide spilling out into the country. The horrors only grew. The Valkaran forces, seeing the citizens of Kingshelm rush at them, were stirred from their camp. Unsure if an enemy force was charging them, they began to take up arms. Geralt watched as his forces began to cut down the fleeing civilians. "We are all guilty of this madness," he said to himself with horror. He ran to the front as fast as he could and shouted at the top of his lungs.

"STOP!!! I ORDER YOU TO STOP!!"

Some Valkaran soldiers around him paused and recognized him, but the order came too late for many who had tried to flee the city. It became a never-ending nightmare in which it felt the sun would never rise again. The sights of untold carnage and needless death would haunt Geralt all his days, the burning of Kingshelm a terror without end.

After endless hours the sun still did not pierce the rising smoke. It wasn't until what Geralt could only assume was early morning that he found Ferir, wandering the massacre. He grabbed him by the shoulders and shook him.

"Ferir, you're alive."

The man stood in stunned horror.

"What..what have we done Geralt?" he mumbled. His face was covered in blackened ash. His entire demeanor a reflection of the scene around him.

Geralt had no answer for him.

"What do we do now?" Ferir asked looking him in the eyes.

"We have no choice. If we want to live, we only have one option," Geralt answered.

"Leviantanas?" asked Ferir.

"Leviantanas," Geralt said nodding.

14

IMARI

He had vanished. Fahim had just disappeared. The small group of them couldn't shake the shock of what had just happened.

How..how is that possible? Do you know, Nabila?" Imari asked.

"I've only seen that once by the man of shadows. It can only be the work of that sinister monster," she snarled.

He turned and looked at the space where Fahim had been. Something else strange had happened. The dark taint that had once covered his spear was gone returning it to normal. He pulled the spear from the glass, the wind whistling loudly from the hole now created.

He looked the spear over. Everything was as it should be.

"What is going on?" he said aloud.

"Your spear is nice and all, Imari, but we need to get out of here. Nabila, are there any important parchments or items we need to find while we are here?" Khaleena turned to the young queen.

Nabila nodded her head and moved to the stone table searching through the various documents resting there. Imari took the moment of rest to check on Impatu, the two of them embracing.

"My young friend, I never thought I would see you again," Imari said with a grin.

"You lacked that much faith in me?" teased Impatu.

"How were you captured?" Imari asked.

"The Sycar began searching from house to house. It wasn't long till they found us holed up in that storehouse. An injured Khalan was a dead give away."

"How did you recover so quickly?" Imari inquired examining his wound.

Impatu shot a glance over at Riah.

"Riah truly does know her herbs. She cleaned the wound and in a matter of days it was beginning to heal."

Riah smiled with a blush, but it soon faded back to sorrow as Imari quickly realized she was kneeling over the body of Moheem. The weight of tragedy at the lives lost flooded him. His mind rushed back to his brother.

"Khaleena, come here!" he commanded.

She looked up at him puzzled,

"What, brother?"

"You need to see something." He motioned with his head to look.

She saw it, the body of her brother Imbaku, lying still on the ground. She rushed down, wailing as she went. She collapsed over him her shoulders heaving up and down.

"That lacka, that shuka, I…"

Imari came behind her placing his hand on her shoulder and kneeled next to her.

"He gave his life for me, Khaleena. He saved us."

"Why did he always think he needed to prove something?" she said through her tears.

Imari let her have a moment before he responded, "Khaleena, we will mourn him and have a proper burial when this is all over."

She sniffed wiping away her tears.

"I didn't get to say goodbye."

"He told me to tell you something," Imari said with a sorrowful smile.

"Yes?"

"He said to tell you to remember who the hero was today."

"Eishh…oh Imbaku."

She began to weep all over again. Imari stood, giving her a time to grieve by herself. His face turned to Nabila and Amira who were staring at a certain parchment.

"Something interesting?" he called out.

They stopped staring for a moment and looked up at him, a sober look in their eyes.

"Not good?" he asked.

"Henry, Imari, you should read it yourselves," responded Amira.

"Me?" Henry asked quizzically. "Alright, if you think it's important."

"It is," was all Nabila said.

Both of them moved behind her, glancing at the letter in her hand.

F,

It has begun. Soon Doran will be off the board. You and your forces should gather with Valkara. Together, you will not find any trouble against Kingshelm. I will do my part in all this. If need be I will intervene, but I prefer a more…distant approach. The young steward king knows nothing of my true plans. We should use this to our advantage. If you can join with Valkara this can all be over quickly. I hear rumblings of dissent growing among your people, led by your daughter. Do not let this throw you off the true prize. If we can defeat Kingshelm, we will usher in a new era. May you have victory in the coming days.

L.

"This is all information we knew already," mused Imari.

"Not everything," corrected Nabila. "Who is this mysterious L?"

Henry motioned to see the letter. He scoured it turning
it over in his hand.

"Was there an envelope with a seal?"

"None that we found," sighed Amira.

Riah spoke up, "When Asad captured us, I overheard him
speaking to Fahim. He said something about trusting serpents
born of the same line as Kingshelm. It seemed strange to me
at the time."

Henry's eyes light up. "It's Leviatanas."

Everyone stopped to look at him.

"What makes you say that? An L could mean a person,
not a place."

"It all makes sense," Henry said to no one in particular.
"Titus being unaware of the betrayal. Leviatanas is Kingshelm's
most trusted ally, so he would trust them above all others.
Besides that, you said serpents born of the same line did you
not?" his gaze fixing on a now nervous Riah.

"I mean, yes, but that could mean anything?"

"The symbol of Leviatanas is the Leviathan, the serpent of
the sea. The only other line from The Founders is…"

"Leviatanas," muttered Imari. "So that means Kingshelm
could be walking into a trap."

"Khosi, I must take this news to Kingshelm. They must
be warned," Henry said resolutely.

"Of course, you have been a faithful friend, Henry. Without
you, we would not have won this victory. I will assist in any
way possible," Imari proclaimed.

"What about Sahra? Or was what Fahim said true?" came
the voice of Khaleena. "Will you come to Kingshelm's aid,
Nabila?"

All eyes fell on Nabila. Imari could see her face begin to
flush.

"Sahra has much rebuilding to do before we can aid anyone. If you have forgotten, there is still a battle raging below us. I must stop the bloodshed of our people first."

"And after?" Khaleena asked not backing down.

"We will see," stated Nabila.

"What about us, Khosi, and our people? They will want to know what has happened," chimed in Impatu. "Would it be best to run off to another land's war before you have even returned to Khala?"

Now the eyes had shifted to him. He recognized the heat Nabila must have felt only a short moment ago as each pair of eyes weighed your decision. He thought a moment before speaking.

"Henry, I believe Impatu speaks wisdom. I must return to Khala before I could do anything to help you. But, Khala is on your way. If you are willing, you may journey with us. Refresh yourself for a few days, then I will join you."

"Khosi, with respect, I will travel with you as far as Khala, after this I cannot say. I feel this is too urgent a matter to wait."

"I understand," said Imari, sad, but understanding.

"Before we make any more plans we should stop this battle below us," advised Nabila to them all.

With a nod they all agreed, and with haste they made their return to the palace entrance beneath them. The sight on the palace stairs was that of a graveyard. In the time it had taken for them to defeat Fahim, many on both sides had been slain. Blood ran like rapids down the steps. A few hundred men still remained locked in combat. Nabila let out a howling cry. Each man, for a moment, locking onto her. In her hand she held up the sword of her father, one item of proof left behind, and in the other the helmet of her brother. No words were needed as one Sycar warrior after another began to drop their weapons each beginning to grasp their new reality. There was a new woman in charge. In short time they were rounded up by the remaining rebel forces. Nabila gave the order to some of the Sycar captains to disperse among the city and tell their remaining forces to stand down. It was over, there would be a new day in Sahra. Imari just hoped it would be a better one. For the first time he was a bit unsure.

After Nabila had given her commands she turned to him, motioning for him to follow. She found a secluded place just inside the palace overhang. They stood, both of them unsure where to start.

"So you will return to Khala now?" she asked.

"If my queen will let me," Imari stated unsure if it was a kind gesture or a subordinate's request.

"You think me a monster like my father now, don't you?" she asked, sorrow in her voice.

"No...but I see your hands are not as clean as I had once hoped." He couldn't tell if that comment would sting even more.

"I had hoped that you and I could rule the south as equals. That is still my hope. Is it so wrong to desire to rule our kingdoms free from far away kings?" she said exhaling.

"Eloy is still a worthy High King. He was faithful to my family and it is Kingshelm who freed us to rule ourselves. It would be a betrayal on my part to take that freedom and use it for my own wishes, Nabila."

"You are noble." She stared off in the distance for a moment. "I suppose returning to the kingdom that held you captive from the beginning does not appeal to you either."

He didn't reply. She knew his answer.

"So you will stay with Kingshelm. But what of us?" her eyes now staring into his, searching for his answer.

"Nabila, I have loved you since the day I met you. I do not place our kingdoms' history on you. I do not place what your father has done on you. You have helped me save my people. Nabila, my promise to you was forever, and as long as you see me as your husband I will keep that promise to you."

Her eyes welled up with tears as she reached to embrace him. They held each other for a moment, letting the responsibilities they carried wash away. Imari gently brushed her hair back.

"Will you come to visit me in Khala?"

"When things are put into order here, yes," she said with a lover's smile.

"How will we do this, Imari, ruling two kingdoms apart from each other?" She buried her face in his chest.

"We will sort these things out in due time," he said resting his chin on her head.

Inside he wrestled with this same question. They held on to each other as long as they could. Nabila looked up at him.

"I will have the port prepare ships ready to transport you and your men back to Khala by tomorrow evening. I will also send with you a royal decree, letting all Sahra's men stationed there know to stand down and allow the Khosi to return. I will come to you as quickly as I can to ensure they don't give you any trouble."

"You have done more for us, love, than you can imagine. Thank you."

He moved his hand under her chin lifting it to embrace her with a kiss. Her smile made the parting moment that much more difficult.

"I love you, my Khosi." she said with a grin.

"I love you, my Sulta."

***

The port smelled of the sea. Gulls filled the air searching for any cheap meals. Shouts from sailors echoed across the docks. Imari had never been of the seafaring persuasion. He preferred the shifting sand beneath his feet. He looked over at Henry who was eager to set out. Ever since the dreary news of Leviatanas betrayal he had been uneasy. Imari could sympathize. Betrayal was a bitter pill, especially when it harms those you love.

He watched as the last of his men, followed by his sister and the young Impatu, boarded. They had all said their goodbyes that morning. The mood was bittersweet. The bonds that they had made with their new allies would be lasting, but there is always something about the idea of returning home. It had been years since Imari had looked upon Khala. He wondered what had changed. Would he even recognize it when he saw it? Khaleena had assured him he would. She had taken a few discreet visits into the city in the past. He would soon find out for himself.

They finally set sail just as the sun was beginning to set, the end of one adventure and the start of another. Their journey was filled with reunion and mourning. Impatu shared in more detail what had taken place after Imari's departure. He shared how the famous markets of Wahah were shut down for the first time in two hundred years due to the riot they started. He also shared of their eventual capture and the perilous journey by sea from Wahah to Sahra. At one point they even attempted to escape and nearly paid with their lives for it.

Khaleena, Lombaku, and the rest of the Masisi took time to mourn over Boani and all the others they had lost. In Masisi fashion this was done in private with no outsiders allowed. It was not spoken of again. After the appropriate time, Imari found Khaleena leaning on the railing overlooking the sea.

"What's next for you?" he asked leaning beside her.

"Ahh yes, the chief of the Masisi," she said in reply. "I suppose I shall return to the rest of the tribe."

"You won't return with me to Khala?"

"The Masisi were not the most welcome in the grand city of the desert, even before Sahra was running things. I won't abandon them after they have given us so much."

"What if you didn't have too?" Imari asked.

"I appreciate the sentiment, Imari, but I don't know if the people of Khala will see things as we do. Traditions can be hard to break, especially defective ones."

"Ahh, but someone must try," he said with a wiry smile. "Why not us? We were able to do all this, were we not?"

Khaleena cracked a smile. "I suppose so. So what about you? Do you truly plan to go to Kingshelm's aid?"

"Yes, we owe them a great debt. Besides that, Henry is a friend and I wish to help him."

"So who will run things while you are gone? Another thing the people are sure to squint at," she said with a chuckle.

"Well…" he replied, " I was hoping you'd be willing to do it. In times like these, Khala needs a royal member on the throne."

"Khosi and Masisi Chieftain? Careful, I might let all that power go to my head," she said with a laugh.

They stared in companionable silence out at the sea for a time. Khaleena took a deep sigh.

"Something else on your mind sister?" Imari asked.

"Will you bury Imbaku before you go?" her eyes staring at the endless sea before them.

"Yes, he deserves that much. More than that. His name will be numbered among the honored warriors of history," proclaimed Imari.

"It still won't bring him back," sniffed Khaleena as tears started welling up in her eyes. "Eisshhh, I am sick of crying."

"Me too, sister," Imari placed his hand on her shoulder. "If it's any comfort, I think we will see him again someday."

With tear-filled eyes they let the waves gently rock them as they reflected on their brother.

It was a little over a day at sea when the ports of Wahah came into view. As they docked, the city, which had previously been a bustling display of exotic goods, now stood cold and quiet. It made Imari wonder if what they had done had been for the better after all. He quickly reminded himself that a beautiful veneer can often hide the grotesque truth beneath. They only stayed one night in the city, as they were keen to keep moving. Sad eyes watched as the strange company of

Khalan and Masisi passed them by. Hopefully, someday soon, business could return to normal.

The road ahead felt so different than the journey they had taken over the last few months. No running for their lives. No hiding off the roads. Sure, there were still bandits and the occasional wild beast, but with a host their size, they needn't worry. The bright sun shown overhead as they traveled the next few days. The familiar scorching sun of Khala there to welcome them home. Imari didn't mind. It reminded them that they were getting ever closer.

The day had arrived almost seven years in the making. The city of Khala gleamed under the midday sun. Four towers stood as sentinels with a large wall connecting them. The palace was a gem glistening in the middle, a large terra-cotta ziggurat. Surrounding the palace was the city and all its inhabitants. From the outside it would look as if a city its size and splendor could never survive in the midst of the desert. The secret was buried underneath. The largest aquifer in all of Islandia sat beneath them, fed from underground rivers. The rivers' source was the great lake of Leviathan herself. The city became an oasis for all travelers in the south. It was a treasure of its people and coveted by her enemies, the latter being Fahim's motivation to take her those many years ago. She was also prized at creating some of the most spectacular gems and jewels in the kingdom. Hard places created beautiful things. For Imari, this was home. As they approached the gate a cry rang out from the nearest watchtower.

"The Khosi returns! The message is true. Prepare the way. Rejoice in celebration. The lost is found. The dead brought back. Our Khosi lives!"

The proclamation took Imari by surprise. As the gates swung open a plethora of people had gathered waving banners of the leopard's paw. Desert flowers were thrown from balconies above. Never in his wildest dreams had he pictured this moment. His eyes filled with tears. Rejoicing was shouted in the streets. Ululating rang in the air. Food and fine goods were presented around every corner as the procession made its way to the palace entry.

No gate surrounded the palace as Khalan's saw themselves as one. A palace for the Khosi, available to the large and small of his people. This was the way, the rising and falling together. The large doors swung open as Imari, Khaleena, and the rest entered within. The doors closed behind them, making the sounds from the streets a muffled roar. Inside, the light from the sun shown down from the hollow top of the ziggurat. Servants busied themselves on the three tiers above them. A small pool reflecting the sun's rays sat in the middle of the open courtyard, a place of refreshment and community. Fresh vegetation was everywhere, creating a cool and humid climate within.

"Welcome home, brother," Khaleena said from behind him.

"Welcome home," he said soaking it all in.

That evening the ceremony for Imbaku took place. Overlooking the city from a terrace extending out of the palace, Imari could see the vast majority of the city coming to mourn the late prince. The main road was a straight path to the city gate filled with Khalans paying their respect. The call of remembrance and reflection was being ushered out to the people. In closing, Imari approached the body of Imbaku displayed for all to see. He cried out in a loud voice.

"Khalans, your Khosi has returned, but not without a price. We must forever remember this moment for it is the moment we reflect on the cost of evil, of war, of betrayal, and restoration. It is a cost that we pay for with the ones we love. Imbaku saved my life. He will forever be in my memory, but let us not forget what he died for. Not just me, but a kingdom. A kingdom honorable, free, and above all, an oasis. A place where weary travelers come, not just to drink the waters, but to be refreshed by a people. A people true, kind, and hopeful that evil will not have the final say. This is the kingdom we must build, and we will build it together."

In closing, Imari nodded to those who orchestrated the ceremony. They bowed and lifted the small platform Imbaku laid upon and moved in a ceremonial procession to the royal tombs beneath the palace. Imari and his sister followed at the end of the line. At the tomb, Imbaku was placed on a shelf next to their mother and father who had been buried with the royal line of Khala, one small kindness Fahim had shown them. With a bowed head, and one last moment of weeping, they left Imbaku to rest.

As Imari was making his way to the king's chambers, Henry stepped from the shadows. A sober look on his face.

"Yes, Henry?" said Imari weary from the day.

"I have grim news to share, Khosi," he said.

"I'm tired of grim news," Imari said rubbing his face. "Go on."

"Kingshelm is destroyed," Henry said choking back tears.

"What?!" Imari blurted in shock. "What do you mean destroyed?"

"Just that, Khosi. It seems it has been burnt to the ground. Titus and the forces of Kingshelm believe they have Valkara trapped. King Titus has been informed that Leviatanas has tricked Valkara to come to Founding Habor. He believes with Leviatanas help they can end this war."

"Only he is the one being deceived…"

"Yes, Khosi. I must beg your pardon, but I need to leave tonight. I may still be able to save them."

"It will take you three days to reach Founding Habor even if you could make it to Kingshelm's port," retorted Imari.

"What choice do I have? I cannot sit idly by as my people are destroyed."

Imari thought for a moment.

"We will ride together. I will have the quickest steeds in all Khala prepared."

"Khosi, I cannot ask this of you. What of Khala? What of your people?"

"There is still a royal princess to lead in my place. Besides, without Kingshelm to aid us in the future, there may not be a Khala in the days to come. Go to the stables. I will inform the necessary people about what should be done in my stead, then I will meet you there."

"We owe you a great debt," Henry said bowing.

"Not until we save the men of Kingshelm," replied Imari.

With that, they moved with haste to their necessary tasks. Imari sighed to himself, "There is no rest for the weary."

15

TITUS

Nothing but ash remained. The rest of Kingshelm's forces had caught up to them, but there was nothing they could do. Only a few buildings, a gutted palace, and a wall remained. Most of those who called the city home had either been killed or fled to other cities and villages within the Riverlands. A small group had stayed and made a tiny relief camp in the meantime. Many of the most vulnerable and weak that still remained occupied it.

Titus wandered with Elorah and Lydia by his side through the rumble hoping beyond hope to wake from the nightmare. No matter how hard he tried, there was no dream to wake from.

"It's all gone," he muttered to no one in particular.

Lydia grabbed his hand squeezing it tight. It was a small comfort, one he was thankful to have.

"Could Valkara truly be capable of this?" Elorah stated in disbelief.

Titus winced at the prospect, looking to see Lydia's reaction. It carried nothing but a shared sorrow of all the tragedies that had transpired. They made their way toward the palace remains. The overall structure was still standing, but every door and window was now an exposed opening. Smoke still rose in certain places, the sky a backdrop of sullen grey, full of smoke and raining bits of ash.

As they entered the palace they searched for any remains. Nothing but charred wood, melted metal, and bones were left to greet them. From what they could tell, the inferno had started in the main lobby before the throne room. Scorch marks revealed flames that had climbed the walls from where tapestries once hung. They followed small indicators until they reached an offshoot hallway. Lying in the middle of the floor were two skeletons, one hunched over next to each other.

"This is a strange sight," Elorah remarked.

"Yes, indeed," Titus said as he examined the scene.

He noticed two small daggers partially melted on the floor beneath them.

"It looks as though these two were in some sort of conflict. Look," he motioned for them to observe the evidence he just discovered.

"Look at the hand," pointed Elorah to one of the skeletons.

On the figure rested a slightly disfigured ring. A sigil ring belonging to the city steward. Eli's ring.

"Eli?!" Titus stood abruptly. "Then who is that?" he said turning to look at the other victim.

Nothing remained to inform them of the other skeleton. They searched the immediate area to find any other clue but none could be found.

"So it would seem Eli was trying to stop this person, maybe someone from Valkara?" proposed Elorah.

"Or an insider," said Lydia.

"What makes you say that?" asked Elorah.

"Whoever it was had access to the palace. I doubt they would let a Valkaran stroll in casually."

None of it made sense. They didn't find any signs of battle within the city. All the corpses in the streets had either been burned or suffocated from the smoke. The only wounds caused by a sword were outside the wall. It was as if whatever started this calamity had been within the city itself. But who? Titus' head was thumping. There was no way of knowing.

The only mystery that had been solved that day was where the Valkaran army had gone. A small group of survivors had informed them that they had set sail from the port, but even that had not made much sense to them. Where would they go? On the other side of Lake Leviathan was all Leviantanas territory, the closest ally of Kingshelm. If King Leon didn't want to get involved before, he would have no choice with an enemy army running around his lands. The puzzle just didn't seem to fit together. Titus was broken from his thoughts when he heard a yell for their attention.

"King Titus! King Titus!" called the messenger from their camp. He approached them, kneeling over to catch his breath. "I have an urgent letter." He held it out for Titus.

"From who?" he asked as he reached for it.

"Leviatanas, sir," he said out of breath.

"Lancelin!" Titus exclaimed as he folded the letter open.

Titus,

I have heard of Kingshelm's burning. You must know that we will not stand for such a horrendous act. My father has been infuriated by this atrocity and has devised a plan. Valkara attempts to enter our lands. We will broker a false alliance with them in order to draw up enough time for you to arrive. Together we can end this madness. You're haste, my friend, is of the utmost importance. We will meet you at Jezero. Together we will march on Valkara near Founding Habor with our armies. Our Kingdom is counting on you, Steward King.

-Lancelin.

Titus handed the letter over to Elorah to read, who in turn handed it to Lydia at Titus' beckoning.

"Then we should set off at once," urged Elorah. "Say the word and I will have the men ready to sail. It should take little more than a day to reach Founding Habor."

It was faint, but something inside Titus felt uneasy about the whole thing. It frustrated him that Leviantanas would wait until their own interests were under threat to act, but Lancelin was a friend and he couldn't leave them to be destroyed.

"The men will want vengeance, they will be ready at your call, my king," Elorah continued.

"I am not here for vengeance, Elorah. We still do not even know the truth of what happened," Titus reminded him.

"Is it not clear, Titus?! I mean, my king," Elorah said in a rare moment of frustration.

"Prepare the men, and send word to any of our allies throughout the kingdom," Titus said.

Elorah bowed and began to leave when Titus grabbed him by the arm, "But make sure they know this is about the whole kingdom, not their personal revenge."

With that, he went to prepare the army. Titus let out a sigh watching him go unsure what was to become of them all or what victory would mean after everything was said and done.

"This doesn't feel right," Lydia said as she moved beside him.

"I agree," he said putting his arm around her waist. "None of this makes any sense anymore. Is not Kingshelm the prize? Yet someone wanted to destroy it." He turned to look her in the eyes.

"I'm sorry," Titus suddenly stated.

"What for?" She asked.

"All this time I have been thinking only of Kingshelm, but your brothers," he stopped at that.

She sat quietly thinking on his words. She bit her lip as she looked back at him.

"My heart and my head tell me two different tales on what I wish to discover."

"How so?"

"On the one hand I wish to see them again, to laugh, sing, and share our old lives. On the other side I know the truth can only be one thing." She sighed deeply. "Either they are dead and I will never see them again, or they are alive which means they likely had a hand in this. Even if that were not true, our old life is dead there is no going back."

Titus reflected on what she must be wrestling with. Once again he found himself searching for the right words and could find none. He pulled her in close.

"Will you make me a promise?" he asked.

She did not reply for a moment as she searched his eyes. "Yes."

"No matter what we find on the other side of this. No matter how horrid, ugly, or dark, we won't give up. Will you promise me that?"

She laid her head into his chest. "I promise."

He smiled a deep and loving smile. Of all the horrendous things that had happened, he was grateful for the one ray of hope he had discovered.

They returned to the encampment outside the city. It was filled with a flurry of activity, Elorah's words proven true. The men were ready to take their anger out on something. The march to the port only a mile away was accomplished in record time. The momentum was quickly stalled as almost all of the larger boats had been used by Valkara as they had crossed the great lake. Elorah and the captains mustered up as many fishing boats and private ships that they could find. It would be just enough to get them all across. It was a motley armada, but it would accomplish the task. It was determined the best course was to wait until the morning to sail.

Titus awoke that morning with a fresh sense of unease. Today Islandia's future would be decided, her fate placed in their hands. It wasn't the task he dreamed would be his. He had been a young, naive prince only a few months prior, and now it was under his command whether there would be a remnant of Kingshelm at all.

The ships set sail, Titus and the commanders aboard one of the few large ships still available. He recounted his first voyage on the lake. It had been a diplomatic trip with his father to Leviantanas. He was swept up in the memory once again.

Birds cried out in glee at the fisherman's catch being brought into port. He could feel the buzz of energy running through the busy harbor. Titus looked up at his father, an example of regal confidence. They had been ushered onto a prestigious looking boat with red paint and golden trim, a lion head at its bow. It boasted a large white sail with a roaring purple lion displayed upon it. Sailors called out to one another as they set sail. Titus and his father watched it all from atop the deck.

"Father, why are you bringing me on this trip?" Titus asked curiously.

His father smiled looking down on his young prince.

"Well, my boy, it's about time you start to get used to such travel. Some day when you are the Steward King, pardoning Eloy's return, you, too, will need to travel."

"But why this trip? Why not somewhere adventurous like Sahra or Valkara!"

"Ahhh, why just boring old Leviatanas, huh? Is that what you're asking me?" Richard jested with a big grin.

Titus nodded eagerly.

"Well, Leviatanas has been our friend for many years. For your first royal trip I think it's important you see their lands. They will be your closest allies someday if you ever need to call on them. Besides all that, I think there may a friend you'd like to meet, a prince much like you."

"Like me?" Titus asked wide-eyed. "Does he like to ride horses?" Titus' favorite activity in those days.

"Ohh, I am sure he does, son." Richard knelt to look his son in the eyes. "Remember, my son, friends are for more than just having an ally in a fight or for joyous occasions. They are the ones you can trust when things get most grim."

"I am counting on that, Father," Titus said as he receded from the memory.

The waves were a bit choppy stirring him from his thoughts, much like that day. He noticed Lydia coming up from behind him. He motioned for her to join him.

"Have you ever been on a boat before?" he asked.

She looked thoroughly offended.

"We have a port city called Thoras, thank you very much!" The feistiness returning to her for the first time in some days. Titus was thankful for that.

"I meant no offense. I just wasn't sure if a pretty maiden like yourself did much adventuring as a child." A teasing smile crept across his face.

"You've really done it now, lad." An equally feisty grin crossed her own.

"Lad? Huh, is that how you address a king?"

"Hmmm, not if you're a proper maiden. Sadly, I am not one," the sarcasm thick in her voice.

"Good, I think this king isn't interested in just any maiden."

"Now don't be gettin all soft on me, Titus," she said punching him in the arm.

"I would never, my lady." He gave her a mocking bow.

In response, she tackled him to the deck. They tumbled down a few feet. Lydia knelt over him as they came to a halt, her deep emerald eyes looking into his. Before he moved to kiss her, he heard Elorah's voice.

"If you two are not too busy, could I have a word?"

Titus blushed with embarrassment as he looked up at him, "Give me one moment."

Elorah gave him a disapproving nod.

"Ahh, I didn't embarrass ya, did I?" smirked Lydia.

"You? Of course not." Titus brushed himself off as he stood up.

"See you later, my king." She gave him a wink as she walked away.

He smiled to himself thinking of that future encounter. She truly had captured his heart. Now to survive long enough to make sure he could have a life to appreciate that fact. He moved into a small room off the deck where they had decided to have their meetings. Elorah, along with a few captains, were discussing the upcoming encounter. At his entry, Elorah motioned for him to join them.

"You see, with Leviantanas forces we could easily encompass Valkara's army. Last we knew they only had some 2,500 men remaining. Surely they have lost some to attrition and the like." stated one of the captains.

"Who knows, they might have hired some mercenaries. We should send our men to a flanking maneuver after the original encounter," argued another of the captains.

"No consensus on the plan?" Titus asked.

"No, we were hoping you might have something to share," Elorah stated.

Titus rubbed his chin in thought. "We should wait until we reach Lancelin. We don't know the size of their force or what troops he will have rallied in such a short time."

"I agree with the King," said Elorah. "We should wait and see what we have to work with."

"Is that all, Elorah?" Titus asked a bit confused.

"One other thing," he signaled for the others to leave.

"May I speak freely?" he asked.

Titus didn't like where this was going. "Yes…"

"It's about Lydia. I share some concerns with our captains."

"What about her? She has been nothing but helpful to us, has she not? Besides that, you are the one who suggested a future union," defended Titus.

"Yes, but things have changed. She is Valkaran and Valkara just burned Kingshelm to the ground, and here you are flaunting an affection for each other in front of your army. Do you not see a problem?" his gaze was stern.

"You have already condemned Valkara? Lydia had nothing to do with that. If we are going to win this war we have got to let go of those grudges."

"Who else could have, Titus? Don't let your affection for her blind you. If we must go to war with her people, you need to be able to lead us. I hold nothing against the girl, but you are king and your people come before your personal feelings."

"You think I would betray Kingshelm?! I have given everything for Kingshelm."

"No, my lord, I know your sacrifice. I fear that your affection for Lydia will stop you from doing what is necessary, to destroy Valkara if necessary."

Titus let his anger pass before replying. "I would hope not to destroy any of the kingdoms when this is done, Elorah, but if you think I won't fight if need be, you're wrong." He stormed out of the room regret sitting in his stomach.

"This shouldn't be how we win. Hating our enemies and destroying those in our way," he sighed to himself.

That evening they could see Jezero, one of Leviatanas' port cities on Lake Leviathan. Within the hour they had landed, the sun just barely clinging to the day. As they unloaded from the ship a single figure stood to greet them. He stood in his familiar jade armor a welcoming smile across his face. Titus rushed down the ramp and embraced his old friend.

"Lancelin, you don't know how good it is to see you!" he exclaimed.

"Wow, you've turned into quite the softy in my absence," chuckled Lancelin. "It's good to see you too. How was the trip?"

"Fair weather, which has brought us to you quickly."

"Good, good. Yes, if you'd like I will direct you to where your men should camp. We can discuss more after you are settled." Lancelin motioned for him to follow.

Ship after ship began to arrive, as men unload supplies for the evening and coming battle. Lancelin instructed them on where they should settle for the evening, a spot just outside the city near his forces. When formalities had finished, he invited Titus, and whoever he wished to join him, in his personal lodging within Jezero.

The sun had set and the room was dimly lit by flickering candles. The suite that Lancelin had taken up residence was the finest in all the city, luxury at every turn. The room itself was one open space. The back half was an open patio overlooking Lake Leviathan. This time of year the cool air wafting off the waters was refreshing as it entered the room. Vibrant green curtains swayed in the window, cups of fine gold were laid out on an ivory table for any who would desire a drink, and alongside them, roasted pork and fresh fish from the lake. The luxury left a bitter taste in Titus' mouth as thoughts of the charred corpse of Kingshelm came to mind. He looked over at the uneasy faces of Elorah, Lydia, and a few of the captains as well. They had no time or need for indulgences. Lancelin sat reclining on a couch, cup in hand.

"Welcome friends. Please, help yourself to anything. I am sure you are weary from your travels," he said standing to greet them.

They hesitantly entered, unsure of what they should or should not partake in. Lancelin, sensing this, set his cup down.

"I'm sorry, I understand you just lost your home. I had hoped maybe this would have eased your hearts. I see it's done the opposite. Please, what can I do to help?" he begged.

"No, no it's fine." Titus turned to the others. "We should not reject such gracious hospitality, eat."

Still a bit unsure, the captains and Elorah sat down and slowly began to pick at the food. Lydia stood off to the side not considering it for a second. Lancelin motioned for Titus to follow him to the patio. They both leaned against the ledge looking out over the lake.

"Many a memory traveling to see one another, huh?" Lancelin mused.

"Yes, there have been a lot of memories made throughout the years," Titus reflected. He turned to Lancelin. "So what is our aim for tomorrow?"

"Straight to business? I suppose so," he shuffled his feet a bit. "I have convinced Valkara that we will join in their fight. They are under the assumption that we will be leading you to Founding Harbor to your doom. Little do they know it will be the reverse."

"Is that the truth Lancelin?" Titus stared into his eyes.

"Of course!" he took a step back a bit offended. "In times like these your allies are the ones you must trust if you are to win the day. Besides, without you here we would be in just as much peril."

"Good. I need friends, Lancelin. Being king isn't all it's cut out to be," he admitted.

"It is lonely at the top," sighed Lancelin. "Thankfully, after tomorrow, we can start afresh. I know Kingshelm is heavy on your heart, but think of it this way, maybe it can be the start of something new." Lancelin clasped his hand on Titus' shoulder. "Come, let's go eat. I am sure you're starving."

As they entered back into the room Titus glanced at Lydia. Her stare warning him of some unforeseen danger. Lancelin ushered him to sit down around the table. Titus sat, but glanced back over at Lydia. She subtly shook her head in a gesture that said don't. He was a bit confused at first until she looked down at the food. Now he understood her.

"Come, friend! Eat," encouraged Lancelin.

"I am sorry," smiled Titus. "I am afraid I had too much before coming here tonight." A clear lie, but Lancelin shrugged it off.

The rest of the night was spent in talks of the battle and happenings within the kingdom. Titus had trouble following any of it, an uneasiness in his stomach. Lancelin wouldn't have poisoned the food, would he? He trusted Lydia, however, she had earned that. She eventually sat next to him, likely an attempt to not draw too much attention. Elorah gave Titus a disconcerting look when she sat. He ignored the clear disapproval.

Lancelin, for the first time, acknowledged the Valkaran princess.

"I am so sorry for your loss, my lady. I am sure all of this has been taxing on you. Are you sure you are up to the task we have tomorrow?"

"I would just worry about yerself. I don't see the need for bloodshed when the truth is revealed to Valkara," she scoffed.

"What truth is that?" he asked quizzically.

"The true monster behind all this. A man named Balzara is the one who manipulated my father and took over our kingdom. When Valkara hears who the true enemy is, they may be willing to join us."

"I see," mused Lancelin. "You have high hopes, my lady."

Lydia turned to hear what the others were discussing obviously annoyed with Lancelin's dismissive response. Titus was unsure what to make of the uneasy conversation. It was around midnight when the small gathering came to a close. Lancelin dismissed them and wished the best of luck for the coming conflict. Titus walked through the camp with Lydia, escorting her to her tent. After a moment of silence she spoke up.

"You don't need to escort me. I am a grown woman, you know."

"I know, that's not why I am doing this," he said as they reached her tent. "I want to know why you were suspicious tonight."

She looked away for a moment, as if she didn't want to say.

"Come now. Tell me," he pressed.

"It's nothing solid. Even a week ago I might dismiss it as a silly feeling." She looked him in the eyes. "There is something dark that has touched him, Titus. He hides it well, but I can see it. It's the same darkness I could see stirring in my father like a sickness yet to spring."

"Do you think he is lying?"

"I cannot say, but I do not trust he has revealed his whole agenda to us," she confessed.

This left Titus even more uneasy. He leaned in and kissed her goodnight.

"Well, it's good I have you by my side then?"

"The best shield-maiden that never fought in a war," she joked.

He smiled and opened the tent flap for her to enter. She looked up at him as she entered.

"Just be careful, Titus, I can't lose you, too."

He nodded exuding a confidence he didn't feel. He weaved his way through the moonlit night dreading the morning's arrival. "The truth will be revealed soon enough," he thought, but was it the truth he wanted to hear.

Early that next morning they were on the march. Titus barely slept, but he was thankful that he no longer had to fight his fatigue. It would only be half a day's journey, and they would reach their destination, the small harbor created from the landing of The Founders. It was a historic location embezzled in memorials, but outdated in its function. The Samudara Port on the southern end of The Spine had become the main ocean trading center reducing Founding Harbor to no more than a pilgrimage site. Titus had only been to the harbor as a small boy. He could recall the many paintings and monuments built representing the great day The Founders had arrived. The view of the vast strip of white sandy shores that stretched down most of the region nicknamed The Spine, and the smell of the great Islandic Ocean stretching out far beyond sight. Those were the memories Titus carried. Now, sadly, they may be replaced with a bloody battlefield.

The morning dragged on forever. They all rode in mutual silence, knowing the seriousness of the moment. This day would decide the future of Islandia for good or ill. They had arrived at the small cliffs that descended onto the long stretch of beach. At the bottom, sat the humble town of Founding Harbor. Just outside its perimeter sat the forces of Valkara their banners flapping in the wind battle lines already drawn.

"It looks as if they knew we were coming," Titus stated.

"The ruse must be kept up until the last, my friend. Don't worry. Together we outnumber them three to one," Lancelin said as he spurred his horse onward.

Titus turned to Elorah and the other captains that had dined with them the night before. None of them looked ill.

"At least Lancelin didn't poison them," he thought to himself. He looked to Lydia who seemed to be reading his mind. Her eyes saying "I still don't trust him".

When the host of their forces had reached the bottom of the cliff's descent, they began to form up into battle lines across from the Valkarans. It was the familiar sight Titus remembered. To his left was the sandy beach with the vast Islandic Ocean lapping up the coast. The unwelcome addition was the host of Valkara arrayed before them, a disheveled looking force. Blistered and scarred shields painted with the familiar crest of the ram were lined before him. Some men carried axes, others swords and spears, their silver masks covering their identity. Two riders came forth from their ranks. One, the man named Geralt who rode on a white horse, was a familiar face. The other, an unfamiliar looking man, was mounted on a painted steed. Titus assumed he was the leader of the Valkaran forces he had never met. Lancelin, Lydia, Elorah, Dios, and he rode to meet them.

"Greetings," said the man Titus did not know.

"Greetings. I have not had the chance to meet you," Titus said cooly.

Geralt had shock written on his face. Titus was unsure if it was due to him or Lydia. A mix of both perhaps.

The man replied, "Ferir, joint commander of Valkaran forces." His eyes flickered over to Lydia. "Lydia…?" he said, his jaw dropping.

"What are you doing?" blurted Geralt, his gaze fixed on her.

"I am assisting the Steward King of Islandia in hopes that we might conquer the true evil plaguing our realms," she said.

A KING'S RETURN

"Girl, you know nothing of war. Are they holding you hostage?" inquired Ferir.

"No, I, in fact, am the one who freed King Titus."

Geralt and Ferir both uttered a sound of bewilderment.

"My Father…my father had been corrupted by a sinister monster, the man named Balzara, but he was betrayed. Balzara has seated Jorn on the throne of Valkara and slain my father," she fought back tears as she said it.

"Your father's dead?" Ferir muttered.

Lydia continued. "So it is my hope, my desire, that you and my brothers, wherever they are," she looked around confused as to why they would not be there, "would lead our forces with King Titus to conquer the real plague on our lands, this Balzara the corrupter."

Both men sat silent for a moment.

"Where are my brothers?" she asked.

"Lydia…they are dead," Geralt said somberly.

Ferir pointed a finger toward Titus. "By the hands of these ilks! Do you think this king benevolent? It is by his men that your brothers were tortured to the point of madness. Brayan's mind was so broken, he burned the whole of Kingshelm to the ground."

"Ferir!" barked Geralt his gaze turning to Lydia.

She melted in her saddle.

"It is true. Their minds had been broken. I am so sorry, Lydia…Brayan was slain at the hands of Eli, Kingshelm's temporary steward. Aiden…" he paused briefly, "we can only assume the worst," explained Geralt.

"That means…the body in the hall was…" she wiped away tears filling her eyes as she brought her hand to her mouth.

"How do you answer for your evils?" said Ferir, pointing to Titus.

Titus quickly looked to Lydia whose eyes questioned if it was true.

"I had nothing to do with such evils! When I left I made sure they were held as royal prisoners should be."

"You may not have given the order, but you placed that cretan Eli in charge, did you not?" Ferir snarled.

"Eli...did that?" muttered Titus.

"There's more," Geralt's eyes now flickering to Lancelin.

Lancelin took a deep sigh, but before he could speak a horn rang in the air. They all turned their attention to two riders coming from the west. One, a man dressed as one from Kingshelm, the other, a Khalan? With thunderous speed they approached.

"My King! My King!" cried the Kingshelm soldier.

"Who are you, soldier, this is a private council," Elorah asked.

"I beg your pardon, commander. My name is Henry and this is the esteemed Khosi of Khala, Imari."

The man named Imari bowed in respect.

"King Titus, my message is urgent, may I speak with you privately?"

"As Khosi, I can confirm, Steward King, you should hear what he has to say," Imari said.

"Is it a matter of the Riverlands?" Elorah asked.

"It is a matter of all lands, sir," his eyes shifting to Lancelin.

"There is no need for all the show anymore." Lancelin interrupted. He dismounted from his steed.

"Titus, you want to know of his message? I will tell you what he is about to say."

Titus' eyes narrowed as he looked at Lancelin. "So you have betrayed us."

Lancelin sighed, "It is Kingshelm that has betrayed us. For too long each of us has lived under the rule of an empty throne. Sure, in the days of Eloy and before, the central rule had brought peace and a veneer of stability, but look around Titus. You truly think you know what is best for us," he motioned at the realms represented on the field. "Yes, I am the one who plotted against your father. He was a good man, but one that would see us restrained and held back for the good of Kingshelm, not Islandia. I knew something must be done, so I convinced Fahim to aid me in ridding Islandia of your father's rule. Of course Fahim understood the oppression of Kingshelm and was happy to oblige," he looked over at Imari, "but I knew just two realms would not do. If we truly were going to create a new Islandia of our own, I would need all the realms onboard. That is when I sought Jorn and Lokir, two men eager for change. Doran was a decent enough king, but I was unsure if he could change his ways to a new line of thinking. So, I had extra precautions in place, Jorn and Lokir. Either way, Valkara would be joined to our plan by delivering the poison to me." He glanced at Lydia. "The loss of your family was a tragedy I wish did not have to occur."

A venomous scowl filled her face, but before she could reply, Lancelin continued. "With Khala under Sahra rule that left only one realm, The Riverlands. I knew you would be loyal to your father's way of thinking. Besides, if you knew that I was the one who killed your father you would never come around to see my perspective. That is when I contacted Eli. I offered him power, and the greedy man that he is grasped at the opportunity. Of course there were complications, your little rebellion to start," he looked toward Imari.

"Not so little now," scowled Imari.

"Yes, indeed. Jorn and Lokir's failure also complicated things...but Balzara does have a way of convincing people to see reason."

"So this Balzara is the one who has twisted you so!" Titus roared.

"He is the one that showed me how broken Islandia truly was. How it needed a new way of rule, one where each kingdom could rule its own people. Titus, don't you see that it is time? Why should you speak for all of us?"

"What of Eloy? What of the unbroken line of Kings? Does none of that mean a thing? Are they not just? Have they not held the balance of power in check?" stammered Titus.

"What of him?" scoffed Lancelin. "The king who chases a fantasy. The king who abandons us? You actually think he will return? You're more naive than me, friend," scoffed Lancelin.

"That sounds too familiar," sighed Titus. "This Balzara is a plague."

"Balzara? You mean the one who wished to free Islandia from Eloy and all those who have tried to rule over us? You may call him a monster, but this King Eloy, if he is so great and grand, where was he when my father's mind fractured into madness? Where was he when your mother and sibling were slaughtered by the barbarians?" he cried pointing a finger toward Lydia. "If he is the one we need, why has he not returned now that his kingdom is tearing at the seams? No! It is those like you who will destroy us. You who wait for a fantasy to fix things. It is we, the realists, who will save Islandia, not you," said Lancelin.

"You've done a fine job of it so far. Can you not see, Lancelin, what you have brought by listening to this madness. Your new age has filled our land with corpses," Titus said.

"There has to be sacrifice for Islandia to step forward into a new dawn."

"Lancelin, my friend is this truly who you've become?"

"It is, and if you cannot see the truth of my words, then I have no choice," Lancelin said shaking his head. "It's time, do it," he lifted his hand to give an order.

Several arrows came flying in, striking many of the captains down. Elorah was also caught by one of the arrows in his shoulder dropping him from his mount.

Ferir gave a shouted order, "Valkara! At arms!"

With that cry his forces rushed forward in a furious charge. Titus and the others with him, scrambled back to their men, but then he saw that they, too, were now being attacked from the Leviantanas army. Soon they would be pressed between in a swirling whirlpool of chaos. Without thinking or hesitation Titus made for the rest of the mounted men who stood at Kingshelm's flank. He lifted his sword to rally them hoping to send a counter-attack toward the oncoming storm.

He roared a battle cry, "To me, riders of the Riverlands!"

A tide of horsemen answered his call, creating a thunderous noise. His horse reared as he gave it the order to charge. They were now wrapped up fully in the fog of battle. There was no time to observe the opposition, no awareness of what was taking place around them. The host of calvary followed their king toward the Valkaran army.

It was a collision of storms. Men flung from horses, and those on the ground were trampled under hoof and spear. Titus felt the weight of humanity crash beneath him as they broke through Valkara's line. Soon momentum was halted. He looked around him. Madness reigned. Around him was an ocean of violence and visceral cries. He was an unsteady boat amid that ocean. Only then did he realize he could not find Lydia, Elorah, or the rest.

He sent his sword crashing down on the helmet of a soldier beneath him. The man letting out a cry of anguish as he fell under the murky waters of the battle. Men began climbing over corpses as an attempt to break free from suffocation in the smothering collision. Titus could see they were close to breaking through the back end of the Valkaran army. A goal, if reached, that would divide their forces in two. That's when he saw the thundering wave rising to meet them. A host of calvary bearing the insignia of the Leviathan came sweeping from behind the Valkaran army. At their head rode Lancelin, now adorning a helmet shaped like a serpent's mouth, leviathan scales spreading out from the sides.

"I see you have a taste for gaudy helmets after all," he muttered to himself as he tried to steer his horse toward the oncoming charge. Once again he raised his sword to rally the calvary. He could sense the presence of several horsemen riding beside him now. His sword dropped, giving the command to charge. Valkarans left and right parted for them, doing all they could to avoid being caught in the middle.

Lancelin drew closer and closer. The two forces crashed like tidal waves coming to greet one another. Horse and rider were thrown asunder. Titus could feel his mount being pulled away from him. Next came the sickening thud he heard, then came the pain. It shot from his back down to his legs. A flurry of images raced over him, flashes of steel, legs, and violent motion. He felt as though it would consume him. It was only when he had nearly embraced that this would be his fate that the fury ended. It looked as if the charge had ended. It was only when he caught his bearings that he realized that his mount had partially fallen on him, preventing him from being trampled to death. He pushed with all the strength he had in him, his dead horse moving just enough for him to slip free. As he stood to his feet he saw that he was just outside of the raging conflict. The battle had turned into a large crest of Valkaran and Leviatanas' forces slowly engulfing the dwindling Kingshelm army. He took notice that a small detachment from the Leviatanas' calvary was headed for him, Lancelin leading them directly toward him. It wasn't until then that Titus saw he wasn't alone. The survivors of the charge were gathering to him, the ragtag remains standing against impending doom. Lancelin bellowed as he drew near.

"For the kingdom! End the Steward King!"

Titus held his ground unwilling to give an inch. When Lancelin came within a few feet, he dropped to his knees, sending a devastating slash at Lancelin's mount. It tumbled headfirst crashing into the ground, throwing Lancelin several yards away. The small forces he had brought with him swept by trying their best to slow momentum to turn for another strike. This was Titus' chance.

Every emotion rose to the surface. There was the betrayal caused by the poisoning of his father, the sorrow of Kingshelm's destruction, the fear of loss, and the rage of everything he loved being ripped from him. He let out an agonizing cry rushing at the dazed Lancelin. Bringing his sword high above his head, he sent a powerful strike downward. Lancelin deflected it. The impact sent his sword flying from his hands. Fear seized his eyes. Titus did not hesitate. He sent another slash, Lancelin blocking it with his armored bracer. The blow dented the armor and sent a howl from Lancelin. Again he sent a strike, catching him across the chest, denting his armor. Again and again he hacked away, unleashing his pent up fury.

Lancelin pulled out a small dagger in faint hope of deflecting the onslaught. He was able to block a few but the strikes kept coming one after another denting his armor, and at times, piercing it. The blows were adding up and soon he would succumb to them. Titus could see him weakening. That's when the cry rang out.

"Ships coming to port, look!" rang out the anonymous voice.

Titus looked to the sea. It was true, half a dozen ships could be spotted. One had already docked unknowingly during the chaos...and their sails, each sail was stamped with the symbol of the seven-pointed star. From pure instinct, Titus reached for the pendant around his neck.

Some distance away a small band of men were moving toward the battle, the banners they carried flapping in the wind. Banners that bore a silver field, a white lion and white star alternating on each. Titus dropped his sword in shock. Lancelin, bloodied and beaten, moved in anguish to see what Titus was staring at. A slight gasp left his lips.

"Is that?" he said in a hushed tone.

"High King Eloy," Titus finished for him.

As the small company approached, Titus could see a man distinguished at their head. He wore a silver breastplate with a shining star on the center. His face was a light olive complexion which carried a thick brown beard. His hair was a shorter cut and, on his head, sat a simple and elegant crown. A bleached white cape flowed from his shoulders. He carried himself in a regal, yet humble, manner. Titus could not help but stare. He had waged everything on this moment. His hopes had been realized. The King had returned.

EPILOGUE

The proclamation spread throughout the battlefield. Among the carnage men began to throw down their arms at the sight of the king's return. Ferir could be seen leading the Valkaran army in a retreat to the south. Like locusts, after devouring all they could, retreating away. Leviatanas forces threw down their arms at the sight of the true king. Titus still stood over Lancelin, but was unable to move. The sword slipped from his hand. An envoy approached them, King Eloy with a handful of high-ranking men. The chief of these men, dressed in full silver armor, came forward.

"What is taking place? I see banners of Valkara, Leviatanas, and Kingshelm itself. What is this madness?" interrogated the man.

Titus' head sank. "My King, it is as you see. The kingdom has fallen into war. We have failed you."

"Who is this who speaks?" barked the captain.

Eloy gave a gesturing wave to calm him.

"This young man carries the look of someone close to me. You are Richard's son are you not?" Eloy asked in a calming voice.

"I am, my king," Titus dropped to a knee.

"Where is my friend Richard, is he here as well?" Eloy asked.

Tears began to well up in Titus' eyes.

"I am afraid, my king, his death is part of the reason you see this conflict before you."

His failures all rising before his eyes in the sight of the king. To his shock, as he slowly rose to look at Eloy once more, he saw something strange. He saw tears forming in Eloy's eyes as well.

"That is sorrowful news indeed. So you are the new Steward King, I assume?" As if just noticing, he looked down at the young man on the ground before him. "The Leviathan...you. Does this mean Leon is dead as well?" the bitter taste of the words evident on his face.

Lancelin bloodied and bruised rose to a knee. "No, my lord, he is alive, but not well. I am his son, Lancelin, heir to Leviatanas."

"It would seem you two are at odds," observed the captain.

Titus and Lancelin stayed silent, unsure where to start. Titus was mustering up what to say when Eloy spoke again.

"There will be time for that. Look, Cebrail, the conflict has ended. Send for the men to come ashore. It is of the utmost urgency that we divulge what we have learned."

Without reply, Cebrail turned to go back to the port. Eloy turned his gaze back to Titus and Lancelin.

"We will settle whatever this dispute may be, but you must know whatever it is, it must be put aside. There is unspeakable darkness coming, and if we do not stand together it will destroy us all."

Titus took a deep breath, "My king, I am afraid it may have already arrived."

To Be Continued...

ILLUSTRATIONS

By Igor Olszewski

KINGSHELM

VALKARA

SAHRA

KHALA

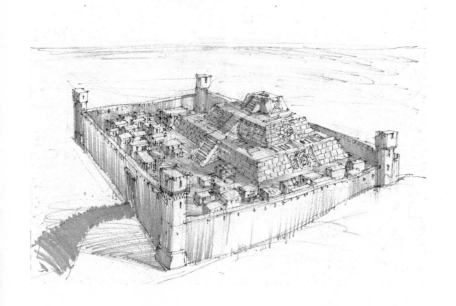

LEVIATANAS

ABOUT THE AUTHOR

Jacob Johnson is a Career Missionary with Assemblies of God World Missions. He along with his wife Vanessa and daughter Kynleigh serves in Botswana, Africa partnering with the national church to empower university students. Jacob has the heart to see students discipled with a deep understanding of God's love and purpose for their lives. He believes that it is only through living life together as a community can we truly be a light shining out into the world.

CPSIA information can be obtained
at www.ICGtesting.com
Printed in the USA
LVHW010720100820
662780LV00005B/226